In the Mayor's

In the Mayor's Parlour

by J. S. Fletcher

Copyright © 10/2/2015
Jefferson Publication

ISBN-13: 978-1517634377

Printed in the United States of America

All rights reserved. No part of this book may be reprinted or reproduced or utilized in any form or by any electronic, mechanical, or other means, now known or hereafter invented, including photocopying and recording, or in any form of storage or retrieval system, without prior permission in writing from the publisher.'

Table of Contents

CHAPTER I 4
   THE MAYOR'S PARLOUR *4*
CHAPTER II 9
   THE CAMBRIC HANDKERCHIEF *9*
CHAPTER III 15
   THE TANNERY HOUSE *15*
CHAPTER IV 21
   BULL'S SNUG *21*
CHAPTER V 26
   SLEEPING FIRES *26*
CHAPTER VI 31
   THE ANCIENT OFFICE OF CORONER *31*
CHAPTER VII 36
   THE VOLUNTARY WITNESS *36*
CHAPTER VIII 42
   MRS. SAUMAREZ *42*
CHAPTER IX 47
   THE RIGHT TO INTERVENE *47*
CHAPTER X 53
   THE CAT IN THE BAG *53*
CHAPTER XI 58
   THE NINETEEN MINUTES' INTERVAL *58*
CHAPTER XII 63
   CIRCUMSTANTIAL EVIDENCE *63*
CHAPTER XIII 68
   A WOMAN INTERVENES *68*
CHAPTER XIV 73
   WHOSE VOICES? *73*
CHAPTER XV 78
   THE SPECIAL EDITION *78*
CHAPTER XVI 83
   THE CASTLE WALL *83*

CHAPTER XVII 88
   IMPREGNABLE 88
CHAPTER XVIII 92
   LOOSE STRANDS 92
CHAPTER XIX 98
   BLACK SECRETS AND RED TAPE 98
CHAPTER XX 103
   THE FELL HAND 103
CHAPTER XXI 108
   CORRUPTION 108
CHAPTER XXII 113
   THE PARLOUR-MAID 113
CHAPTER XXIII 118
   THE CONNECTING WALL 118
CHAPTER XXIV 124
   BEHIND THE PANEL 124
CHAPTER XXV 128
   THE EMPTY ROOM 128
   THE END. 131

CHAPTER I

THE MAYOR'S PARLOUR

H athelsborough market-place lies in the middle of the town—a long, somewhat narrow parallelogram, enclosed on its longer side by old gabled houses; shut in on its western end by the massive bulk of the great parish church of St. Hathelswide, Virgin and Martyr, and at its eastern by the ancient walls and high roofs of its mediæval Moot Hall. The inner surface of this space is paved with cobble-stones, worn smooth by centuries of usage: it is only of late years that the conservative spirit of the old borough has so far accommodated itself to modern requirements as to provide foot-paths in front of the shops and houses. But there that same spirit has stopped; the utilitarian of to-day would sweep away, as being serious hindrances to wheeled traffic, the two picturesque fifteenth-century erections which stand in this market-place; these, High Cross and Low Cross, one at the east end, in front of the Moot Hall, the other at the west, facing the chancel of the church, remain, to the delight of the archæologist, as instances of the fashion in which our forefathers built gathering places in the very midst of narrow thoroughfares.

Under the graceful cupola and the flying buttresses of High Cross the countryfolk still expose for sale on market-days their butter and their eggs; around the base of the slender shaft called Low Cross they still offer their poultry and rabbits; on other than market-days High Cross and Low Cross alike make central, open-air clubs, for the patriarchs of the place, who there assemble in the lazy afternoons and still lazier eventides, to gossip over the latest items of local news; conscious that as they are doing so their ancestors have done for many a generation, and that old as they may be themselves, in their septuagenarian or octogenarian states, they are as infants in comparison with the age of the stones and bricks and timbers about them, grey and fragrant with the antiquity of at least three hundred years.

Of all this mass of venerable material, still sound and uncrumbled, the great tall-towered church at one end of the market-place, and the square, heavily fashioned Moot Hall at the other, go farthest back, through association, into the mists of the Middle Ages. The church dates from the thirteenth century and, though it has been skilfully restored on more than one occasion, there is nothing in its cathedral-like proportions that suggests modernity; the Moot Hall, erected a hundred years later, remains precisely as when it was first fashioned, and though it, too, has passed under the hand of the restorer its renovation has only taken the shape of strengthening an already formidably strong building. Extending across nearly the whole eastern end of the market-place, and flanked on one side by an ancient dwelling-house—once the official residence of the Mayors of Hathelsborough—and on the other by a more modern but still old-world building, long used as a bank, Hathelsborough Moot Hall presents the appearance of a mediæval fortress, as though its original builders had meant it to be a possible refuge for the townsfolk against masterful Baron or marauding Scot. From the market-place itself there is but one entrance to it; an arched doorway opening upon a low-roofed stone hall; in place of a door there are heavy gates of iron, with a smaller wicket-gate set in their midst; from the stone hall a stone stair leads to the various chambers above; in the outer walls the windows are high and narrow; each is filled with old painted glass. A strong, grim building, this; and when the iron gates are locked, as they are every night when the curfew bell—an ancient institution jealously kept up in Hathelsborough—rings from St. Hathelswide's tower, a man might safely wager his all to nothing that only modern artillery could effect an entrance to its dark and gloomy interior.

On a certain April evening, the time being within an hour of curfew—which, to be exact, is rung in Hathelsborough every night, all the year round, sixty minutes after sunset, despite the fact that it is nowadays but a meaningless if time-honoured ceremony—Bunning, caretaker and custodian of the Moot Hall, stood without its gates, smoking his pipe and looking around him. He was an ex-Army man, Bunning, who had seen service in many parts of the world, and was frequently heard to declare that although he had set eyes on many men and many cities he had never found the equal of Hathelsborough folk, nor seen a fairer prospect than that on which he now gazed. The truth was that Bunning was a Hathelsborough man, and having wandered about a good deal during his military service, from Aldershot to Gibraltar, and Gibraltar to Malta, and Malta to Cairo, and Cairo to Peshawar, was well content to settle down in a comfortable berth amidst the familiar scenes of his childhood. But anyone who loves the ancient country towns of England would have agreed with Bunning that Hathelsborough market-place made an unusually attractive picture on a spring evening. There were the old gabled houses, quaintly roofed and timbered; there the lace-like masonry of High Cross; there the slender proportions of Low Cross; there the mighty bulk of the great church built over the very spot whereon the virgin saint suffered martyrdom; there, towering above the gables on the north side, the well-preserved masonry of the massive Norman Keep of Hathelsborough Castle; there a score of places and signs with which Bunning had kept up a close acquaintance in youth and borne in mind when far away under other skies. And around the church tower, and at the base of the tall keep, were the elms for which the town was famous; mighty giants of the tree world, just now bursting into leaf, and above them the rooks and jackdaws circling and calling above the hum and murmur of the town.

To Bunning's right and left, going away from the eastern corner of the market-place, lay two narrow streets, called respectively River Gate and Meadow Gate—one led downwards to the little river on the southern edge of the town; the other ran towards the wide-spread grass-lands that stretched on its northern boundary. And as he stood looking about him, he saw a man turn the corner of Meadow Gate—a man who came hurrying along in his direction, walking sharply, his eyes bent on the flags beneath his feet, his whole attitude that of one in deep reflection. At sight of him Bunning put his pipe in his pocket, gave himself the soldier's shake and, as the man drew near, stood smartly to attention. The man looked up—Bunning's right hand went up to his cap in the old familiar fashion; that was how, for many a long year of service, he had saluted his superiors.

There was nothing very awe-compelling about the person whom the caretaker thus greeted with so much punctilious ceremony. He was a little, somewhat insignificant-looking man—at first sight. His clothes were well-worn and carelessly put on; the collar of his under-coat projected high above that of his overcoat; his necktie had slipped round towards one ear; his linen was frayed; his felt hat, worn anyway, needed brushing; he wore cotton gloves, too big for him. He carried a mass of papers and books under one arm; the other hand grasped an umbrella which had grown green and grey in service. He might have been all sorts of insignificant things: a clerk, going homeward from his work; a tax-gatherer, carrying his documents; a rent-collector, anxious about a defaulting tenant—anything of that sort. But Bunning knew him for Mr. Councillor John Wallingford, at that time Mayor of Hathelsborough. He knew something else too—that Wallingford, in spite of his careless attire and very ordinary appearance, was a remarkable man. He was not a native of the old town; although he was, for twelve months at any rate, its first magistrate, and consequently the most important person in the place, Hathelsborough folk still ranked him as a stranger, for he had only been amongst them for some twelve years. But during that time he had made his mark in the town—coming there as managing clerk to a firm of solicitors, he had ultimately succeeded to the practice which he had formerly managed for its two elderly partners, now retired. At an early period of his Hathelsborough career he had taken keen and deep interest in the municipal affairs of his adopted town and had succeeded in getting a seat on the Council, where he had quickly made his influence felt. And in the previous November he had been elected—by a majority of one vote—to the Mayoralty and had so become the four hundred and eighty-first burgess of the ancient borough to wear the furred mantle and gold chain which symbolized his dignity. He looked very different in these grandeurs to what he did in his everyday attire, but whether in the Mayoral robes or in his carelessly worn clothes any close observer would have seen that Wallingford was a sharp, shrewd man with all his wits about him—a close-seeing, concentrated man, likely to go through, no matter what obstacles rose in his path, with anything that he took in hand.

Bunning was becoming accustomed to these evening visits of the Mayor to the Moot Hall. Of late, Wallingford had come there often, going upstairs to the Mayor's Parlour and remaining there alone until ten or eleven o'clock. Always he brought books and papers with him; always, as he entered, he gave the custodian the same command—no one was to disturb him, on any pretext whatever. But on this occasion, Bunning heard a different order.

"Oh, Bunning," said the Mayor, as he came up to the iron gates before which the ex-sergeant-major stood, still at attention, "I shall be in the Mayor's Parlour for some time to-night, and I'm not to be disturbed, as usual. Except, however, for this—I'm expecting my cousin, Mr. Brent, from London, this evening, and I left word at my rooms that if he came any time before ten he was to be sent on here. So, if he comes, show him up to me. But nobody else, Bunning."

"Very good, your Worship," replied Bunning. "I'll see to it. Mr. Brent, from London."

"You've seen him before," said the Mayor. "He was here last Christmas—tall young fellow, clean-shaven. You'll know him."

He hurried inside the stone hall and went away by the stairs to the upper regions of the gloomy old place, and Bunning, with another salute, turned from him, pulled out his pipe and began to smoke again. He was never tired of looking out on that old market-place; even in the quietest hours of the evening there was always something going on, something to be seen, trivial things, no doubt, but full of interest to Bunning: folks coming and going; young people sweethearting; acquaintances passing and re-passing; these things were of more importance to his essentially parochial mind than affairs of State.

Presently came along another Corporation official, whom Bunning knew as well as he knew the Mayor, an official who, indeed, was known all over the town, and familiar to everybody, from the mere fact that he was always attired in a livery the like of which he and his predecessors had been wearing for at least two hundred years. This was Spizey, a consequential person who, in the borough rolls for the time being, was entered as Bellman, Town Crier, and Mace Bearer. Spizey was a big, fleshy man, with a large solemn face, a ponderous manner, and small eyes. His ample figure was habited at all seasons of the year in a voluminous cloak which had much gold lace on its front and cuffs and many capes about the shoulders; he wore a three-cornered laced hat on his bullet head, and carried a tall staff, not unlike a wand, in his hand. There were a few—very few—progressive folk in Hathelsborough who regarded Spizey and his semi-theatrical attire as an anachronism, and openly derided both, but so far nobody had dared to advocate the abolition of him and his livery. He was part and parcel of the high tradition, a reminder of the fact that Hathelsborough possessed a Charter of Incorporation centuries before its now more popular and important neighbouring boroughs gained theirs, and in his own opinion the discontinuance of his symbols of office would have been little less serious than the sale of the Mayor's purple robe and chain of solid gold: Spizey, thus attired, was Hathelsborough. And, as he was not slow to remind awe-stricken audiences at his favourite tavern, Mayors, Aldermen and Councillors were, so to speak, creatures of the moment—the Mayor, for example, was His Worship for twelve months and plain Mr. Chipps the grocer ever after—but he, Spizey, was a Permanent Institution, and not to be moved.

Spizey was on his way to his favourite tavern now, to smoke his pipe—which it was beneath his dignity to do in public—and drink his glass amongst his cronies, but he stopped to exchange the time of day with Bunning, whom he regarded with patronizing condescension, as being a lesser light than himself. And having remarked that this was a fine evening, after the usual fashion of British folk, who are for ever wasting time and breath in drawing each other's attention to obvious facts, he cocked one of his small eyes at the stairs behind the iron gates.

"Worship up there?" he asked, transferring his gaze to Bunning.

"Just gone up," answered Bunning. "Five minutes ago."

The Mace-Bearer looked up the market-place, down River Gate and along Meadow Gate. Having assured himself that there was nobody within fifty yards, he sank his mellow voice to a melodious whisper, and poked Bunning in the ribs with a pudgy forefinger.

"Ah!" he said confidingly. "Just so! Again! Now, as a Corporation official—though not, to be sure, of the long standing that I am—what do you make of it?"

"Make of what?" demanded the caretaker.

Spizey came still nearer to his companion. He was one of those men who when disposed to confidential communication have a trick of getting as close as possible to their victims, and of poking and prodding them. Again he stuck his finger into Bunning's ribs.

"Make of what, says you!" he breathed. "Ay, to be sure! Why, of all this here coming up at night to the Moot Hall, and sitting, all alone, in that there Mayor's Parlour, not to be disturbed by nobody, whosomever! What's it all mean?"

"No business of mine," replied Bunning. "Nor of anybody's but his own. That is, so far as I'm aware of. What about it?"

Spizey removed his three-cornered hat, took a many-coloured handkerchief out of it, and wiped his forehead—he was in a state of perpetual warmth, and had a habit of mopping his brow when called on for mental effort.

"Ah!" he said. "That's just it—what about it, do you say? Well, what I say is this here—'taint in accordance with precedent! Precedent, mark you!—which is what a ancient Corporation of this sort goes by. Where should we all be if what was done by our fathers before us wasn't done by us? What has been, must be! Take me, don't I do what's been done in this here town of Hathelsborough for time immemorial? Well, then!"

"That's just it," said Bunning. "Well, then? Why shouldn't his Worship come here at night and stick up there as long as he likes? What's against it?"

"Precedent!" retorted Spizey. "Ain't never been done before—never! Haven't I been in the office I hold nigh on to forty years? Seen a many mayors, aldermen and common councillors come and go in my time. But never do I remember a Mayor coming here to this Moot Hall of a night, with books and papers—which is dangerous matters at any time, except in their proper place, such as my proclamations and the town dockyments—and sitting there for hours, doing—what?"

Bunning shook his head. He was pulling steadily at his pipe as he listened, and he gazed meditatively at the smoke curling away from it and his pipe.

"Well?" he said, after a pause. "And what do you make of it? You'll have some idea, I reckon, a man of your importance."

Once more the Mace-Bearer looked round, and once more applied his forefinger to Bunning's waistline. His voice grew deep with confidence.

"Mischief!" he whispered. "Mischief! That's what I make of it! He's up to something—something what'll be dangerous to the vested interests in this here ancient borough. Ain't he allus been one o' them Radicals—what wants to pull down everything that's made this here country what it is? Didn't he put in his last election address, when he was a candidate for the Council, for the Castle Ward, that he was all for retrenchment and reform? Didn't he say, when he was elected Mayor—by a majority of one vote!—that he intended to go thoroughly into the financial affairs of the town, and do away with a lot of expenses which in his opinion wasn't necessary? Oh, I've heard talk—men in high office, like me, hears a deal. Why, I've heard it said that he's been heard to say, in private, that it was high time to abolish me!"

Bunning's mouth opened a little. He was a man of simple nature, and the picture of Hathelsborough without Spizey and his livery appalled him.

"Bless me!" he exclaimed.

"To be sure!" said Spizey. "It's beyond comprehension! To abolish me!—what, in a manner of speaking, has existed I don't know how long. I ain't a man—I'm a office! Who'd cry things that was lost—at that there Cross? Who'd pull the big bell on great occasions, and carry round the little 'un when there was proclamations to be made? Who'd walk in front o' the Mayor's procession, with the Mace—what was give to this here town by King Henry VII, his very self? Abolish me? Why, it's as bad as talking about abolishing the Bible!"

"It's the age for that sort of thing," remarked Bunning. "I seen a deal of it in the Army. Abolished all sorts o' things, they have, there. I never seen no good come of it, neither. I'm all for keeping up the good old things—can't better 'em, in my opinion. And, as you say, that there mace of ours—'tis ancient!"

"Nobody but one o' these here Radicals and levellers could talk o' doing away with such proper institutions," affirmed Spizey. "But I tell yer—I've heard of it. He said—but you'd scarce believe it!—there was no need for a town crier, nor a bellman, and, as for this mace, it could be carried on Mayor's Day by a policeman! Fancy that, now—our mace carried by a policeman!"

"Dear, dear!" said Bunning. "Don't seem to fit in, that! However," he added consolingly, "if they did abolish you, you'd no doubt get a handsome pension."

"Pension!" exclaimed Spizey. "That's a detail!—it's the office I'm a-considering of. What this here free and ancient borough 'ud look like, without me, I cannot think!"

He shook his head and went sadly away, and Bunning, suddenly remembering that it was about his supper-time, prepared to retreat into the room which he and his wife shared, at the end of the stone hall. But as he entered the gates, a quick firm footstep sounded behind him, and he turned to see a smart, alert-looking young man approaching. Bunning recognized him as a stranger whom he had seen once or twice before, at intervals, in company with Wallingford. For the second time that night he saluted.

"Looking for the Mayor, sir?" he asked, throwing the gate open. "His Worship's upstairs—I was to show you up. Mr. Brent, isn't it, sir?"

"Right!" replied the other. "My cousin left word I was to join him here. Whereabouts is he in this old fortress of yours?"

"This way, sir," said Bunning. "Fortress, you call it, sir, but it's more like a rabbit-warren! No end of twists and turns—that is, once you get inside it."

He preceded Richard Brent up the stone staircase, along narrow corridors and passages, until he came to a door, at which he knocked gently. Receiving no reply he opened it and went in, motioning Brent to follow. But before Bunning had well crossed the threshold he started back with a sharp cry. The Mayor was there, but he was lying face forward across the desk—lifeless.

CHAPTER II

THE CAMBRIC HANDKERCHIEF

In the Mayor's Parlour

Bunning knew the Mayor was dead before that cry of surprise had passed his lips. In his time he had seen many dead men—sometimes it was a bullet, sometimes a bayonet; he knew the signs of what follows on the swift passage of one and the sharp thrust of the other. In his first glance into the room he had been quick to notice the limp hand hanging across the edge of the desk, the way in which Wallingford's head lay athwart the mass of papers over which he had collapsed in falling forward from his chair—that meant death. And the old soldier's observant eye had seen more than that—over the litter of documents which lay around the still figure were great crimson stains. The caretaker's cry changed to articulated speech.

"Murder! The Mayor's been murdered!"

Brent, a strongly-built and active man, pushed by, and made for the desk. He was going to lay a hand on his cousin's shoulder, but Bunning stopped him.

"For God's sake, Mr. Brent, don't touch him!" he exclaimed. "Let him be, sir, till the police——" He paused, staring round the gloomy, oak-panelled room from the walls of which the portraits of various dignitaries looked down. "Who on earth can have done it?" he muttered. "It's—it's not three-quarters of an hour since he came up here!"

"Alone?" asked Brent.

"Alone, sir! And I'll take my solemn oath that nobody was here, waiting for him. I'd been in this room myself, not five minutes before he came," said Dunning. "It was empty of course."

Brent disregarded the caretaker's admonition and laid a finger on the dead man's forehead. But Bunning pointed to a dark stain, still spreading, on the back of the Mayor's coat—a well-worn garment of grey tweed.

"Look there, sir," he whispered. "He's been run through the body from behind—right through the heart!—as he sat in his chair. Murder!"

"Who should murder him?" demanded Brent.

Bunning made no answer. He was looking round. There were three doors into that room; he glanced at each, shaking his head after each glance.

"We'd best get the police, at once, Mr. Brent," he said. "The police station's just at the back—there's a way down to it from outside this parlour. I'll run down now. You, sir——"

"I'll stop here," answered Brent. "But get a doctor, will you? I want to know——"

"Dr. Wellesley, the police-surgeon, is next door," replied Brent. "The police'll get him. But he's beyond all doctors, Mr. Brent! Instantaneous—that! I know!"

He hurried out of the room, and Brent, left alone with the dead man, looked at him once again wonderingly. Cousins though they were, he and Wallingford knew little of each other; their acquaintance, such as it was, had not been deep enough to establish any particular affection between them. But since Wallingford's election as Mayor of Hathelsborough Brent, by profession a journalist in London, had twice spent a week-end with him in the old town, and had learnt something of his plans for a reform of certain matters connected with the administration of its affairs. They had discussed these things on the occasion of his last visit, and now, as he stood by the dead man, Brent remembered certain words which Wallingford had spoken.

"There are things that I can do," Wallingford had said, with some confidence. And then he had added, with a cynical laugh, "But there are other things that—why, it would be, literally, as much as my life's worth to even try to undermine them!"

That was now four months since, but Brent remembered. And as he stood there, waiting for help which would be useless, he began to wonder if Wallingford, eager for reform, had attempted anything likely to bring him into personal danger. Certainly, from all that

Brent knew of him, he was the sort of man who, having set himself to a task, would let nothing stop him in accomplishing it; he was the sort of man too, Brent thought, who had a genius for making enemies: such men always have. But murder? Cold-blooded, deliberate, apparently well-planned murder! Yet there it was, before him. The Mayor of Hathelsborough had walked up into that room, sacred to his official uses and suggestive in its atmosphere and furniture of his great dignity, and had settled down to his desk, only to be assassinated by some enemy who had taken good care to perform his crime with swiftness and thoroughness.

The sound of heavy footsteps on the stairs outside the half-open door aroused Brent from these melancholy speculations; he turned to see Bunning coming back, attended by several men, and foremost among them, Hawthwaite, superintendent of the borough police, whom Brent had met once or twice on his previous visits to the town. Hawthwaite, a big, bearded man, was obviously upset, if not actually frightened; his ruddy face had paled under the caretaker's startling news, and he drew his breath sharply as he entered the Mayor's Parlour and caught sight of the still figure lying across the big desk in the—middle.

"God bless my life and soul, Mr. Brent!" he exclaimed in hushed tones as he tiptoed nearer to the dead and the living. "What's all this? You found the Mayor dead—you and Bunning? Why—why——"

"We found him as you see him," answered Brent. "He's been murdered! There's no doubt about this, superintendent."

Hawthwaite bent down fearfully towards the dead man, and then looked round at Bunning.

"When did he come up here?" he asked sharply.

"About three-quarters of an hour before Mr. Brent came, sir," replied Bunning. "He came up to me as I was standing outside the gates, smoking my pipe, and said that he was going up to the Mayor's Parlour, and nobody was to be allowed to disturb him, but that if his cousin, Mr. Brent, came, he was to be shown up. Mr. Brent came and I brought him up, and we found his Worship as you see."

"Somebody's been lying in wait for him," muttered Hawthwaite. "Hid in this room!"

"Nobody here five minutes before he came up, sir," affirmed Bunning. "I was up here myself. There was nobody in here, and nobody in this part of the building."

Hawthwaite looked round the room, and Brent looked with him. It was a big room, panelled in old oak to half the height of its walls; above the panelling hung numerous portraits of past occupants of the Mayoral chair and some old engravings of scenes in the town. A wide, old-fashioned fire-place stood to the right of the massive desk; on either side of it were recesses, in each of which there was a door. Hawthwaite stepped across to these in turn and tried them; each was locked from the inside; he silently pointed to the keys.

"The door to the stairs was open, sir," remarked Bunning. "I mean his Worship hadn't locked himself in, as I have known him do."

Hawthwaite nodded. Then he nudged Brent's elbow, looking sideways at the dead man.

"Been done as he sat writing in his chair," he muttered. "Look—the pen's fallen from his fingers as he fell forward. Queer!"

A policeman came hurrying into the room, pulling himself up as he saw what was there. His voice instinctively hushed.

"Dr. Wellesley's just gone down Meadow Gate, sir," he announced. "They've sent for him to come here at once."

In the Mayor's Parlour

"Unless!" murmured the superintendent. "Still——"

Then the five or six men present stood, silently waiting. Some stared about the room, as if wondering at its secret: some occasionally took covert glances at its central figure. One of the three high, narrow windows was open: Brent distinctly heard the murmur of children playing in the streets outside. And suddenly, from the tower of St. Hathelswide, at the other end of the market-place, curfew began to ring.

"He's coming, sir!" whispered the policeman who stood near the door. "On the stairs, sir."

Brent turned as Dr. Wellesley came hurrying into the room; a tall, clean-shaven, fresh-coloured man, who went straight to the desk, looked at what he found there, and turned quickly on the men grouped around.

"How long is it since he was found?" he asked abruptly.

"Ten or twelve minutes," answered Brent.

"Dead then?"

"Yes," said Brent. "I should say—of course, I don't speak professionally—but I should think he'd been dead at least half an hour."

The doctor glanced at the superintendent.

"We must have him taken down to the mortuary," he said. "Let some of you men stay here with me, and send another for my assistant and for Dr. Barber."

The superintendent gave some orders, and touching Brent's arm motioned him to follow outside the room.

"This is a bad business, Mr. Brent!" he said as they paused at the head of the stair. "That's murder, sir! But how on earth did the murderer get in there? Bunning tells me that he himself was standing outside the iron gates at the entrance to the Moot Hall from the time the Mayor entered until you came. He asserts that nobody entered the place by those gates."

"I suppose there are other means of entrance?" suggested Brent.

"Doubtful if anybody could get in by them at this hour of the evening," answered the superintendent. "But there are two ways by which anybody could get to the Mayor's Parlour. They're both what you might call complicated. I'll show you them. Come this way."

He led Brent across a corridor that branched off from the head of the stone staircase, and presently stopped at a big double door.

"This is the Council Chamber," he said, as they entered a spacious apartment. "You see that door in the far corner, over there? There's a staircase leads down from that to the rooms that Bunning and his wife occupy as caretakers—a back stairs, in fact. But nobody can come up it, and through the Council Chamber, and along the corridor to the Mayor's Parlour without first coming through Bunning's rooms, that's flat. As for the other—well, it's still more unlikely."

He led Brent out of the Council Chamber and farther along to another door, which he flung open as he motioned his companion to enter.

"This is the Borough Court," he said. "Magistrates' bench, solicitors' table, and all the rest of it. And there's the dock, where we put the prisoners. Now, Mr. Brent, there's a staircase—a corkscrew staircase, modern, of ironwork—in the corner of that dock which leads down to the cells. And that's the second way by which you could get to the Mayor's Parlour. But just fancy what that means! A man who wanted to reach the Mayor's Parlour by that means of approach would have to enter the police station from St. Laurence Lane, at the back of the Moot Hall, pass the charge office, pass my office, go along a passage in which he'd be pretty certain to meet somebody, come up that stairs into the dock there, cross the court and—so on. That's not likely! And yet, those are the only ways by which there's access to the Mayor's Parlour except by the big staircase from the iron gates."

"What is certain," observed Brent, "is that the murderer did get to the Mayor's Parlour. And what seems more important just now is the question—how did he get away from it, unobserved? If Bunning is certain that no one entered by the front between my cousin's arrival and my coming, he is equally certain that no one left. Is it possible that anyone left by the police station entrance?"

"We'll soon settle that point!" answered Hawthwaite. "Come down there."

He opened the door of the dock and led Brent down an iron staircase into an arched and vaulted hall at its foot, whence they proceeded along various gloomy passages towards a heavy, iron-studded door. Near this, a police constable stood writing at a tall desk; the superintendent approached and spoke to him. Presently he turned back to Brent.

"There's nobody that he doesn't know has been in or out of this place during the whole of the evening," he said. "He's been on duty there since six o'clock. Nobody has entered—or left—during the time that's elapsed."

"I never supposed they had," remarked Brent. "The thing's been done in much cleverer fashion than that! As I said before, what we do know is that the murderer got to the Mayor's Parlour, and that he got away from it!"

Hawthwaite shook his head, with a puzzled expression overspreading his somewhat heavy and unimaginative features.

"Ay, but how?" he said. "How?"

"That's a job for you," replied Brent, with a suggestive glance. "And, if I might suggest it, why not make a thorough examination of the Moot Hall? My cousin showed me over it when I was here last, and I remember some queer places in it."

"There are queer places in it," admitted Hawthwaite. "But it's hardly likely the murderer would hang about after doing what he did. Of course I'll have the whole place searched thoroughly—every inch of it!—for any possible clues and traces. We shall neglect nothing in a case of this sort, I can assure you, Mr. Brent. I—But come into my office."

He led the way into a drab-walled, official-looking apartment, curiously suggestive of the lesser and meaner forms of crime, and pointed to a chair.

"Sit down," he said. "As I was about to say——"

"Oughtn't one to be doing something?" interrupted Brent, refusing the chair. "That's what I feel anyway. Only what can one do?"

"Ah, that's just it!" exclaimed Hawthwaite. "You may feel as energetic as you will, but what can you do? The doctors are doing the absolutely necessary things at present; as for me, all I can do is to search for clues and traces, as I suggested, and make all possible inquiries. But there you are, we've nothing to go on—nothing, I mean, that would identify."

Brent gave the superintendent a keen glance.

"Between ourselves," he said, "have you any reason for suspecting anyone?"

Hawthwaite started. His surprise was genuine enough.

"For suspecting anyone?" he exclaimed. "Good Lord, no, Mr. Brent! His Worship, poor man, wasn't exactly popular in the town—with a certain section, that is—but I couldn't believe that there's man or woman in the place would wish him harm! No, sir—in my opinion this is outside work!"

"Somewhat doubtful whether any outsider could obtain the apparently very accurate knowledge of Hathelsborough Moot Hall which the murderer of my cousin evidently possessed, isn't it?" suggested Brent. "I should say the guilty person is some one who knows the place extremely well!"

Before the superintendent could reply, his partly-open door was further opened, and a little, bustling, eager-faced man, who wore large spectacles and carried a pencil behind his right ear, looked in. Brent recognized him as another of the half-dozen Hathelsborough men whose acquaintance he had made on former visits—Peppermore, the hard-worked editor-reporter of the one local newspaper. Wallingford had introduced him to Peppermore in the smoking-room of the *Chancellor* Hotel, and Peppermore, who rarely got the chance of talking to London journalists, had been loquacious and ingratiating. His expressive eyebrows—prominent features of his somewhat odd countenance—went up now as he caught sight of Brent standing on the superintendent's hearth-rug. He came quickly into the room.

"Mr. Brent!" he exclaimed. "No idea you were here, sir. My profound sympathy, Mr. Brent! Dear, dear! what a truly terrible affair!" Then, his professional instincts getting the better of him, he turned on Hawthwaite, at the same time pulling out a note-book. "What are the details, Mr. Superintendent?" he asked. "I just met one of your officers, going for Dr. Barber; he gave me the scantiest information, so I hurried to see you."

"And I can't give you any more," replied Hawthwaite. "There are no details yet, my lad! All we know is that the Mayor was found dead in the Mayor's Parlour half an hour ago, and that he's been murdered. You'll have to wait for the rest."

"We don't go to press till 12.30," remarked Peppermore, unperturbed by this curtness. "Perhaps by then you can give me more news, Mr. Superintendent? Murdered! The Mayor of Hathelsborough! Now that's something that's unique in the history of the town, I believe. I was looking over the records not so long since, and I don't remember coming across any entry of such an event as this. Unparalleled!"

Hawthwaite made no reply. At that moment a policeman put his head inside the door and asked him to go to Dr. Wellesley, and he went off, leaving the two newspaper men together. Brent looked at Peppermore and suddenly put an abrupt question to him.

"I guess you'll know," he said meaningly. "Was my cousin unpopular in this place?"

Peppermore turned his big spectacles on his questioner and sank his voice to a whisper.

"Between ourselves," he answered, "in some quarters—very!"

"Of late, I suppose?" suggested Brent.

"Become—gradually—more and more so, Mr. Brent," said Peppermore. "You see, he only got elected Mayor by one vote. That meant that half the Council was against him. Against his policy and ideas, you know. Of course he was a reformer. Those who didn't like him called him a meddler. And in my experience of this place—ten years—it's a bad thing to meddle in Hathelsborough affairs. Too many vested interests, sir! Certainly—amongst some people—Mr. Wallingford was not at all popular. But—murder!"

"There are plenty of people who don't stick at that," remarked Brent. "But you wanted information. I'll give you some." He went on to tell how he and Bunning had found Wallingford, and of the difficulties of access to the Mayor's Parlour. "The thing is," he concluded, "how did the murderer get in, and how did he get away?"

"Queer!" admitted Peppermore, scribbling fast in his note-book. "That's a nice job for the detectives. Looks like a skilfully-planned, premeditated job too——"

Hawthwaite came in again, carrying something in his hand, concealed by a piece of brown paper. His face betokened a discovery.

In the Mayor's Parlour

"Look here!" he said. "No secret about it—you can mention it, Peppermore. Just after you and I had gone out of the Mayor's Parlour, Mr. Brent, Bunning picked something out of the hearth, where it was half-burnt, and what's left charred, and gave it to Dr. Wellesley. See!"

He laid the brown paper on his desk, turned back the edges, and revealed part of a fine cambric pocket-handkerchief, crumpled and blood-stained, charred and blackened.

"Without a doubt," he whispered confidentially, "this belonged to the murderer! He got blood on his hands—he wiped them on this, and threw it away on the fire, to burn. And this half is not burned!"

CHAPTER III

THE TANNERY HOUSE

During a moment's impressive silence the three men, standing side by side at Hawthwaite's desk, stared at the blood-stained memento of the crime. Each was thinking the same thought—there, before them, was the life-blood of the man who little more than an hour previously had been full of energy, forcefulness, ambition. It was Peppermore who first spoke, in an awe-stricken voice.

"You'll take care of that, Mr. Superintendent?" he said. "A clue!"

"I should just think so!" exclaimed Hawthwaite. He picked up a box of letter-paper which lay close by, emptied it of its contents, and lifted the fragment of handkerchief by a corner. "That goes into my safe," he continued, as he placed his find in the box. "A clue, as you say, and an important one. That, as you may observe, is no common article; it's a gentleman's handkerchief—fine cambric. If it had only been the other part of it, now, there'd probably have been a name on it, or initials wove into it: there's nothing of that sort, you see, on what's left. But it's something, and it may lead to a good deal."

He put the cardboard box away in a safe and locked it up; putting the key in his pocket, he gave Brent an informing glance.

"I've had a word or two with the medical men while I was out there," he said confidentially. "They say there's no doubt as to how he was killed. The murderer, they're confident, was standing behind him as he himself was either writing or looking over the papers on his desk, and suddenly thrust a knife clean through his shoulders. They say death would be instantaneous."

"A knife!" muttered Brent.

"Well," continued Hawthwaite, "as regards that, there are all sorts of knives. It would be a long, thin weapon, said Dr. Wellesley; and Dr. Barber, he suggested that it was the sort of wound that would be caused by one of those old-fashioned rapiers. And they did say, both of them, that it had been used—whatever the weapon was—with great force: gone clean through."

Peppermore was listening to these gruesome details with all the ardour of the born news-seeker. But Brent turned away.

"Is there anything I can do?" he asked.

"Why, there isn't," replied Hawthwaite. "The fact is, there is nothing to do outside our work. The doctors are doing theirs, and there'll have to be an inquest of course. I've sent to notify Mr. Seagrave, the coroner, already, and I'm having a thorough search made of the Moot Hall, and making inquiries about his Worship's last movements. There's nothing more can be done, at present. One of my men has gone round to tell his landlady. It's a fortunate thing, Mr. Brent," he added with a knowing look, "that your cousin wasn't a married man! This would have been a fine thing to have to break to a man's wife and family! About relations, now, Mr. Brent, you'll know what to do? I know nothing about his private affairs."

"Yes," answered Brent. "But I'm much more concerned, just now, about his public affairs. It seems to me—indeed, it's no use trying to disguise it—that this has arisen out of the fact that as Mayor of Hathelsborough he was concerning himself in bringing about some drastic reforms in the town. You probably know yourself that he wasn't popular——"

"Yes, yes, Mr. Brent," interrupted Hawthwaite.

"But then, you know, murder——! I can't think there's anybody in this place would carry their likes to that length! Murder!"

"You don't know," said Brent. "But, at any rate, I'm my cousin's nearest blood-relation, and I'm going to find out who killed him, if it's humanly possible. Now who is there in the town who knows most about his public affairs—who is there who's most conversant with whatever it was that he had in hand?"

Hawthwaite seemed to consider matters.

"Well, Alderman Crood, the tanner, is the Deputy-Mayor," he replied at last. "I should say he's as good a man to go to as anybody, Mr. Brent. He's chairman of the Financial Committee too; and it was in financial matters that Mr. Wallingford was wanting to make these reforms you've mentioned. If there's anything known—I mean that I don't know—Alderman Crood's the most likely man to know it."

"Alderman Crood," remarked Peppermore softly, "knows everything that goes on in Hathelsborough—everything!"

"So to speak; so to speak!" said Hawthwaite. "There are things of course——"

"Where does Alderman Crood live?" asked Brent. Already he was moving towards the door. "As I can do nothing here, I'll go to him at once. I'm not going to leave a stone unturned in this matter, superintendent."

"Quite right, Mr. Brent, quite right! Neither will I," asserted Hawthwaite. "Alderman Crood lives by his tannery—the far end of the town. Anybody'll show you the place, once you're past the big church."

"I'm going that way," remarked Peppermore. "Come with me, Mr. Brent." He led Brent out into St. Lawrence Lane, a narrow thoroughfare at the back of the Moot Hall, and turning a corner, emerged on the market-place, over which the night shadows had now fallen. "A terrible affair, this, Mr. Brent!" he said as they walked along. "And a most extraordinary one too—it'll be more than a nine days' wonder here. A deep mystery, sir, and I question if you'll get much light on it where you're going."

"You said that Alderman Crood knew everything," observed Brent.

"Ay!" answered Peppermore, with a short laugh. "But that isn't to say that he'll tell everything—or anything! Alderman Crood, Mr. Brent, is the closest man in this town—which is saying a good deal. Since I came here, sir, ten years ago, I've learnt much—and if you'll drop in at the *Monitor* office any time you like, Mr. Brent—mornings preferable—I'll give you the benefit of my experience: Hathelsborough folk, sir, are, in my opinion, the queerest lot in all England. But you want to see Alderman Crood—now, go to the end of the market-place, turn down Barley Market, and drop a hundred yards or so down the hill at the end—then you'll smell Crood's tan-yard, even if you don't see it. His is the big, solid-looking house at the side—you can't miss it."

The editor-reporter shot up an alley at his left, at the head of which was a lighted window with Monitor Office on it in black letters; and Brent went on his way to seek the Deputy-Mayor. As he passed Low Cross, and the east end of the great church, and turned into the wide, irregular space called Barley Market, he tried to analyse his feelings about the tragic event on which he had chanced without warning. He had left Fleet Street early that afternoon, thinking of nothing but a few days' pleasant change, and here he was, in that quiet, old-world town, faced with the fact that his kinsman and host had been brutally murdered at the very hour of his arrival. He was conscious of a fierce if dull resentment—the resentment of a tribesman who finds one of his clan done to death, and knows that the avenging of blood is on his shoulders from henceforth. He had no particular affection for his cousin, and therefore no great sense of personal loss, but Wallingford after all was of his breed, and he must bring his murderer to justice.

Alderman Crood's house, big, broad, high, loomed up across him as the odours of the tan-yard at its side and rear assailed his nostrils. As he went towards it, the front door opened a little, and a man came out. He and Brent met in the light of a street lamp, and Brent recognized a policeman whom he had seen in the Mayor's Parlour. The man recognized him, and touched his helmet. Brent stopped.

"Oh," he said, "have you been to tell Mr. Crood of what has happened?"

"Just that, sir," replied the policeman. "He's Deputy-Mayor, sir."

"I know," said Brent. "Then, he's at home?"

"Yes, sir."

Brent was going forward, but a sudden curiosity seized on him. He paused, glancing at the policeman suggestively.

"Did—did Mr. Crood say anything?" he asked.

The policeman shook his head.

"Nothing, sir, except that he supposed Superintendent Hawthwaite was seeing to everything."

"Did you happen to tell him that I was here?"

"I did, sir; I said his Worship's cousin from London had just come. No harm, sir, I hope?"

"Not a bit—glad you did," said Brent. "He'll expect me."

He said good night to the man and walked forward to Alderman Crood's door. It was like the house to which it gave entrance—very high and broad, a massive affair, topped by a glass transom, behind which a light, very dim and feeble, was burning. Brent felt for and rang a bell, and heard it ring somewhere far off in the house. Then he waited; waited so long that he was about to ring again, when he heard a bolt being withdrawn inside the big door; then another. Each creaked in a fashion that suggested small use, and the need of a little oil. The door opened, and he found himself confronting a girl, who stood holding a small lamp in her hand; behind her, at the far end of a gloomy, cavernous hall a swinging lamp, turned low, silhouetted her figure.

Something about the girl made Brent look at her with more attention than he would ordinarily have given. She was a tallish girl, whose figure would have been unusually good had it been properly filled out; as it was, she was thin, but only too thin for her proportions—her thinness, had she been three inches shorter, would have passed for a graceful slenderness. But Brent took this in at a glance; his attention was more particularly concentrated on the girl's face—a delicate oval, framed in a mass of dark hair. She was all dark—dark hair, an olive complexion, large, unusually lustrous dark eyes, fringed by long soft lashes, an almost dark rose-tint on her cheeks. And in the look which she gave him there was something as soft as her eyes, which were those of a shy animal—something appealing, pathetic. He glanced hastily at her attire—simple, even to plainness—and wondered who she was, and what was her exact status in that big house, which seemed to require the services of a staff of domestics.

Brent asked for Alderman Crood. The girl glanced towards the end of the hall and then looked at him doubtfully.

"What name?" she inquired in tones that were little above a whisper.

"My name's Brent," the caller answered, in a clear, loud voice. Somehow, he had a suspicion that Crood was listening at the other end of the cavernous hall. "I am Mr. Wallingford's cousin."

The girl gave him a curious glance and motioning him to wait, went away up the hall to a door which stood partly open, revealing a lighted interior. She disappeared within; came out again, walked a little way towards Brent, and spoke with a timid smile.

"Will you please come this way?" she said. "Mr. Crood will see you."

Brent strode up the hall, the girl, preceding him, pushed open the door which she had just left. He walked into a big room and, through a fog of tobacco smoke, saw that he was in the presence of three men, who sat in arm-chairs round a hearth whereon a big fire of logs blazed. Behind their chairs a table was set out with decanters and glasses, a tobacco-jar and cigar-boxes: clearly he had interrupted a symposium of a friendly and social sort.

The visitor's eyes went straight to the obvious master of the house, a big, heavily-built, massive-framed man of sixty or thereabouts, who sat in state on the right-hand side of the hearth. Brent took in certain details of his appearance at a glance: the broad, flabby, parchment-hued face, wide mouth, square jaw, and small, shrewd eyes; the suit of dead-black broadcloth, and the ample black neckcloth swathed about an old-fashioned collar; he noted, too, the fob which dangled from Alderman Crood's waist, and its ancient seals and ornaments. A survival of the past, Alderman Crood, he thought, in outward seeming, but there was that in his watchful expression which has belonged to man in every age.

The small shrewd eyes, in their turn, measured up Brent as he crossed the threshold, and Crood, seeing what he would have described as a well-dressed young gentleman who was evidently used to superior society, did what he would certainly not have done for any man in Hathelsborough—he rose from his chair and stretched out a hand.

"How do you do, sir?" he said in a fat, unctuous voice. "The cousin of our lamented Mayor, poor gentleman, of whose terrible fate we have this moment learned, sir. I can assure you, Mr.—Brent, I think?—and whatever other relations there may be, of our sincere sympathy, sir—I never knew a more deplorable thing in my life. And to happen just as you should arrive on a visit to your cousin, Mr. Brent—dear, dear! The constable who came to inform me of what had happened mentioned that you'd come, and we were just talking—But I'll introduce you to these gentlemen, sir; allow me—Mr. Mallett, our esteemed bank manager. Mr. Coppinger, our respected borough treasurer."

Brent silently shook hands with the two other men; just as silently he made a sharp inspection of them as they resettled themselves in their chairs. Mallett, a spick-and-span sort of man, very precise as to the cut of his clothes and particular as to the quality of his linen and the trimming of his old-fashioned side-whiskers, he set down at once as the personification of sly watchfulness: he was the type of person who would hear all and say no more than was necessary or obligatory. Coppinger, a younger man, had that same watchful look; a moment later, Brent saw it in Crood's big face too. They were all watchful, all sly, these men, he decided: the sort who would sit by and listen, and admit nothing and tell nothing; already, before even he asked the questions which he had come to put, he knew that he would get no answer other than noncommittal, evasive ones. He saw that all three men, instead of being anxious to give him information, were actuated by the same desire—to find out what he knew, to hear what he had to say.

Crood, as Brent seated himself, waved a hand towards the decanters on the table.

"You'll try a little drop o' something, Mr. Brent?" he said, with insinuating hospitality. "A taste of whisky, now? Do you no harm after what you've just been through." He turned to the girl, who had followed Brent into the room and, picking up her needlework, had seated herself near the master of the house. "Queenie, my love," he continued, "give the gentleman a whisky and soda—say the word, sir. My niece, sir—Miss Queenie Crood—all my establishment, Mr. Brent; quiet, old-fashioned folk we are, but glad to see you, sir; though I wish the occasion had been a merrier one—dear, dear!"

Brent made the girl a polite bow and, not wishing to show himself stand-offish, took the glass which she mixed and handed to him. He turned to Crood.

"It's not a pleasant occasion for me, sir," he said. "I am my cousin's nearest blood-relative, and it lies with me to do what I can to find out who's responsible for his death. I understand that you are Deputy-Mayor, so naturally you're conversant with his public affairs. Now, I've learnt within the last hour that he had become unpopular in the town—made enemies. Is that so, Mr. Crood?"

Crood, who was smoking a long churchwarden pipe, took its stem from his lips, and waved it in the air with an expressive motion.

"Well, well!" he said soothingly. "There might ha' been a little of something of that sort, you know, Mr. Brent, but in a purely political sense, sir, an entirely political sense only. No personal feeling, you know, sir. I'm sure Mr. Mallett there will agree with me—and Mr. Coppinger too."

"Absolutely!" said Mallett.

"Unreservedly!" said Coppinger.

"Your cousin, sir, our late lamented Mayor, was much respected in the town," continued Crood. "He was the hardest-working Mayor we've had for many years, Mr. Brent."

"A first-rate man of business!" observed Mallett.

"A particularly clever hand at figures!" remarked Coppinger.

"A man as tried hard to do his duty," said Crood. "Of course I'll not say that everybody saw eye to eye with him. They didn't. Wherever there's public bodies, Mr. Brent, there'll be parties. Your poor cousin had his party—and there was, to be sure, a party against him and his. But you'll be well aware, sir, as a London gentleman, that no doubt often visits Parliament, that here in England men is enemies in politics that's firm friends outside 'em. I believe I may say that that's a fact, sir?"

"Oh, no doubt!" agreed Brent. He was already feeling at a loss, and he scarcely knew what to say next. "I heard, though, that my cousin, as Mayor, was proposing such drastic reforms in the administration of your borough affairs, that—well, in short, that personal feeling had been imported."

Crood shook his head more solemnly than ever.

"I think you've been misinformed on that point, Mr. Brent," he said. "There may be—no doubt are—mischievous persons that would say such things, but I never heard nothing of the sort, sir. Political feeling, perhaps; but personal feeling—no!"

"Certainly not!" said Mallett.

"Nothing of the sort!" said Coppinger.

"Now, I should say," remarked Crood, waving his pipe again, "that our late lamented Mayor, as an individual, was much thought of amongst the townspeople. I believe Mr. Mallett will agree with that—and Mr. Coppinger."

"A great deal thought of," answered Mallett.

"By, I should say, everybody," added Coppinger.

"He was, of course, a comparative stranger," continued Crood. "Twelve years only had he been amongst us—and now cut off, sudden and malicious, at the beginning of his career! But well thought of, sir, well thought of!"

"Then you feel sure that this crime has not sprung out of his public affairs?" suggested Brent. "It's not what you'd call a political murder?"

"Of that, sir, I would take my solemn oath!" declared Crood. "The idea, sir, is ridiculous."

"Absurd!" said Mallett.

"Out of the question!" affirmed Coppinger.

"Why then, has he been murdered?" asked Brent. "What's at the bottom of it?"

All three men shook their heads. They looked at each other. They looked at Brent.

"Ay—what?" said Crood.

"Just so!" agreed Mallett.

"That's precisely where it is," concluded Coppinger. "Exactly!"

"More in it than anyone knows of—most probably—at present, Mr. Brent," observed Crood, with solemn significance. "Time, sir, time! Time, sir, may tell—may!"

Brent saw that he was not going to get any information under that roof, and after a further brief exchange of trite observations he rose to take his leave. Alderman Crood wrung his hand.

"Sorry I am, sir, that your first visit to my establishment should be under such painful circumstances," he said unctuously. "I hope you'll favour me with another talk, sir—always pleased to see a London gentleman, I'm sure—we're behind, perhaps, in these parts, Mr. Brent, but honest and hearty, sir, honest and hearty. Queenie, my love, you'll open the door for the young gentleman?"

The girl took Brent into the gloomy hall. Halfway along its shadows, she suddenly turned on him with a half shy, half daring expression.

"You are from London?" she whispered.

"From London?—yes," said Brent. "Why?"

"I want to—to talk to somebody about London," she went on, with a nervous, backward glance at the door they had just left. "May I—will you let me talk to—you?"

"To be sure!" answered Brent. "But when—where?"

"I go into the Castle grounds every afternoon," she answered timidly. "Could—could you come there—some time?"

"To-morrow afternoon?" suggested Brent. "Say three o'clock? Would that do?"

"Yes," she whispered. "Thank you—I'll be there. It seems—queer, but I'll tell you. Thank you again—you'll understand to-morrow."

She had her hand on the big street door by then. Without more words she let him out into the night; he heard the door close heavily behind him. He went back towards the heart of the little town, wondering. Only a few hours before, he had been in the rush and bustle of Fleet Street, and now, here he was, two hundred miles away, out of the world, and faced with an atmosphere of murder and mystery.

CHAPTER IV

BULL'S SNUG

When Brent came again to the centre of the town he found that Hathelsborough, instead of sinking to sleep within an hour of curfew, according to long-established custom, had awakened to new life. There were groups at every corner, and little knots of folk at doors, and men in twos and threes on the pavement, and it needed no particular stretching of his ears to inform him that everybody was talking of the murder of his cousin. He caught fragmentary bits of surmise and comment as he walked along; near a shadowy corner of the great church he purposely paused, pretending to tie his shoe-lace, in order to overhear a conversation between three or four men who had just emerged from the door of an adjacent tavern, and were talking in loud, somewhat excited tones: working men, these, whose speech was in the vernacular.

"You can bet your life 'at this job's been done by them whose little game Wallingford were going to checkmate!" declared one man. "I've allus said 'at he were running a rare old risk. We know what t' old saying is about new brooms sweeping clean—all very well, is that, but ye can smash a new broom if ye use it over vigorously. Wallingford were going a bit too deeply into t' abuses o' this town—an' he's paid t' penalty. Put out o' t' way—that's t' truth on it!"

"Happen it may be," said a second man. "And happen not. There's no denying 'at t' Mayor were what they call a man o' mystery. A mysterious chap, d'ye see, in his comings and goings. Ye don't know 'at he mayn't ha' had secret enemies; after all, he were nowt but a stranger i' t' town—nobbut been here twelve year or so. How do we know owt about him? It may be summat to do wi' t' past, this here affair. I'm none going t' believe 'at there's anybody i' Hathelsborough 'ud stick a knife into him just because he were cleaning up t' town money affairs, like."

"Never ye mind!" asserted the former speaker. "He were going to touch t' pockets o' some on 'em, pretty considerable, were t' Mayor. And ye know what Hathelsborough folk is when their pockets is touched—they'll stick at nowt! He's been put away, has Wallingford, 'cause he were interfering over much."

Brent walked on, reflecting. His own opinions coincided, uncomfortably but decidedly, with those of the last speaker, and a rapidly-growing feeling of indignation and desire for vengeance welled up within him. He looked round at the dark-walled, closely shuttered old houses about him with a sense of dull anger—surely they were typical of the reserve, the cunning watchfulness, the suggestive silences of the folk who lived in them, of whom he had just left three excellent specimens in Crood, Mallett and Coppinger. How was he, a stranger, going to unearth the truth about his cousin's brutal murder, amongst people like these, endowed, it seemed to him, with an Eastern-like quality of secretiveness? But he would!

He went on to the rooms in which Wallingford had lived ever since his first coming to the town. They were good, roomy, old-fashioned apartments in a big house, cosy and comfortable, but the sight of Wallingford's study, of his desk, his books and papers, of his favourite chair and his slippers at the fire, of the supper-table already spread for him and Brent in an inner parlour, turned Brent sick at heart. He turned hastily to Wallingford's landlady, who had let him in and followed him into the dead man's room.

"It's no use, Mrs. Appleyard," he said. "I can't stop here to-night, anyway. It would be too much! I'll go to the *Chancellor*, and send on for my luggage."

The woman nodded, staring at him wonderingly. The news had evidently wrought a curious change in her; usually, she was a cheery, good-natured, rather garrulous woman, but she looked at Brent now as if something had dazed her.

"Mr. Brent," she whispered, in awe-stricken accents, "you could have knocked me down with a feather when they came here and told me. He was that well—and cheerful—when he went out!"

"Yes," said Brent dully. "Yes." He let his eyes run over the room again—he had looked forward to having a long, intimate chat with Wallingford that night over the bright fire, still crackling and glowing in readiness for host and guest. "Ay, well!" he added. "It's done now!"

"Them police fellows, Mr. Brent," said the landlady, "have they any idea who did it?"

"I don't think they've the least idea yet," replied Brent. "I suppose you haven't, either?"

Mrs. Appleyard, thus spurred to reminiscence, recovered something of her customary loquaciousness.

"No, to be sure I haven't," she answered. "But I've heard things, and I wish—eh, I do wish!—that I'd warned him! I ought to ha' done."

"What about?" asked Brent. "And what things?"

The landlady hesitated a little, shaking her head.

"Well, you know, Mr. Brent," she said at last, "in a little town like this, folk will talk—Hathelsborough's a particular bad place for talk and gossip; for all that, Hathelsborough people's as secret as the grave when they like, about their own affairs. And, as I say, I've heard things. There's a woman comes here to work for me at odd times, a woman that sometimes goes to put in a day or two at Marriner's Laundry, where a lot of women works, and I recollect her telling me not so long since that there was talk amongst those women about the Mayor and his interfering with things, and she'd heard some of 'em remark that he'd best keep his fingers out o' the pie or he'd pay for it. No more, Mr. Brent; but a straw'll show which way the wind blows. I'm sure there was them in the town that wanted to get rid of him. All the same—murder!"

"Just so," said Brent. "Well, I've got to find it all out."

He went away to the *Chancellor* Hotel, made his arrangements, sent to Mrs. Appleyard's for his luggage, and eventually turned into bed.

But it was little sleep that Brent got that night, and he was thankful when morning came and he could leave his bed and find relief in activity. He was out and about while the grey mists still hung around the Hathelsborough elms, and at eight o'clock walked into the police-station, anxious for news.

Hawthwaite had no news for him. Late the previous night, and early that morning, the police had carried out an exhaustive search of the old Moot Hall, and had failed to discover anything that seemed to bear relation to the crime. Also they had made themselves acquainted with the murdered man's movements immediately previous to his arrival at the Moot Hall; there was nothing whatever in them that afforded any clue.

"We know all that he did from five o'clock yesterday afternoon to the time you found him, Mr. Brent," said Hawthwaite. "He left his office at five o'clock, and went home to his rooms. He was there till nearly seven o'clock. He went out then and walked round by Abbey Lodge, where he left some books—novels, or something of the sort—for Mrs. Saumarez. Then——"

"Who's Mrs. Saumarez?" asked Brent.

"She's a young widow lady, very wealthy, it's understood, who came to live in the town some two years ago," replied Hawthwaite. "Very handsome young woman—you'll be seeing her. Between you and me," he added, with a knowing glance, "his Worship—late Worship, I should say—had been showing her great attention, and I don't think she was indifferent to him—he used to go and dine with her a good deal anyway. However, that's neither here nor there, just now. He called, I say, at Abbey Lodge, left these books, and then came on to the Moot Hall, as Bunning said. That's the plain truth about his movements."

"I don't think his movements matter," observed Brent. "What does matter is—what were the movements of the murderer, and how did he get into the Mayor's Parlour? Or was he concealed there when my cousin entered and, if so, how did he get out and away?"

"Ay, just so, Mr. Brent," agreed Hawthwaite. "As to that, we know nothing—so far. But it was of importance to find out about your cousin's own movements, because, you see, he might have been seen, for instance, in conversation with some stranger, or—or something of that sort, and it all helps."

"You don't know anything about the presence of any strangers in the town last night?" inquired Brent.

"Oh, we've satisfied ourselves about that," replied Hawthwaite. "We made full inquiries last night at the railway station and at the hotels. There were no strangers came into the town last night, or evening, or afternoon, barring yourself and a couple of commercial travellers who are well known here. We saw to that particular at once."

"Then you've really found out—nothing?" suggested Brent.

"Nothing!" asserted Hawthwaite. "But the inquest won't be held until to-morrow morning, and by then we may know something. And, in the meantime, there's something you might do, Mr. Brent—I gather that you're his next-of-kin? Very well, sir, then you might examine his papers—private papers and so on. You never know what bit of sidelight you might come upon."

"Very good," said Brent. "But I shall want help—large help—in that. Can you recommend a solicitor, now?"

"There's Mr. Tansley," replied Hawthwaite. "His office is next door to his late Worship's—a sound man, Tansley, Mr. Brent. And, if I were you, I should get Tansley to represent you at the inquest to-morrow—legal assistance is a good thing to have, sir, at an affair of that sort."

Brent nodded his acquiescence and went back to his hotel. He was thankful that there were few guests in the house—he had no wish to be stared at as a principal actor in the unfolding drama. Yet he speedily realized that he had better lay aside all squeamish feelings of that sort; he foresaw that the murder of its Mayor would throw Hathelsborough into the fever of a nine-days' wonder, and that his own activities would perforce draw attention to himself. And there were things to be done, and after he had breakfasted he set resolutely and systematically about doing them. Tansley's office first—he made an arrangement with Tansley to meet him at Wallingford's rooms that afternoon, to go through any private papers that might be found there. Then his cousin's office—there were clerks there awaiting instructions. Brent had to consult with them as to what was to be done about business. And that over, there was another and still more difficult task—the arrangements for Wallingford's interment. Of one thing Brent was determined—whatever Alderman Crood, as Deputy-Mayor, or whatever the Aldermen and Councillors of Hathelsborough desired, he, as the murdered man's next-of-kin, was not going to have any public funeral or demonstration; it roused his anger to white heat to think of even the bare possibility of Wallingford's murderer following him in smug hypocrisy to his grave. And in Brent's decided opinion that murderer was a Hathelsborough man, and one of high place.

It was nearly noon when he had completed these arrangements, and then, having no more to do at the moment, he remembered the little newspaper man, Peppermore, and his invitation to call at the *Monitor* office. So, as twelve o'clock chimed and struck from the tower of St. Hathelswide, he walked up the narrow entry from the market-place, along which the editor-reporter had shot the previous night, and, after a preliminary reconnoitring of the premises, tapped at a door marked "Editorial." A shrill voice bade him enter, and he turned the handle to find himself inspecting an unusually untidy and littered room, the atmosphere of which seemed chiefly to be derived from a mixture of gas, paste and printers' ink. Somewhere beyond sounded the monotonous rumble of what was probably an old-fashioned printing machine.

A small-figured, sharp-faced, red-haired youngster of apparently fifteen or sixteen years was the sole occupant of this unsavoury sanctum. He was very busy—so busy that he had divested himself of his jacket, and had rolled up his shirt-sleeves. In his right hand he wielded a pair of scissors; with them he was industriously clipping paragraphs from a pile of newspapers which lay before him on a side-table. It was evident that he had a sharp eye for telling stuff, for in the moment which elapsed after Brent's entrance he had run it over a column, swooped on a likely item, snipped it out and added it to a heap of similar gleanings at his elbow. He glanced at his caller with an expression which was of the sort that discourages wasting of time.

"Mr. Peppermore?" inquired Brent, taking his cue. "In?"

"Out," answered the boy.

"Long?" demanded Brent.

"Can't say," said the busy one. "Might be and mightn't." Then he gave Brent a close inspection. "If it's news," he added, "I can take it. Is it?"

"No news," replied Brent. "Mr. Peppermore asked me to call. I'll wait." He perched himself on the counter, and watched the scissors. "You're the sub-editor, I reckon?" he said at last with a smile. "Eh?"

"I'm all sorts of things in this blooming office," answered the boy. "We're short-handed here, I can tell you! Takes me and Mr. P. all our time to get the paper out. Why, last week, Mr. P. he didn't have time to write his Editorial! We had to shove an old one in. But lor' bless you, I don't believe anybody reads 'em! Liveliness, and something about turnips—that's what our folks likes. However, they'll have some good stuff this week. We'd a real first-class murder in this town last night. The Mayor! Heard about it?"

"I've heard," said Brent. "Um! And how long have you been at that job?"

"Twelve months," replied the boy. "I was in the law before that—six months. But the law didn't suit me. Slow! There's some go in this—bit too much now and then. What we want is another reporter. Comes hard on me and Mr. Peppermore, times. I did two cricket matches, a fire, a lost child, and a drowning case last Saturday."

"Good!" said Brent. "Know any shorthand?"

"I can do a fair bit," answered the man-of-all-work. "Learning. Can you?"

"Some," replied Brent. "Did a lot—once. What system?"

But just then Peppermore, more in a hurry than ever, came bustling in, to beam brightly through his spectacles at sight of his visitor.

"Mr. Brent!" he exclaimed. "Delighted, my dear sir, charmed! Not often our humble roof is extended over a distinguished visitor. Take a chair, sir—but no! stop! I've an idea." He seized Brent by the lapel of his coat and became whispering and mysterious. "Step outside," he said. "Twelve o'clock—we'll go over to Bull's."

"What's Bull's?" asked Brent, as they went out into the entry.

Peppermore laughed and wagged his finger.

"Bull's, sir?" he said. "Bull's?—centre of all the gossip in Hathelsborough. Come across there and have a quiet glass with me, and keep your eyes and ears open. I've been trying all the morning to get some news, ideas, impressions, about the sad event of last night, Mr. Brent—now, for current criticism, Bull's is the place. All the gossips of the town congregate there, sir."

"All right," agreed Brent. "Show the way!"

Peppermore led him down the narrow entry, across the market-place, and into an equally narrow passage that opened between two shops near High Cross. There Brent found himself confronted by what seemed to be a high, blank, doorless and windowless wall; Peppermore perceived his astonishment and laughed.

"Some queer, odd nooks and corners in Hathelsborough, Mr. Brent!" he said knowingly. "It would take a stranger a long time to find out all the twists and turns in this old town. But everybody knows the way to Bull's Snug—and here we are!"

He suddenly made a sharp turn to the right and into another passage, where he pushed open a door, steered his companion by the elbow through a dark entry, and thrusting aside a heavy curtain ushered him into as queer a place as Brent had ever seen. It was a big, roomy apartment, lavishly ornamented with old sporting prints and trophies of the rustic chase; its light came from the top through a skylight of coloured glass; its floor was sawdusted; there were shadowy nooks and recesses in it, and on one side ran a bar, presided over by two hefty men in their shirt-sleeves. And here, about the bar, and in knots up and down the room and at the little tables in the corners, was a noontide assemblage, every man with a glass in his hand or at his elbow. Peppermore drew Brent into a vacant alcove and gave him a significant glance.

"I guess there isn't a man in this room, Mr. Brent, that hasn't got his own theory about what happened last night," he murmured. "I don't suppose any of 'em know you—they're not the sort of men you'd meet when you were here before—these are all chiefly tradesmen, betting men, sportsmen, and so on. But as I say, if you want the gossip of the town, here's the place! There never was a rumour in Hathelsborough but it was known and canvassed and debated and improved upon in Bull's, within an hour. Every scandalmonger and talebearer comes here—and here's," he continued, suddenly dropping his voice to a whisper, "one of the biggest of 'em—watch him, and listen to him, if he comes near us. That tall, thin man, in the grey suit, the man with the grizzled moustache. Listen, Mr. Brent; I'll tell you who that chap is, for he's one of the queerest and at the same time most interesting characters in the town. That, sir, is Krevin Crood, the ne'er-do-weel brother of Mr. Alderman Crood—watch him!"

CHAPTER V

SLEEPING FIRES

Already interested in the Crood family because of what he had seen of Simon Crood and his niece on the previous evening, Brent looked closely at the man whom Peppermore pointed out. There was no resemblance in him to his brother, the Alderman. He was a tall, spare, fresh-coloured man, apparently about fifty years of age, well-bred of feature, carefully groomed; something in his erect carriage, slightly swaggering air and defiant eye suggested the military man. Closer inspection showed Brent that the grey tweed suit, though clean and scrupulously pressed, was much worn, that the brilliantly polished shoes were patched, that the linen, freshly-laundered though it was, was far from new—everything, indeed, about Krevin Crood, suggested a well-kept man of former grandeur.

"Decayed old swell—that's what he looks like, eh, Mr. Brent?" whispered Peppermore, following his companion's thoughts. "Ah, they say that once upon a time Krevin Crood was the biggest buck in Hathelsborough—used to drive his horses and ride his horses, and all the rest of it. And now—come down to that."

He winked significantly as he glanced across the room, and Brent knew what he meant. Krevin Crood, lofty and even haughty in manner as he was, had lounged near the bar and stood looking around him, nodding here and there as he met the eye of an acquaintance.

"Waiting till somebody asks him to drink," muttered Peppermore. "Regular sponge, he is! And once used to crack his bottle of champagne with the best!"

"What's the story?" asked Brent, still quietly watching the subject of Peppermore's remarks.

"Oh, the old one," said Peppermore. "Krevin Crood was once a solicitor, and Town Clerk, and, as I say, the biggest swell in the place. Making his couple of thousand a year, I should think. Come down in the usual fashion—drink, gambling, extravagance and so on. And in the end they had to get rid of him—as Magistrates' Clerk, I mean: it was impossible to keep him on any longer. He'd frittered away his solicitor's practice too by that time, and come to the end of his resources. But Simon was already a powerful man in the town, so they—he and some others—cooked things nicely for Krevin. Krevin Crood, Mr. Brent, is one of the Hathelsborough abuses that your poor cousin meant to rid the ratepayers of—fact, sir!"

"How?" asked Brent.

"Well," continued Peppermore, "I said that Simon and some others cooked things for him. Instead of dismissing Krevin for incompetence and inattention to his duties, they retired him—with a pension. Krevin Crood, sir, draws a hundred and fifty-six pounds a year out of the revenues of this rotten little borough—all because he's Simon's brother. Been drawing that—three pounds a week—for fifteen years now. It's a scandal! However, as I say, he once had two thousand a year."

"A difference," remarked Brent.

"Ay, well, he adds a bit to his three pound," said Peppermore. "He does odd jobs for people. For one thing, he carries out all Dr. Wellesley's medicines for him. And he shows strangers round the place—he knows all about the history and antiquities of the Castle, St. Hathelswide, and St. Laurence, and the Moot Hall, and so on. A hanger-on, and a sponge—that's what he is, Mr. Brent. But clever—as clever, sir, as he's unprincipled."

"The Croods seem to be an interesting family," observed Brent. "Who is that girl that I saw last night—the Alderman's niece? Is she, by any chance, this chap's daughter?"

"Queenie," said Peppermore. "Pretty girl too, that, Mr. Brent. No, sir; she's this chap's niece, and Simon's. She's the daughter of another Crood. Ben Crood. Ben's dead—he never made anything out, either—died, I believe, as poor as a church mouse. Simon's the moneyed man of the Crood family—the old rascal rolls in brass, as they call it here. So he took Queenie out of charity, and I'll bet my Sunday hat that he gets out of her the full equivalent of all that he gives her! Catch him giving anything for nothing!"

"You don't love Alderman Crood?" suggested Brent.

Peppermore picked up his glass of bitter ale and drank off what remained. He set down the glass with a bang.

"Wouldn't trust him any farther than I could throw his big carcase!" he said with decision. "Nor any more than I would Krevin there—bad 'uns, both of 'em. But hullo! as nobody's come forward this morning, Krevin's treating himself to a drink! That's his way—he'll get his drink for nothing, if he can, but, if he can't, he's always got money. Old cadger!"

Brent was watching Krevin Crood. As Peppermore had just said, nobody had joined Krevin at the bar. And now he was superintending the mixing of a drink which one of the shirt-sleeved barmen was preparing for him. Presently, glass in hand, he drew near a little knot of men, who, in the centre of the room, were gossiping in whispers. One of the men turned on him.

"Well, and what's Sir Oracle got to say about it?" he demanded, with something like a covert sneer. "You'll know all about it, Krevin, I reckon! What's your opinion?"

Krevin Crood looked over the speaker with a quiet glance of conscious superiority. However much he might have come down in the world, he still retained the manners of a well-bred and educated man, and Brent was not surprised to hear a refined and cultured accent when he presently spoke.

"If you are referring to the unfortunate and lamentable occurrence of last night, Mr. Spelliker," he answered, "I prefer to express no opinion. The matter is *sub judice*."

"Latin!" sneered the questioner. "Ay! you can hide a deal o' truth away behind Latin, you old limbs o' the law! But I reckon the truth'll come out, all the same."

"It is not a legal maxim, but a sound old English saying that murder will out," remarked Krevin quietly. "I think you may take it, Mr. Spelliker, that in this case, as in most others, the truth will be arrived at."

"Ay, well, if all accounts be true, it's a good job for such as you that the Mayor is removed," said Spelliker half-insolently. "They say he was going to be down on all you pensioned gentlemen—what?"

"That, again, is a matter which I do not care to discuss," replied Krevin. He turned away, approaching a horsy-looking individual who stood near. "Good-morning, Mr. Gates," he said pleasantly. "Got rid of your brown cob yet? If not, I was talking to Simpson, the vet, yesterday—I rather fancy you'd find a customer in him."

Peppermore nudged his companion's arm. Brent leaned nearer to him.

"Not get any change out of him!" whispered Peppermore. "Cool old customer, isn't he? *Sub judice*, eh? Good! And yet—if there's a man in all Hathelsborough that's likely to know what straws are sailing on the undercurrent, Mr. Brent, Krevin Crood's the man! But you'll come across him before you're here long—nobody can be long in Hathelsborough without knowing Krevin!"

They left Bull's then, and after a little talk in the market-place about the matter of paramount importance Brent returned to the *Chancellor*, thinking about what he had just seen and heard. It seemed to him, now more assuredly than ever, that he was in the midst of a peculiarly difficult maze, in a network of chicanery and deceit, in an underground burrow full of twistings and turnings that led he could not tell whither. An idea had flashed through his mind as he looked at Krevin Crood in the broken man's brief interchange of remarks with the half-insolent tradesman: an idea which he had been careful not to mention to Peppermore. Krevin Crood, said Peppermore, was mainly dependent on his pension of three pounds a week from the borough authorities—a pension which, of course, was terminable at the pleasure of those authorities; Wallingford had let it be known, plainly and unmistakably, that he was going to advocate the discontinuance of these drains on the town's resources: Krevin Crood, accordingly, would be one of the first to suffer if Wallingford got his way, as he was likely to do. And Peppermore had said further that Krevin Crood knew all about the antiquities of Hathelsborough—knew so much, indeed, that he acted as cicerone to people who wanted to explore the Castle, and the church, and the Moot Hall. Now, supposing that Krevin Crood, with his profound knowledge of the older parts of the town, knew of some mysterious and secret way into the Mayor's Parlour, and had laid in wait there, resolved on killing the man who was threatening by his reforming actions to deprive him of his pension? It was not an impossible theory. And others branched out of it. It was already evident to Brent that Simon Crood, big man though he was in the affairs of the borough, was a schemer and a contriver of mole's work: supposing that he and his gang had employed Krevin Crood as their emissary? That, too, was possible. Underground work! There was underground work all round.

Then, thinking of Alderman Crood, he remembered Alderman Crood's niece; her request to him; his promise to her. He had been puzzled, not a little taken aback by the girl's eager, anxious manner. She had been quiet and demure enough as she sat by Simon Crood's fire, sewing, in silence, a veritable modest mouse, timid and bashful; but in that big, gloomy hall her attitude had changed altogether—she had been almost compelling in her eagerness. And Brent had wondered ever since, at intervals, whatever it could be that she wanted with him—a stranger? But it was near three o'clock now, and instead of indulging in further surmise, he went off to meet her.

Hathelsborough Castle, once one of the most notable fortresses of the North, still remained in an excellent state of preservation. Its great Norman keep formed a landmark that could be seen over many a mile of the surrounding country; many of its smaller towers were still intact, and its curtain walls, barbican and ancient chapel had escaped the ravages of time. The ground around it had been laid out as a public garden, and its great courtyard turned into a promenade, set out with flowerbeds. It was a great place of resort for the townsfolk on summer evenings and on Sundays, but Brent, coming to it in the middle of the afternoon, found it deserted, save for a few nursemaids and children. He went wandering around it and suddenly caught sight of Queenie Crood. She was sitting on a rustic bench in an angle of the walls, a book in her hand; it needed little of Brent's perception to convince him that the book was unread: she was anxiously expecting him.

"Here I am!" he said, with an encouraging smile, as he sat down beside her. "Punctual to the minute, you see!"

He looked closely at her. In the clearer light of day he saw that she was not only a much prettier girl than he had fancied the night before, but that she had more fire and character in her eyes and lips than he had imagined. And though she glanced at him with evident shyness as he came up, and the colour came into her cheeks as she gave him her hand, he was quick to see that she was going to say whatever it was that was in her mind. It was Brent's way to go straight to the point.

"You wanted to speak to me," he said, smiling again. "Fire away!—and don't be afraid."

The girl threw her book aside, and turned to him with obvious candour.

"I won't!" she exclaimed. "I'm not a bit afraid—though I don't know whatever you'll think of me, Mr. Brent, asking advice from a stranger in this barefaced fashion!"

"I've had to seek advice from strangers more than once in my time," said Brent, with a gentle laugh. "Go ahead!"

"It was knowing that you came from London," said Queenie. "You mightn't think it but I never met anybody before who came from London. And—I want to go to London. I will go!"

"Well," remarked Brent slowly, "if young people say they want to go to London, and declare that they will go to London, why, in my experience they end up by going. But, in your case, why not?"

The girl sat silent for a moment, staring straight in front of her at the blue smoke that circled up from the quaint chimney stacks of the town beneath the Castle. Her eyes grew dreamy.

"I want to go on the stage," she said at last. "That's it, Mr. Brent."

Brent turned and looked at her. Under his calm and critical inspection she blushed, but as she blushed she shook her head.

"Perhaps you think I'm one of the stage-struck young women?" she said. "Perhaps you're wondering if I can act? Perhaps——"

"What I'm wondering," interrupted Brent, "is—if you know anything about it? Not about acting, but about the practical side of the thing—the profession? A pretty stiff proposition, you know."

"What I know," said Queenie Crood determinedly, "is that I've got a natural talent for acting. And I'd get on—if only I could get away from this place. I will get away!—if only somebody would give me a bit of advice about going to London and getting—you know—getting put in the way of it. I don't care how hard the life is, nor how hard I'd have to work—it would be what I want, and better than this anyway!"

"You aren't happy in this town?" suggested Brent.

Queenie gave an eloquent glance out of her dark eyes.

"Happy!" she exclaimed scornfully. "Shut up in that house with Simon Crood! Would you be? You saw something of it last night. Would you like to be mewed up there, day in, day out, year in, year out, with no company beyond him and those two cronies of his, who are as bad as himself—mean, selfish, money-grubbers! Oh!"

"Isn't your uncle good to you?" asked Brent with simple directness.

"He's been good enough in giving me bed and board and clothing since my father and mother died six years ago," answered the girl, "and in return I've saved him the wages of the two servants he ought to have. But do you think I want to spend all my life there, doing that sort of thing? I don't—and I won't! And I thought, when I heard that you were a London man, and a journalist, that you'd be able to tell me what to do—to get to London. Help me, Mr. Brent!"

She involuntarily held out her hands to him, and Brent just as involuntarily took them in his. He was a cool and not easily impressed young man, but his pulses thrilled as he felt the warm fingers against his own.

"By George!" he exclaimed. "If—if you can act like that——"

"I'm not acting!" she said quickly.

29

"Well, well, I didn't say you were," he answered with a laugh. "Only if you could—but of course I'll help you! I'll find out a thing or two for you: I don't know much myself, but I know people who do know. I'll do what I can."

The girl pressed his hands and withdrew her own.

"Thank you, thank you!" she said impulsively. "Oh, if you only knew how I want to get away—and breathe! That house——"

"Look here," interrupted Brent, "you're very candid. I like that—it suits me. Now, frankly you don't like that old uncle of yours? And just why?"

Queenie looked round. There was no one near them, no one indeed in sight, except a nursemaid who wheeled a perambulator along one of the paths, but she sunk her voice to something near a whisper.

"Mr. Brent," she said, "Simon Crood's the biggest hypocrite in this town—and that's implying a good deal more than you'd ever think. He and those friends of his, Mallett and Coppinger, who are always there with him—ah, they think I know nothing, and understand nothing, but I hear their schemings and their talk, veiled as it is. They're deep and subtle, those three—and dangerous. Didn't you see last night that if you'd sat there till midnight or till morning you'd never have had a word out of them—a word, that is, that you wanted? You wouldn't!—they knew better!"

"I got nothing out of them," admitted Brent. He sat thinking in silence for a time. "Look here," he said at last, "you know what I want to find out—who killed my cousin. Help me! Keep your eyes and ears open to anything you see and hear—understand?"

"I will!" answered Queenie. "But you've got a big task before you! You can be certain of this—if the Mayor was murdered for what you called political reasons——"

"Well?" asked Brent, as she paused. "Well?"

"It would all be arranged so cleverly that there's small chance of discovery," she went on. "I know this town—rotten to the core! But I'll help you all I can, and——"

A policeman suddenly came round the corner of the wall, and at sight of Brent touched his peaked cap.

"Looking for you, Mr. Brent," he said. "I heard you'd been seen coming up here. The superintendent would be obliged if you'd step round, sir; he wants to see you at once, particularly."

"Follow you in a moment," answered Brent. He turned to Queenie as the man went away. "When shall I see you again?" he asked.

"I always come here every afternoon," she answered. "It's the only change I get. I come here to read."

"Till to-morrow—or the next day, then," said Brent. He nodded and laughed. "Keep smiling! You'll maybe play Juliet, or some other of those old games, yet."

The girl smiled gratefully, and Brent strode away after the policeman. In a few minutes he was in Hawthwaite's office. The superintendent closed the door, gave him a mysterious glance, and going over to a cupboard produced a long, narrow parcel, done up in brown paper.

"A discovery!" he whispered. "It occurred to me this afternoon to have all the heavy furniture in the Mayor's Parlour examined. No light job, Mr. Brent—but we found this."

And with a jerk of his wrist he drew from the brown paper a long, thin, highly polished rapier, the highly burnished steel of which was dulled along half its length, as if it had been first dimmed and then hastily rubbed.

"I make no doubt that this was what it was done with," continued Hawthwaite. "We found it thrust away between the wainscoting and a heavy bookcase which it took six men to move. And our deputy Town Clerk says that a few days ago he saw this lying on a side table in the Mayor's Parlour—his late Worship observed to him that it was an old Spanish rapier that he'd picked up at some old curiosity shop cheap."

"You'll go into that, and bring it in evidence?" suggested Brent.

"You bet!" replied Hawthwaite grimly. "Oh, we're not going to sleep, Mr. Brent—we'll get at something yet! Slow and sure, sir, slow but sure."

Brent went away presently, and calling on Tansley, the solicitor, walked with him to Wallingford's rooms. During the next two hours they carefully examined all the dead man's private papers. They found nothing that threw any light whatever on his murder. But they came upon his will. Wallingford had left all he possessed to his cousin, Richard Brent, and by the tragedy of the previous night Brent found that he had benefited to the extent of some fifteen thousand pounds.

CHAPTER VI

THE ANCIENT OFFICE OF CORONER

The discovery of Wallingford's will, which lay uppermost amongst a small collection of private papers in a drawer of the dead man's desk, led Brent and Tansley into a new train of thought. Tansley, with the ready perception and acumen of a man trained in the law, was quick to point out two or three matters which in view of Wallingford's murder seemed to be of high importance, perhaps of deep significance. Appended to the will was a schedule of the testator's properties and possessions, with the total value of the estate estimated and given in precise figures—that was how Brent suddenly became aware that he had come into a small fortune. Then the will itself was in holograph, written out in Wallingford's own hand on a single sheet of paper, in the briefest possible fashion, and witnessed by his two clerks. And, most important and significant of all, it had been executed only a week previously.

"Do you know how that strikes me?" observed Tansley in a low voice, as if he feared to be overheard. "It just looks to me as if Wallingford had anticipated that something was about to happen. Had he ever given you any idea in his letters that he was going to do this?"

"Never!" replied Brent. "Still—I'm the only very near relative that he had."

"Well," said Tansley, "it may be mere coincidence, but it's a bit odd that he should be murdered within a week of that will's being made. I'd just like to know if he'd been threatened—openly, anonymously, any way. Looks like it."

"I suppose we shall get into things at the inquest?" asked Brent.

Tansley shrugged his shoulders.

"Maybe," he answered. "I've no great faith in inquests myself. But sometimes things do come out. And our coroner, Seagrave, is a painstaking and thorough-going sort of old chap—the leading solicitor in the town too. But it all depends on what evidence can be brought forward. I've always an uneasy feeling, as regards a coroner's inquiry, that the very people who really could tell something never come forward."

"Doesn't that look as if such people were keeping something back that would incriminate themselves?" suggested Brent.

"Not necessarily," replied Tansley. "But it often means that it might incriminate others. And in an old town like this, where the folk are very clannish and closely connected one with another by, literally, centuries of intermarriage between families, you're not going to get one man to give another away."

"You think that even if the murderer is known, or if some one suspected, he would be shielded?" asked Brent.

"In certain eventualities, yes," answered Tansley. "We all know that rumours about your cousin's murder are afloat in the town now—and spreading. Well, the more they spread, the closer and more secretive will those people become who are in the know; that is, of course, if anybody is in the know. That's a fact!"

"What do you think yourself?" said Brent suddenly. "Come now?"

"I think the Mayor was got rid of—and very cleverly," replied Tansley. "So cleverly that I'm doubtful if to-morrow's inquest will reveal anything. However, it's got to be held."

"Well, you'll watch it for me?" said Brent. "I'm going to spare no expense and no pains to get at the truth."

He sat at Tansley's side when the inquest was opened next morning in the principal court of the old Moot Hall. It struck him as rather a curious fact that, although he had followed the profession of journalist for several years, he had never until then been present at the holding of this—one of the most ancient forms of inquiry known to English law. But he was familiar with the history of the thing—he knew that ever since the days of Edward IV the Coroner had held his sitting, *super visum corporis*, with the aid of at least twelve jurymen, *probi et legales homines*, there was scarcely in all the range of English legal economy an office more ancient. He inspected the Coroner and his jury with curious interest—Seagrave, Coroner of the Honour of Hathelsborough, was a keen-faced old lawyer, whose astute looks were relieved by a kindly expression; his twelve good men and true were tradesmen of the town, whose exterior promised a variety of character and temperament, from the sharply alert to the dully unimaginative.

There were other people there in whom Brent was speedily interested, and at whom he gazed with speculative attention in the opening stages of the proceedings. The court was crowded: by the time Seagrave, as Coroner, took his seat, there was not a square foot of even standing space. Brent recognized a good many folk. There was Peppermore, with his sharp-eyed boy assistant; there, ranged alongside of them, were many other reporters, from the various county newspapers, and at least one man whom Brent recognized as being from the Press Association in London. And there was a big array of police, with Hawthwaite at its head, and there were doctors, and officials of the Moot Hall, and, amongst the general public, many men whom Brent remembered seeing the previous day in Bull's Snug. Krevin Crood was among these; in a privileged seat, not far away, sat his brother, the Alderman, with Queenie half-hidden at his side, and his satellites, Mallett and Coppinger, in close attendance. And near them, in another privileged place, sat a very pretty woman, of a distinct and superior type, attired in semi-mourning, and accompanied by her elderly female companion. Brent was looking at these two when Tansley nudged his elbow.

"You see that handsome woman over there—next to the older one?" he whispered. "That's the Mrs. Saumarez you've heard of—that your unfortunate cousin was very friendly with. Rich young widow, she is, and deuced pretty and attractive—Wallingford used to dine with her a good deal. I wonder if she's any ideas about this mystery? However, I guess we shall hear many things before the day's out; of course I haven't the slightest notion what evidence is going to be given. But I've a pretty good idea that Seagrave means to say some pretty straight things to the jury!"

Here Tansley proved to be right. The Coroner, in opening the proceedings, made some forcible remarks on their unusual gravity and importance. Here was a case in which the chief magistrate of one of the most ancient boroughs in England had been found dead in his official room under circumstances which clearly seemed to point to murder. Already there were rumours in the town and neighbourhood of the darkest and most disgraceful sort—that the Mayor of Hathelsborough had been done to death, in a peculiarly brutal fashion, by a man or men who disagreed with the municipal reforms which he was intent on carrying out. It would be a lasting, an indelible blot on the old town's fair fame, never tarnished before in this way, if this inquiry came to naught, if no definite verdict was given, he earnestly hoped that by the time it concluded they would be in possession of facts which would, so to speak, clear the town, and any political party in the town. He begged them to give the closest attention to all that would be put before them, and to keep open minds until they heard all the available evidence.

"A fairly easy matter in this particular case!" muttered Tansley, as the jurymen went out to discharge their distasteful, preliminary task of viewing the body of the murdered man. "I don't suppose there's a single man there who has the ghost of a theory, and I'm doubtful if he'll know much more to-night than he knows now—unless something startling is sprung upon us."

Brent was the first witness called into the box when the court settled down to its business. He formally identified the body of the deceased as that of his cousin, John Wallingford: at the time of his death, Mayor of Hathelsborough, and forty-one years of age. He detailed the particulars of his own coming to the town on the evening of the murder, and told how he and Bunning, going upstairs to the Mayor's Parlour, had found Wallingford lying across his desk, dead. All this every man and woman in the court knew already—but the Coroner desired to know more.

"I believe, Mr. Brent," he said, when the witness had given these particulars, "that you are the deceased's nearest blood-relative?"

"I am," replied Brent.

"Then you can give us some information which may be of use. Although the Mayor had lived in Hathelsborough some twelve years or so, he was neither a native of the town nor of these parts. Now, can you give us some particulars about him—about his family and his life before he came to this borough?"

"Yes," said Brent. "My cousin was the only son—only child, in fact—of the Reverend Septimus Wallingford, who was sometime Vicar of Market Meadow, in Berkshire. He is dead—many years ago—so is his wife. My cousin was educated at Reading Grammar School, and on leaving it he was articled to a firm of solicitors in that town. After qualifying as a solicitor, he remained with that firm for some time. About twelve years ago he came to this place as managing clerk to a Hathelsborough firm; its partners eventually retired, and he bought their practice."

"Was he ever married?"

"Never!"

"You knew him well?"

"He was some twelve years my senior," answered Brent, "so I was a mere boy when he was a young man. But of late years we have seen a good deal of each other—he has frequently visited me in London, and this would have been my third visit to him here. We corresponded regularly."

"You were on good terms?"

"We were on very good terms."

"And confidential terms?"

"As far as I know—yes. He took great interest in my work as a journalist, and I took great interest in his career in this town."

"And I understand that he has marked his sense of—shall we say, kinship for you by leaving you all his property?"

"He has!"

"Now, did he ever say anything to you, by word of mouth or letter, about any private troubles?"

"No, never!"

"Or about any public ones?"

"Well, some months ago, soon after he became Mayor of Hathelsborough, he made a sort of joking reference, in a letter, to something that might come under that head."

"Yes? What, now?"

"He said that he had started on his task of cleaning out the Augean stable of Hathelsborough, and that the old task of Hercules was child's play compared to his."

"I believe, Mr. Brent, that you visited your cousin here in the town about Christmas last? Did he say anything to you about Hathelsborough at that time? I mean, as regards what he called his Augean stables task?"

Brent hesitated. He glanced at the eagerly-listening spectators, and he smiled a little.

"Well," he replied half-hesitatingly, "he did! He said that in his opinion Hathelsborough was the rottenest and most corrupt little town in all England!"

"Did you take that as a seriously meant statement, Mr. Brent?"

"Oh, well—he laughed as he made it. I took it as a specimen of his rather heightened way of putting things."

"Did he say anything that led you to think that he believed himself to have bitter enemies in the town?"

"No," said Brent, "he did not."

"Neither then nor at any other time?"

"Neither then nor at any other time."

The Coroner asked no further questions, and Brent sat down again by Tansley, and settled himself to consider whatever evidence might follow. He tried to imagine himself a Coroner or juryman, and to estimate and weigh the testimony of each succeeding witness in its relation to the matter into which the court was inquiring. Some of it, he thought, was relevant; some had little in it that carried affairs any further. Yet he began to see that even the apparently irrelevant evidence was not without its importance. They were links, these statements, these answers; links that went to the making of a chain.

He was already familiar with most of the evidence: he knew what each witness was likely to tell before one or other entered the box. Bunning came next after himself; Bunning had nothing new to tell. Nor was there anything new in the medical evidence given by Dr. Wellesley and Dr. Barber—all the town knew how the Mayor had been murdered, and the purely scientific explanations as to the cause of death were merely details. More interest came when Hawthwaite produced the fragment of handkerchief picked up on the hearth of the Mayor's Parlour, half-burnt; and when he brought forward the rapier which had been discovered behind the bookcase; still more when a man who kept an old curiosity shop in a back street of the town proved that he had sold the rapier to Wallingford only a few days before the murder. But interest died down again while the Borough Surveyor produced elaborate plans and diagrams, illustrating the various corridors, passages, entrances and exits of the Moot Hall, with a view to showing the difficulty of access to the Mayor's Parlour. It revived once more when the policeman who had been on duty at the office in the basement stepped into the box and was questioned as to the possibilities of entrance to the Moot Hall through the door near which his desk was posted. For on pressure by the Coroner he admitted that between six and eight o'clock on the fateful evening he had twice been absent from the neighbourhood of that door for intervals of five or six minutes—it was therefore possible that the murderer had slipped in and slipped out without attracting attention.

This admission produced the first element of distinct sensation which had so far materialized. As almost every person present was already fairly well acquainted with the details of what had transpired on the evening of the murder—Peppermore having published every scrap of information he could rake up, in successive editions of his *Monitor*—the constable's belated revelation came as a surprise. Hawthwaite turned on the witness with an irate, astonished look; the Coroner glanced at Hawthwaite as if he were puzzled; then looked down at certain memoranda lying before him. He turned from this to the witness, a somewhat raw, youthful policeman.

"I understood that you were never away from that door between six and eight o'clock on the evening in question?" he said. "Now you admit that you were twice away from it?"

"Yes, sir. I'm sorry, sir, I clean forgot that when—when the superintendent asked me at first. I—I was a bit flustered like."

"Now let us get a clear statement about this," said the Coroner, after a pause. "We know quite well from the plans, and from our own knowledge, that anyone could get up to the Mayor's Parlour through the police office in the basement at the rear of the Moot Hall. What time did you go on duty at the door that opens into the office, from St. Laurence Lane?"

"Six o'clock, sir."

"And you were about the door—at a desk there, eh?—until when?"

"Till after eight, sir."

"But you say you were absent for a short time, twice?"

"Yes, sir, I remember now that I was."

"What were the times of those two absences?"

"Well, sir, about ten minutes to seven I went along to the charge office for a few minutes—five or six minutes. Then at about a quarter to eight I went downstairs into the cellar to get some paraffin for a lamp—I might be away as long, then, sir."

"And, of course, during your absence anybody could have left or entered—unnoticed?"

"Well, they could, sir, but I don't think anybody did."

"Why, now?"

"Because, sir, the door opening into St. Laurence Lane is a very heavy one, and I never heard it either open or close. The latch is a heavy one, too, sir, and uncommon stiff."

"Still, anybody might," observed the Coroner. "Now, what is the length of the passage between that door, the door at the foot of the stairs leading to this court—by which anybody would have to come to get that way to the Mayor's Parlour?"

The witness reflected for a moment.

"Well, about ten yards, sir," he answered.

In the Mayor's Parlour

The Coroner looked at the plan which the Borough Surveyor had placed before him and the jury a few minutes previously. Before he could say anything further, Hawthwaite rose from his seat and making his way to him exchanged a few whispered remarks with him. Presently the Coroner nodded, as if in assent to some suggestions.

"Oh, very well," he said. "Then perhaps we'd better have her at once. Call—what's her name, did you say? Oh, yes—Sarah Jane Spizey!"

From amidst a heterogeneous collection of folk, men and women, congregated at the rear of the witness-box, a woman came forward—one of the most extraordinary looking creatures that he had ever seen, thought Brent. She was nearly six feet in height; she was correspondingly built; her arms appeared to be as brawny as a navvy's; her face was of the shape and roundness of a full moon; her mouth was a wide slit, her nose a button; her eyes were as shrewd and hard as they were small and close-set. A very Grenadier of a woman!—and apparently quite unmoved by the knowledge that everybody was staring at her.

Sarah Jane Spizey—yes. Wife of the Town Bellman. Resident in St. Laurence Lane. Went out charing sometimes; sometimes worked at Marriner's Laundry. Odd-job woman, in fact.

"Mrs. Spizey," said the Coroner, "I understand that on the evening of Mr. Wallingford's death you were engaged in some work in the Moot Hall. Is that so?"

"Yes, sir. Which I was a-washing the floor of this very court."

"What time was that, Mrs. Spizey?"

"Which I was at it, your Worshipful, from six o'clock to eight."

"Did you leave this place at all during that time?"

"Not once, sir; not for a minute."

"Now during the whole of that time, Mrs. Spizey, did you see anybody come up those stairs, cross the court, and go towards the Mayor's Parlour?"

"Which I never did, sir! I never see a soul of any sort. Which the place was empty, sir, for all but me and my work, sir."

The Coroner motioned Mrs. Spizey to stand down, and glanced at Hawthwaite.

"I think this would be a convenient point at which to adjourn," he said. "I——"

But Hawthwaite's eyes were turned elsewhere. In the body of the court an elderly man had risen.

CHAPTER VII

THE VOLUNTARY WITNESS

E verybody present, not excluding Brent, knew the man at whom the Superintendent of Police was staring, and who evidently wished to address the Coroner. He was Mr. Samuel John Epplewhite, an elderly, highly respectable tradesman of the town, and closely associated with that Forward Party in the Town Council of which the late Mayor had become the acknowledged leader; a man of substance and repute, who would not break in without serious reason upon proceedings of the sort then going on. The Coroner, following Hawthwaite's glance, nodded to him.

"You wish to make some observation, Mr. Epplewhite?" he inquired.

"Before you adjourn, sir, if you please," replied Epplewhite, "I should like to make a statement—evidence, in fact, sir. I think, after what we've heard, that it's highly necessary that I should."

"Certainly," answered the Coroner. "Anything you can tell, of course. Then, perhaps you'll step into the witness-box?"

The folk who crowded the court to its very doors looked on impatiently while Epplewhite went through the legal formalities. Laying down the Testament on which he had taken the oath, he turned to the Coroner. But the Coroner again nodded to him.

"You had better tell us what is in your mind in your own way, Mr. Epplewhite," he said. "We are, of course, in utter ignorance of what it is you can tell. Put it in your own fashion."

Epplewhite folded his hands on the ledge of the witness-box and looked around the court before finally settling his eyes on the Coroner: it seemed to Brent as if he were carefully considering the composition, severally and collectively, of his audience.

"Well, sir," he began, in slow, measured accents, "what I have to say, as briefly as I can, is this: everybody here, I believe, is aware that our late Mayor and myself were on particularly friendly terms. We'd always been more or less of friends since his first coming to the town: we'd similar tastes and interests. But our friendship had been on an even more intimate basis during the last year or two, and especially of recent months, owing, no doubt, to the fact that we belonged to the same party on the Town Council, and were both equally anxious to bring about a thorough reform in the municipal administration of the borough. When Mr. Wallingford was elected Mayor last November, he and I, and our supporters on the Council, resolved that during his year of office we would do our best to sweep away certain crying abuses and generally get the affairs of Hathelsborough placed on a more modern and a better footing. We were all——"

The Coroner held up his hand.

"Let us have a clear understanding," he said. "I am gathering—officially, of course—from what you are saying that in Hathelsborough Town Council there are two parties, opposed to each other: a party pledged to Reform, and another that is opposed to Reform. Is that so, Mr. Epplewhite?"

"Precisely so," answered the witness. "And of the Reform party, the late Mayor was the leader. This is well known in the town—it's a matter of common gossip. It is also well known to members of the Town Council that Mr. Wallingford's proposals for reform were of a very serious and drastic nature, that we of his party were going to support them through thick and thin, and that they were bitterly opposed by the other party, whose members were resolved to fight them tooth and nail."

"It may be as well to know what these abuses were which you proposed to reform?" suggested the Coroner. "I want to get a thorough clearing-up of everything."

"Well," responded the witness, with another glance around the court, "the late Mayor had a rooted and particular objection to the system of payments and pensions in force at present, which, without doubt, owes its existence to favouritism and jobbery. There are numerous people in the town drawing money from the borough funds who have no right to it on any ground whatever. There are others who draw salaries for what are really sinecures. A great deal of the ratepayers' money has gone in this way—men in high places in the Corporation have used their power to benefit relations and favourites: I

In the Mayor's Parlour

question if there's another town in the country in which such a state of things would be permitted. But there is a more serious matter than that, one which Mr. Wallingford was absolutely determined, with the help of his party, and backed by public opinion, if he could win it over—no easy thing, for we had centuries of usage and tradition against us!—to bring to an end. That is, the fact that the financial affairs of this town are entirely controlled by what is virtually a self-constituted body, called the Town Trustees. They are three in number. If one dies, the surviving two select his successor—needless to say, they take good care that they choose a man who is in thorough sympathy with their own ideas. Now the late Mayor was convinced that this system led to nothing but—well, to put it mildly, to nothing but highly undesirable results, and he claimed that the Corporation had the right to deprive the existing Town Trustees of their power, and to take into its own hands the full administration of the borough finances. And of course there was much bitter animosity aroused by this proposal, because the Town Trustees have had a free hand and done what they liked with the town's money for a couple of centuries!"

The Coroner, who was making elaborate notes, lifted his pen.

"Who are the Town Trustees at present, Mr. Epplewhite?" he inquired.

Epplewhite smiled, as a man might smile who knows that a question is only asked as a mere formality.

"The Town Trustees at present, sir," he answered quietly, "are Mr. Alderman Crood, Deputy Mayor; Mr. Councillor Mallett, Borough Auditor; and Mr. Councillor Coppinger, Borough Treasurer."

Amidst a curious silence, broken only by the scratching of the Coroner's pen, Alderman Crood rose heavily in his place amongst the spectators.

"Mr. Coroner," he said, with some show of injured feeling, "I object, sir, to my name being mentioned in connection with this here matter. You're inquiring, sir——"

"I'm inquiring, Mr. Crood, into the circumstances surrounding the death of John Wallingford," said the Coroner. "If you can throw any light on them, I shall be glad to take your evidence. At present I am taking the evidence of another witness. Yes, Mr. Epplewhite?"

"Well, sir, I come to recent events," continued Epplewhite, smiling grimly as the Deputy-Mayor, flushed and indignant, resumed his seat. "The late Mayor was very well aware that his proposals were regarded, not merely with great dislike, but with positive enmity. He, and those of us who agreed with him, were constantly asked in the Council Chamber what right we had to be endeavouring to interfere with a system that had suited our fathers and grandfathers? We were warned too, in the Council Chamber, that we should get ourselves into trouble——"

"Do you refer to actual threats?" asked the Coroner.

"Scarcely that, sir—hints, and so on," replied the witness. "But of late, in the case of the late Mayor, actual threats have been used. And to bring my evidence to a point, Mr. Coroner, I now wish to make a certain statement, on my oath, and to produce a certain piece of evidence, to show that Mr. Wallingford's personal safety was threatened only a few days before his murder!"

Thus saying, Epplewhite thrust a hand into the inner pocket of his coat, and, producing a letter, held it out at arm's length, so that every one could see it. So holding it, he turned to the Coroner.

"It is just a week ago, sir," he proceeded, "that Mr. Wallingford came to supper at my house. After supper, he and I, being alone, began talking about the subject which was uppermost in our minds—municipal reform. That day I had had considerable talk with two or three fellow-members of the Council who belonged to the opposite party, and as a result I showed to Wallingford that opposition to our plans was growing more concentrated, determined and bitter. He laughed a little satirically. 'It's gone beyond even that stage with me, personally, Epplewhite,' he said. 'Don't you ever be surprised, my friend, if you hear of my being found with a bullet through my head or a knife between my ribs!' 'What do you mean?' said I. 'Nonsense!' He laughed again, and pulled out this envelope. 'All right,' he answered. 'You read that!' I read what was in the envelope, sir—and I now pass it to you!"

The Coroner silently took the letter which was passed across to him from the witness, withdrew a sheet of paper from it, and read the contents with an inscrutable face and amidst a dead silence. It seemed a long time before he turned to the jury. Then, he held up the sheet of paper and the envelope which had contained it.

"Gentlemen!" he said. "I shall have to draw your particular attention to this matter. This is an anonymous letter. From the date on the postmark, it was received by the late Mayor about a week before he showed it to Mr. Epplewhite. It is a typewritten communication. The address on the envelope is typewritten; the letter itself is typewritten. I will now read the letter to you. It is as follows:

"'Mr. Mayor,

"'You are a young man in an old town, but you are old enough and sharp enough to take a hint. Take one now, and mind your own business. What business is it of yours to interfere with good old customs in a place to which you don't belong and where you're still a comparative stranger? You only got elected to the Mayoral chair by one vote, and if you are fool enough to think that you and those behind you are strong enough to upset things you'll find yourself wrong, for you won't be allowed. There's something a deal stronger in this town than what you and them are, and that you'll see proved—or happen you won't see it, for if you go on as you are doing, putting your nose in where you've no right, you'll be made so that you'll never see nor hear again. Things is not going to be upset here for want of putting upsetters out of the way; there's been better men than you quietly sided for less. So take a quiet warning, leave things alone. It would become you a deal better if you'd be a bit more hospitable to the Council and give them a glass of decent wine instead of the teetotal stuff you disgraced the table with when you gave your Mayoral banquet—first time any Mayor of this good old borough ever did such a thing. There's them that's had quite enough of such goings-on, and doesn't mind how soon you're shifted. So mend your ways before somebody makes them as they'll never need mending any more.'

"Now, gentlemen," continued the Coroner, as he laid down the letter, "there are one or two things about that communication to which I wish to draw your attention. First of all, it is the composition of a vulgar and illiterate, or, at any rate, semi-illiterate person. I don't think its phrasing and illiteracy are affected; I think it has been written in its present colloquial form without art or design, by whoever wrote it; it is written, phrased, expressed, precisely as a vulgar, coarse sort of person would speak. That is the first point. The second is—it is typewritten. Now, in these days, there are a great many typewriting machines in use in the town; small as the town is, we know there are a great many, in offices, shops, institutions, banks, even private houses. It is not at all likely that the sender of this letter would employ a professional typist to write it, not even a clerk, nor any employé—therefore he typed it himself. I will invite your attention to the letter, which I now hand to you, and then I will place it in the custody of the police, who will, of course, use their best endeavours to trace it."

He passed the letter over to the foreman of the jury, and turned to the witness-box.

"I conclude, Mr. Epplewhite, that the late Mayor left that letter in your possession?" he asked.

"He did, sir," replied Epplewhite. "He said, half jokingly, 'You can keep that, Epplewhite! If they sacrifice me on the altar of vested interests, it'll be a bit of evidence.' So I locked up the letter in my safe there and then, and it has remained there until this morning."

"You, of course, have no idea as to the identity of the sender?"

"None, sir!"

"Had Mr. Wallingford?"

"Neither of us, sir, formed any conclusion. But we both thought that the letter emanated from some member of the opposition."

"Did Mr. Wallingford take it as a serious threat?"

Epplewhite looked doubtful.

"I scarcely know," he said. "He seemed half-minded about it. To regard it, you know, as half a joke and half serious. But I feel certain that he knew he had enemies who might become—well, deadly. That's my distinct impression, Mr. Coroner."

The typewritten letter went its round of the jury and presently came back to the Coroner. He replaced it in its envelope and handed the envelope to Hawthwaite.

"You must leave no stone unturned in your effort to trace that letter to its source," he said. "That's of the highest importance. And now I think we had better adjourn for——"

But Tansley rose from his seat at Brent's elbow.

"I should like to draw attention to a somewhat pertinent fact, Mr. Coroner," he said. "It seems to have a distinct bearing on what has just transpired. During a search of the deceased's private papers, made by Mr. Brent and myself, yesterday afternoon, we found Mr. Wallingford's will. It was drawn up by himself, in very concise terms, and duly executed, only a few days before his death. It suggests itself to me that he was impelled to this by the threat which is distinctly made in the letter you have just read."

"I think we may take it that the late Mayor felt that he was in some personal danger," answered the Coroner. "What you say, Mr. Tansley, appears to corroborate that."

Then with a few words of counsel to the jury, he adjourned the inquest for ten days, and presently the folk who had listened to the proceedings streamed out into the market-place, excited and voluble. Instead of going away, the greater number of those who had been present lingered around the entrance, and Brent, leaving in Tansley's company a few minutes later, found high words being spoken between Alderman Crood and Epplewhite, who, prominent on the pavement, were haranguing each other amidst a ring of open-mouthed bystanders.

"You were at that game all through what you called your evidence!" vociferated Alderman Crood, who was obviously excited and angry far beyond his wont. "Nice evidence, indeed! Naught is it but trying to fasten blame on to innocent folk!"

"Suggesting!" sneered Mallett, close on his leader's right elbow. "Insinuating!"

"Hinting at things!" said Coppinger, close on the left. "Implying!"

"Dirty work!" shouted Alderman Crood. "Such as nobody but the likes o' you—Radicals and teetotallers and chapel folk!—'ud ever think o' doing. You say straight out before the town what's in your mind, Sam Epplewhite, and I'll see what the law has to say to you! I'm none going to have my character taken away by a fellow o' your sort. Say your say, here in public——"

"I'll say my say at the right time and place, Alderman Crood!" retorted Epplewhite. "This thing's going through! We'll find out who murdered John Wallingford yet—there's no need to go far away to find the murderer!"

Crood's big face grew livid with anger, and his long upper lip began to quiver. He raised his hand, as if to command the attention of the crowd, but just then Hawthwaite and a couple of policemen appeared in the open doorway behind, and Mallett and Coppinger, nudging the big man from either side, led him away along the market-place. And suddenly, from amongst the dispersing crowd, distinct murmurs of disapproval and dislike arose, crystallized in a sharp cry from some man on its outer edge.

"Down wi' the Town Trustees!—they're at t' bottom o' this! Down wi' 'em!"

The Town Trustees retreated before a suddenly awakened chorus of hooting. They disappeared into Mallett's private door at the Bank. Brent, watching and listening with speculative curiosity, felt Tansley touch his arm. He turned, to find the solicitor shaking his head, and with a grave countenance.

"Bad, bad!" muttered Tansley. "Very bad!—once get public opinion set on like that, and——"

"And what?" demanded Brent. He was already so convinced that his cousin had fallen a victim to political hatred that he was rather welcoming the revengeful outburst of feeling. "What, now?"

"There'll be an end of all sensible and practical proceedings in connection with the affair," answered Tansley. "There's a big following of the Reform party in the town amongst the working folk, and if they once get it into their heads that the Conservative lot put your cousin away—well, there'll be hell to pay!"

"Personally," said Brent, with a hardening of his square jaw, "I don't care if there is! If we can only put our hands on the murderers, I don't care if the people hang 'em to those lamp-posts! I shouldn't be sorry to see a little lynch law!"

"Then we shall never get at the truth," retorted Tansley. "We may—only may, mind you!—have got a bit towards it this morning, but not far. If at all—perhaps!"

"That threatening letter?" suggested Brent.

"I attach very little importance to it," said Tansley, "though I wasn't going to say so much in court. In my experience in this town, if I've seen one anonymous letter I've seen a hundred. Hathelsborough folk are given to that sort of thing. No, sir—there's a tremendous lot to come out yet. Don't you be surprised if all sorts of extraordinary developments materialize—perhaps when you're least expecting 'em!"

Brent made no answer. He was not easily surprised, and from the moment of his discovery of the crime he had realized that this was a mystery in the unravelling of which time and trouble would have to be expended freely. But he had a moment of genuine surprise that evening, when, as he sat in his private sitting-room at the *Chancellor*, he received a note, written in a delicate feminine hand on crested and scented paper, wherein he was requested, in somewhat guarded and mysterious fashion, to step round to the private residence of Mrs. Saumarez.

CHAPTER VIII

MRS. SAUMAREZ

B rent, at that moment, was in a state of mind which made every fibre of his being particularly sensitive to suspicions and speculative ideas—he had no sooner slipped Mrs. Saumarez's note into his pocket than he began to wonder why she had sent for him? Of course, it had something to do with Wallingford's murder, but what? If Mrs. Saumarez knew anything, why did she not speak at the inquest? She had been present all through the proceedings. Brent had frequently turned his eyes on her; always he had seen her in the same watchful, keen-eyed attitude, apparently deeply absorbed in the evidence, and, it seemed to him, showing signs of a certain amount of anxiety. Anxiety—yes, that was it, anxiety. The other spectators were curious, morbidly curious, most of them, but Mrs. Saumarez he felt sure was anxious. And about what? He wondered, but wondering was no good. He must go and see her of course; and presently he made himself ready and set out. But as he crossed the hall of the hotel he encountered Tansley, who was just emerging from the smoking-room. A thought occurred to him, and he motioned Tansley back into the room he had just quitted, and led him to a quiet corner.

"I say," said Brent, "between ourselves, I've just had a note from that Mrs. Saumarez we saw this morning in the Coroner's Court. She wants me to go round to her house at once."

Tansley showed his interest.

"Ah!" he exclaimed. "Then, she's something to tell."

"Why to me?" demanded Brent.

"You're Wallingford's next of kin," said the solicitor laconically. "That's why."

"Wonder what it is?" muttered Brent. "Some feminine fancy maybe."

"Go and find out, man!" laughed Tansley.

"Just so," replied Brent. "I'm going now. But look here—who and what is this Mrs. Saumarez? Post me up."

Tansley waved his cigar in the air, as if implying that you could draw a circle around his field of knowledge.

"Oh, well," he said, "you saw her to-day. So you're already aware that she's young and pretty and charming—and all that. As for the rest, she's a widow, and a wealthy one. Relict, as we say in the law, of a naval officer of high rank, who, I fancy, was some years older than herself. She came here about two years ago and rents a picturesque old place that was built, long since, out of the ruins of the old Benedictine Abbey that used to stand at the rear of what's now called Abbey Gate—some of the ruins, as you know, are still there. Clever woman—reads a lot and all that sort of thing. Not at all a society woman, in spite of her prettiness—bit of a blue-stocking, I fancy. Scarcely know her myself."

"I think you said my cousin knew her?" suggested Brent.

"Your cousin and she, latterly, were very thick," asserted Tansley. "He spent a lot of time at her house. During nearly all last autumn and winter, though, she was away in the South of France. Oh, yes, Wallingford often went to dine with her. She has a companion who lives with her—that elderly woman we saw this morning. Yes, I suppose Wallingford went there, oh, two or three evenings a week. In fact, there were people—gossipers—who firmly believed that he and Mrs. Saumarez were going to make a match of it. Might be so; but up to about the end of last summer the same people used to say that she was going to marry the doctor—Wellesley."

Brent pricked his ears—he scarcely knew why.

"Wellesley?" he said. "What? Was he a—a suitor?"

"Oh, well," answered Tansley, "I think the lady's one of the sort that's much fonder of men's society than of women's, you know. Anyway, after she came here, she and Wellesley seemed to take to each other, and she used to be in his company a good deal—used to go out driving with him, a lot, and so on. And he used to go to the Abbey House at that time just as much as your cousin did of late. But about the end of last summer Mrs. Saumarez seemed to cool off with Wellesley and take on with Wallingford—fact! The doctor got his nose put out by the lawyer! There's no doubt about it; and there's no doubt, either, that the result was a distinct coolness, not to say dislike, between Wellesley and Wallingford, for up to then those two had been rather close friends. But they certainly weren't after Mrs. Saumarez plainly showed a preference for Wallingford. Yet, in spite of that," continued Tansley, as if some after-thought struck him, "I'll say this for Wellesley: he's never allowed his undoubted jealousy of Wallingford to prevent him from supporting Wallingford on the Town Council. Wellesley, indeed, has always been one of his staunchest and most consistent supporters."

"Oh, Dr. Wellesley's on the Town Council, is he?" asked Brent. "And a Reform man?"

"He's Councillor for the Riverside Ward," answered Tansley, "and a regular Radical. In fact he, Wallingford, and that chap Epplewhite, were the three recognized leaders of the Reform party. Yes, Wellesley stuck to Wallingford as leader even when it became pretty evident that Wallingford had ousted him in Mrs. Saumarez's affections—fact!"

"Affections, eh?" surmised Brent. "You think it had come to as much as that?"

"I do!" affirmed Tansley. "Lord bless you, she and Wallingford were as thick as thieves, as our local saying goes. Oh, yes, I'm sure she threw Wellesley over for Wallingford."

Brent heard all this in silence, and remained for a time in further silence.

"Um!" he remarked at last. "Odd! Mrs. Saumarez is an unusually pretty woman. Dr. Wellesley is a very handsome man. Now, my cousin was about as plain and insignificant a chap to look at as ever I came across—poor fellow!"

"Your cousin was a damned clever chap!" said Tansley incisively. "He'd got brains, my dear sir, and where women—cleverish women, anyhow—are concerned, brains are going to win all the way and come in winners by as many lengths as you please! Mrs. Saumarez, I understand, is a woman who dabbles in politics, and your cousin interested her. And when a woman gets deeply interested in a man——?"

"I guess you're right," assented Brent. "Well, I'll step along and see her."

He left Tansley in the hotel and went away along the market-place, wondering a good deal about the information just given to him. So there was a coolness between his cousin and Wellesley, was there, a coolness that amounted, said Tansley, to something stronger? Did it amount to jealousy? Did the jealousy lead to——? But at that point Brent gave up speculating. If there was anything in this new suggestion, Mrs. Saumarez would hold the key. Once more he was face to face with the fact that had steadily obtruded itself upon him during the last two days: that here in this time-worn old place there were folks who had secrets and did things in a curiously secret fashion.

Mrs. Saumarez's house stood a little way back from the street called Abbey Gate, an old, apparently Early Jacobean mansion, set amidst the elms for which Hathelsborough was famous, so profusely and to such a height did they grow all over the town. A smart parlour-maid, who looked inquisitively at him, and was evidently expecting his arrival, admitted Brent, and led him at once along a half-lighted hall into a little room, where the light of a shaded lamp shone on a snug and comfortable interior and on rows of more books than young and pretty women generally possess. Left alone for a few minutes, Brent glanced round the well-filled shelves, and formed the opinion that Mrs. Saumarez went in for very solid reading, chiefly in the way of social and political economy. He began to see now why she and the murdered Mayor had been such close friends—the subjects that apparently interested her had been those in which Wallingford had always been deeply absorbed. Maybe, then, Mrs. Saumarez had been behind the Reform party in Hathelsborough?—there was a woman wire-puller at the back of these matters as a rule, he believed—that sort of thing, perhaps, was Mrs. Saumarez's little hobby. He turned from these speculations to find her at his elbow.

"Thank you for coming, Mr. Brent," she said softly.

Brent looked attentively at her as he took the hand which she held out to him. Seen at closer quarters he saw that she was a much prettier woman than he had fancied; he saw too that, whatever her tastes might be in the way of politics and sociology, she was wholly feminine, and not above enhancing her charms by punctilious attention to her general appearance and setting. She had been very quietly and even sombrely dressed at the inquest that morning, but she was now in evening dress, and her smart gown, her wealth of fair hair, her violet eyes, and the rose tint of her delicate cheek somewhat dazzled Brent, who was not greatly used to women's society. He felt a little shy and a little awkward.

"Yes, yes, I came at once," he said. "I—of course, I gathered that you wanted me."

Mrs. Saumarez smiled, and pointing to an easy chair in front of the bright fire dropped into another close by it.

"Sit down, Mr. Brent," she said. "Yes, I wanted you. And I couldn't very well go to the *Chancellor*, could I? So thank you again for coming so promptly. Perhaps"—she turned and looked at him steadily—"you're already aware that your cousin and I were great friends?"

"I've heard it," answered Brent. He nodded at one of the book-cases at which she had found him looking. "Similar tastes, I suppose? He was a great hand at that sort of thing."

"Yes," she said. "We had a good deal in common; I was much interested in all his plans, and so on. He was a very clever man, a deeply interesting man, and I have felt—this—more than I'm going to say. And—but I think I'd better tell you why I sent for you."

"Yes," assented Brent.

"I gathered from what was said at the inquest this morning that you are your cousin's sole executor?" she asked.

"I am," replied Brent. "Sole everything."

"Then, of course, you have entire charge and custody of his papers?" she suggested.

"That's so," answered Brent. "Everything's in my possession."

Mrs. Saumarez sighed gently; it seemed to Brent that there was something of relief in the sigh.

"Last autumn and winter," she continued presently, "I was away from home a long time; I was in the South of France. Mr. Wallingford and I kept up a regular, and frequent, correspondence: it was just then, you know, that he became Mayor, and began to formulate his schemes for the regeneration of this rotten little town——"

"You think it's that, eh?" interrupted Brent, emphasizing the personal pronoun. "That's your conviction?"

Mrs. Saumarez's violet eyes flashed, and a queer little smile played for a second round the corner of her pretty lips.

"Rotten to the core!" she said quietly. "Ripe rotten! *He* knew it!—knew more than he ever let anyone know!"

"More than he ever let you know?" asked Brent.

"I knew a good deal," she replied evasively. "But this correspondence. We wrote to each other twice a week all the time I was away. I have all his letters—there, in that safe."

"Yes?" said Brent.

Mrs. Saumarez looked down at the slim fingers which lay in her lap.

"He kept all mine," she continued.

"Yes?" repeated Brent.

"I want them," she murmured, with a sudden lifting of her eyelids in her visitor's direction. "I, naturally, I don't want them to—to fall into anybody else's hands. You understand, Mr. Brent?"

"You want me to find them?" suggested Brent.

"Not to find them, that is, not to search for them," she replied quickly. "I know where they are. I want you, if you please, to give them back to me."

"Where are they?" asked Brent.

"He told me where he kept them," answered Mrs. Saumarez. "They are in a cedar-wood cabinet, in a drawer in his bedroom."

"All right," said Brent. "I'll get them."

Was he mistaken in thinking that it was an unmistakable sigh of relief that left Mrs. Saumarez's delicate red lips and that an additional little flush of colour came into her cheeks? But her voice was calm and even enough.

"Thank you," she said. "So good of you. Of course, they aren't of the faintest interest to anybody. I can have them, then—when?"

Brent rose to his feet.

"When I was taught my business," he said, with a dry smile, "I'd a motto drummed into my head day in and day out. DO IT NOW! So I guess I'll just go round to my cousin's old rooms and get you that cabinet at once."

Mrs. Saumarez smiled. It was a smile that would have thrilled most men. But Brent merely got a deepened impression of her prettiness.

"I like your way of doing things," she said. "That's business. You ought to stop here, Mr. Brent, and take up your cousin's work."

"It would be a fitting tribute to his memory, wouldn't it?" answered Brent. "Well, I don't know. But this letter business is the thing to do now. I'll be back in ten minutes, Mrs. Saumarez."

"Let yourself in, and come straight here," she said. "I'll wait for you."

Wallingford's old rooms were close at hand—only round the corner, in fact—and Brent went straight to them and into the bedroom. He found the cedar cabinet at once; he had, in fact, seen it the day before, but finding it locked had made no attempt to open it. He carried it back to Mrs. Saumarez, set it on her desk, and laid beside it a bunch of keys.

"I suppose you'll find this key amongst those," he said. "They're all the private keys of his that I have anyway."

"Perhaps you will find it?" she suggested. "I'm a bad hand at that sort of thing."

Brent had little difficulty in finding the right key. Unthinkingly, he raised the lid of the cabinet—and quickly closed it again. In that momentary glimpse of the contents it seemed to him that he had unearthed a dead man's secret. For in addition to a pile of letters he had seen a woman's glove; a knot of ribbon; some faded flowers.

"That's it," he said hurriedly, shutting down the lid and affecting to have seen nothing. "I'll take the key off the bunch."

Mrs. Saumarez took the key from him in silence, relocked the cabinet, and carried it over to a safe let in to the wall of the room.

"Thank you, Mr. Brent," she said. "I'm glad to have those letters."

Brent made as if to leave. But he suddenly turned on her.

"You know a lot," he remarked brusquely. "What's your opinion about my cousin's murder?"

Mrs. Saumarez remained silent so long that he spoke again.

"Do you think, from what you've seen of things in this town, that it was what we may call political?" he asked. "A—removal?"

He was watching her closely, and he saw the violet eyes grow sombre, and a certain hardness settle about the lines of the well-shaped mouth and chin.

"It's this!" she said suddenly. "I told you just now that this town is rotten—rotten and corrupt, as so many of these little old-world English boroughs are! *He* knew it, poor fellow; he's steadily been finding it out ever since he came here. I dare say you, coming from London, a great city, wouldn't understand, but it's this way: this town is run by a gang, the members of which manœuvre everything for their own and their friends' benefit, their friends and their hangers-on, their associates, their toadies. They——"

"Do you mean the Town Trustees?" asked Brent.

"Not wholly," replied Mrs. Saumarez. "But all that Epplewhite said to-day about the Town Trustees is true. The three men control the financial affairs of the borough. Wallingford, by long and patient investigation, had come to know *how* they controlled them, and how utterly corrupt and rotten the whole financial administration is. If you could see some of the letters of his which I have in that safe——"

"Wouldn't it be well to produce them?" suggested Brent.

"Not yet anyway," she said. "I'll consider that—much of it's general statement, not particular accusation. But the Town Trustees question is not all. Until very recently, when a Reform party gradually got into being and increased steadily—though it's still in a minority—the whole representation and administration of the borough was hopelessly bad and unprincipled. For what do you suppose men went into the Town Council? To represent the ratepayer, the townspeople? No, but to look after their own interests; to safeguard themselves; to get what they could out of it: the whole policy of the old councils was one of—there's only one word for it, Mr. Brent, and that's only just becoming Anglicized—Graft! Now, the Corporation of a town is supposed to exist for the good, the welfare, the protection of a town, but the whole idea of these Hathelsborough men, in the past, has been to use their power and privileges as administrators, for their own ends. So here you've had, on the one hand, the unfortunate ratepayer and, on the other, a close Corporation, a privileged band of pirates, battening on them. In plain words, there are about a hundred men in Hathelsborough who have used the seven or eight thousand other folk as a means to their own ends. The town has been a helpless, defenceless thing, from which these harpies have picked whatever they could lay their talons on!"

"That's the conclusion he'd come to?" asked Brent.

"He couldn't come to any other after many years of patient investigation," declared Mrs. Saumarez. "And he was the sort of man who had an inborn hatred of abuses and shams and hypocrisy! And now put it to yourself—when a man stands up against vested interests, such as exist here, and says plainly that he's never going to rest, nor leave a stone unturned, until he's made a radical and thorough reformation, do you think he's going to have a primrose path of it? Bah! But *he* knew! He knew his danger."

"But—murder?" said Brent. "Murder!"

Mrs. Saumarez shook her head.

"Yes," she answered. "But there are men in this place who wouldn't stick at even that! You don't know. If Wallingford had done all the things he'd vowed to do, there would have been such an exposure of affairs here as would have made the whole country agape. And some men would have been ruined—literally. I know! And things will come out and be tracked down, if no red herrings are drawn across the trail. You're going to get at the truth?"

"By God, yes!" exclaimed Brent, with sudden fervour. "I am so!"

"Look for his murderers amongst the men he intended to show up, then!" she said, with a certain fierce intensity. "And look closely—and secretly! There's no other way!"

Brent presently left her and went off wondering about the contents of the little cabinet. He would have wondered still more if he had been able to look back into the cosy room which he had just left. For when he had gone, Mrs. Saumarez took the cabinet from the safe and carefully emptied the whole of its contents into the glowing heart of the fire. She stood watching as the flames licked round them, and until there was nothing left there but black ash.

CHAPTER IX

THE RIGHT TO INTERVENE

Brent went back to his hotel to find the Town Clerk of Hathelsborough waiting for him in his private sitting-room. His visitor, a sharp-eyed man whose profession was suggested in every look and movement, greeted him with a suavity of manner which set Brent on his guard.

"I am here, Mr. Brent," he said, with an almost deprecating smile, "as—well, as a sort of informal deputation—informal."

"Deputations represent somebody or something," retorted Brent, in his brusquest fashion. "Whom do you represent?"

"The borough authorities," replied the Town Clerk, with another smile. "That is to say——"

"You'll excuse me for interrupting," said Brent. "I'm a man of plain speech. I take it that by borough authorities you mean, say, Mr. Simon Crood and his fellow Town Trustees? That so?"

"Well, perhaps so," admitted the Town Clerk. "Mr. Alderman Crood, to be sure, is Deputy-Mayor. And he and his brother Town Trustees are certainly men of authority."

"What do you want?" demanded Brent.

The Town Clerk lowered his voice—quite unnecessarily in Brent's opinion. His suave tones became dulcet and mollifying.

"My dear sir," he said, leaning forward, "to-morrow you—you have the sad task of interring your cousin, our late greatly respected Mayor."

"Going to bury him to-morrow," responded Brent. "Just so—well?"

"There is a rumour in the town that you intend the—er—ceremony to be absolutely private," continued the Town Clerk.

"I do," assented Brent. "And it will be!"

The Town Clerk made a little expostulatory sound.

"My dear sir," he said soothingly, "the late Mr. Wallingford was Mayor of Hathelsborough! The four hundred and eighty-first Mayor of Hathelsborough, Mr. Brent!"

Brent, who was leaning against the mantelpiece, looked fixedly at his visitor.

"Supposing he was the nine hundred and ninety-ninth Mayor of Hathelsborough," he asked quietly, "what then?"

"He should have a public funeral," declared the Town Clerk promptly. "My dear sir, to inter a Mayor of Hathelsborough—and the four hundred and eighty-first holder of the ancient and most dignified office—privately, as if he were a—a mere nobody, a common townsman, is—oh, really, it's unheard of!"

"That the notion of the men who sent you here?" asked Brent grimly.

"The notion, as you call it, of the gentlemen who sent me here, Mr. Brent, is that your cousin's funeral obsequies should be of a public nature," answered the Town Clerk. "According to precedent, of course. During my term of office as Town Clerk two Mayors have died during their year of Mayoralty. On such occasions the Corporation has been present in state."

"In state?" said Brent. "What's that amount to? Sort of procession?"

"A duly marshalled one," answered the Town Clerk. "The beadle with his mace; the Deputy-Mayor; the Recorder—the Recorder and Town Clerk, of course, in wigs and gowns—the Aldermen in their furred robes; the Councillors in their violet gowns—a very stately procession, Mr. Brent, preceding the funeral cortège to St. Hathelswide's Church, where the Vicar, as Mayor's Chaplain, would deliver a funeral oration. The procession would return subsequently to the Moot Hall, for wine and cake."

Brent rubbed his square chin, staring hard at his visitor.

"Um!" he said at last. "Well, there isn't going to be anything of that sort to-morrow. I'm just going to bury my cousin quietly and privately, without maces and furred robes and violet gowns. So you can just tell 'em politely—nothing doing!"

"But my dear sir, my good Mr. Brent!" expostulated the visitor. "The Mayor of Hathelsborough! The oldest borough in the country! Why, our charter of incorporation dates from——"

"I'm not particularly interested in archæology, just now anyway," interrupted Brent. "And it's nothing to me in connection with this matter if your old charter was signed by William the Conqueror or Edward the Confessor. I say—nothing doing!"

"But your reasons, my dear sir, your reasons!" exclaimed the Town Clerk. "Such a breaking with established custom and precedent! I really don't know what the neighbouring boroughs will say of us!"

"Let 'em say!" retorted Brent. He laughed contemptuously. But suddenly his mood changed, and he turned on his visitor with what the Town Clerk afterwards described as a very ugly look. "But if you want to know," he added, "I'll tell you why I won't have any

Corporation processing after my cousin's dead body! It's because I believe that his murderer's one of 'em! See?"

The Town Clerk, a rosy-cheeked man, turned pale. His gloves lay on the table at his elbow, and his fingers trembled a little as he picked them up and began fitting them on with meticulous precision.

"My dear sir!" he said, in a tone that suggested his profession more strongly than ever. "That's very grave language. As a solicitor, I should advise you——"

"When I say murderer," continued Brent, "I'm perhaps wrong. I might—and no doubt ought to—use the plural. Murderers! I believe that more than one of your rascally Corporation conspired to murder my cousin! And I'm going to have no blood-stained hypocrites processing after his coffin! You tell 'em to keep away!"

"I had better withdraw," said the Town Clerk.

"No hurry," observed Brent, changing to geniality. He laid his hand on the bell. "Have a whisky-and-soda and a cigar? We've finished our business, and I guess you're a man as well as a lawyer?"

But the visitor was unable to disassociate his personal identity from his office, and he bowed himself out. Brent laughed when he had gone.

"Got the weight of four hundred and eighty-one years of incorporation on him!" he said. "Lord! it's like living with generation after generation of your grandfathers slung round you! Four hundred and eighty-one years! Must have been in the bad old days when this mouldy town got its charter!"

Next morning Brent buried the dead Mayor in St. Hathelswide's Churchyard, privately and quietly. He stayed by the grave until the sexton and his assistants had laid the green turf over it; that done, he went round to the Abbey House and sought out Mrs. Saumarez. After his characteristic fashion he spoke out what was in his mind.

"I've pretty well fixed up, in myself, to do what you suggested last night," he said, giving her one of his direct glances. "You know what I mean—to go on with his work."

Mrs. Saumarez's eyes sparkled.

"That would be splendid!" she exclaimed. "But, if he had opposition, you'll have it a hundred-fold! You're not afraid?"

"Afraid of nothing," said Brent carelessly. "But I just don't know how I'd get any right to do it. I'm not a townsman—I've no *locus standi*. But, then he wasn't, to begin with."

"I'd forgotten that," said Mrs. Saumarez. "And you'd have to give up your work in London—journalism, isn't it?"

"I've thought of that," said Brent. "Well, I've had a pretty good spell at it, and I'm not so keen about keeping on it any longer. There's other work—literary work—I'd prefer. And I'm not dependent on it any way—I've got means of my own, and now Wallingford's left me a good lot of money. No; I guess I wouldn't mind coming here and going on with the job he'd set himself to; I'd like to do it But, then, how to get a footing in the place?"

Mrs. Saumarez considered for a while. Suddenly her face lighted up.

"You've got money," she said. "Why don't you buy a bit of property in the town—a piece of real estate? Then——"

Brent picked up his hat.

"That's a good notion," he said. "I'll step round and see Tansley about it."

Tansley had been one of the very few men whom Brent had invited to be present at his cousin's interment. He had just changed his mourning garments for those of everyday life and was settling down to his professional business when Brent was shown into his private office.

"Busy?" demanded Brent in his usual laconic fashion.

"Give you whatever time you want," answered the solicitor, who knew his man by that time. "What is it now?"

"I've concluded to take up my abode in this old town," said Brent, with something of a sheepish smile. "Seems queer, no doubt, but my mind's fixed. And so, look here, you don't know anybody that's got a bit of real estate to sell—nice little house, or something of that sort? If so——"

Tansley thrust his letters and papers aside, pushed an open box of cigars in his visitor's direction, and lighting one himself became inquisitively attentive.

"What's the game?" he asked.

Brent lighted a cigar and took two or three meditative puffs at it before answering this direct question.

"Well," he said at last, "I don't think that I'm a particularly sentimental sort of person, but all the same I'm not storm-proof against sentiment. And I've just got the conviction that it's up to me to go on with my cousin's job in this place."

Tansley took his cigar from his lips and whistled.

"Tall order, Brent!" he remarked.

"So I reckon," assented Brent. "But I've served an apprenticeship to that sort of thing. And I've always gone through with whatever came in my way."

"Let's be plain," said Tansley. "You mean that you want to settle here in the town, and go on with Wallingford's reform policy?"

"That's just it," replied Brent. "You've got it."

"All I can say is, then, that you're rendering yourself up to—well, not envy, but certainly to hatred, malice and all uncharitableness, as it's phrased in the Prayer Book," declared Tansley. "You'll have a hot old time!"

"Used to 'em!" retorted Brent. "You forget I've been a press-man for some years."

"But you didn't get that sort of thing?" suggested Tansley, half incredulous.

Brent flicked the ash from his cigar and smiled.

"Don't go in for tall talk," he said lazily. "But it was I who tracked down the defaulting directors of the Great Combined Amalgamation affair, and ran to earth that chap who murdered his ward away up in Northumberland, and found the Pembury absconding bank-manager who'd scooted off so cleverly that the detectives couldn't trace even a smile of him! Pretty stiff propositions, all those! And I reckon I can do my bit here in this place, on Wallingford's lines, if I get the right to intervene, as a townsman. That's what I want—*locus standi*."

"And when you've got it?" asked Tansley.

Brent worked his cigar into the corner of his firm lips and folding his arms stared straight in front of him.

"Well," he said slowly, "I think I've fixed that in my own mind, fixed it all out while the parson was putting him away in that old churchyard this morning—I was thinking hard while he was reading his book. I understand that by my cousin's death there's a vacancy in the Town Council—he sat for some ward or other?"

"He sat for the Castle Ward, as Town Councillor," assented Tansley. "So of course there's a vacancy."

"Well," continued Brent, "I reckon I'll put up for that vacancy. I'll be Mr. Councillor Richard Brent!"

"You're a stranger, man!" laughed Tansley.

"I'll not be in a week's time," retorted Brent. "I'll be known to every householder in that ward! But—this *locus standi*? If I bought real estate in the town, I'd be a townsman, wouldn't I? A burgess, I reckon. And then—why legally I'd be as much a Hathelsborough man as, say, Simon Crood?"

Tansley took his hands out of his pockets and began to search amongst his papers.

"Well, you're a go-ahead chap, Brent!" he said. "Evidently not the sort to let grass grow under your feet. And if you want to buy a bit of nice property I've the very goods for you. There's a client of mine, John Chillingham, a retired tradesman, who wants to sell his house—he's desirous of quitting this part of the country and going to live on the South Coast. It's a delightful bit of property, just at the back of the Castle, and it's therefore in the Castle Ward. Acacia Lodge, it's called—nice, roomy, old-fashioned house, in splendid condition, modernized, set in a beautiful old garden, with a magnificent cedar tree on the lawn, and a fine view from its front windows. And, for a quick sale, cheap."

"What's the figure?" asked Brent.

"Two thousand guineas," answered Tansley.

Brent reached for his hat.

"Let's go and look at it," he said.

Within a few hours Brent had settled his purchase of Acacia Lodge from the retired tradesman and Tansley was busy with the legal necessities of the conveyance. That done, and in his new character of townsman and property owner, Brent sought out Peppermore, and into that worthy's itching and astonished ears poured out a confession which the editor of the *Monitor* was to keep secret until next day; after which, retiring to his sitting-room at the *Chancellor*, he took up pen and paper, and proceeded to write a document which occasioned him more thought than he usually gave to his literary productions. It was not a lengthy document, but it had been rewritten and interlineated and corrected several times before Brent carried it to the *Monitor* office and the printing-press. Peppermore, reading it over, grinned with malicious satisfaction.

"That'll make 'em open their mouths and their eyes to-morrow morning, Mr. Brent!" he exclaimed. "We'll have it posted all over the town by ten o'clock, sir. And all that the *Monitor*—powerful organ, Mr. Brent, very powerful organ!—can do on your behalf and in your interest shall be done, sir, it shall be done—*con amore*, as I believe they say in Italy."

"Thank 'ee!" said Brent. "You're the right stuff."

"Don't mention it, sir," replied Peppermore. "Only too pleased. Egad! I wish I could see Mr. Alderman Crood's face when he reads this poster!"

At five minutes past ten next morning, as he, Mallett and Coppinger came together out of the side-door of the bank, where they had been in close conference since half-past nine, on affairs of their own, Mr. Alderman Crood saw the poster on which was set out Brent's election address to the voters of the Castle Ward. The bill-posting people had pasted a copy of it on a blank wall opposite; the three men, open-mouthed and wide-eyed, gathered round and read. Crood grew purple with anger.

"Impudence!" he exclaimed at last. "Sheer brazen impudence! Him—a stranger! Take up his cousin's work, will he? And what's he mean by saying that he's now a Hathelsborough man?"

"I heard about that last night," answered Coppinger. "Tansley told two or three of us at the club. This fellow Brent has bought that property of old Chillingham's—Acacia Lodge. Freehold, you know; bought it right out. He's a Hathelsborough man now, right enough."

Then they both turned and glanced at Mallett, who was re-reading Brent's election address with brooding eyes and lowering brow.

"Well?" demanded Coppinger. "What do you make of it, Mallett?"

Mallett removed his glasses and sniffed.

"Don't let's deceive ourselves," he said, with a hasty glance round. "This chap's out to make trouble. He's no fool, either. If he gets into the Council we shall have an implacable enemy. And he's every chance. So it's all the more necessary than ever that we should bring off to-morrow what we've been talking over this morning."

"We ought to do that," said Coppinger. "We can count on fourteen sure votes."

"Ay!" said Mallett. "But so can they! The thing is—the three votes neither party can count on. We must get at those three men to-day. If we don't carry our point to-morrow, we shall have Sam Epplewhite or Dr. Wellesley as Mayor, and things'll be as bad as they were under Wallingford."

This conversation referred to an extraordinary meeting of the Town Council which had been convened for the next day, in order to elect a new Mayor of Hathelsborough in succession to John Wallingford, deceased. Brent heard of it that afternoon, from Queenie Crood, in the Castle grounds. He had met Queenie there more than once since their first encountering in those sheltered nooks: already he was not quite sure that he was not looking forward with increasing pleasure to these meetings. For with each Queenie came further out of her shell, the more they met, the more she let him see of herself—and he found her interesting. And they had given up talking of Queenie's stage ambitions—not that she had thrown them over, but that she and Brent had begun to find the discussion of their own personalities more to the immediate point than the canvassing of remote possibilities: each, in fact, was in the stage of finding each other a mine worth exploring. Brent began to see a lot in Queenie and her dark eyes; Queenie was beginning to consider Brent, with his grim jaw, his brusque, off-hand speech, and masterful manner, a curiously fascinating person; besides, he was beginning to do things that only strong men do.

"You're in high disgrace at the Tannery House," she remarked archly when they met that afternoon. "I should think your ears must have burned this dinner-time."

"Why, now?" inquired Brent.

"Uncle Simon brought Mallet and Coppinger home to dinner," continued Queenie. "It was lucky there was a big hot joint!—they're all great eaters and drinkers. And they abused you to their hearts' content. This Town Council business—they say it's infernal impudence for you to put up for election. However, Coppinger says you'll not get in."

"Coppinger is a bad prophet," said Brent. "I'll be Town Councillor in a fortnight. Lay anybody ten to one!"

"Well, they'll do everything they can to keep you out," declared Queenie. "You've got to fight an awful lot of opposition."

"Let 'em all come!" retorted Brent. "I'll represent the Castle Ward, and now that I'm a burgess of Hathelsborough I'll be Mayor some old time."

"Not yet, though," said Queenie. "They're going to elect a new Mayor to-morrow. In place of your cousin of course."

Brent started. Nobody had mentioned that to him. Yet he might have thought of it himself—of course there must be a new Mayor of Hathelsborough.

"Gad! I hope it'll not be one of the old gang!" he muttered. "If it is——"

But by noon next day he heard that the old gang had triumphed. Mr. Alderman Crood was elected Mayor of Hathelsborough by a majority of two votes. A couple of the wobblers on the Council had given way at the last moment and thrown in their lot with the reactionary, let-things-alone party.

"Never mind! I'll win my election," said Brent. "The future is with me."

He set to work, in strenuous fashion, to enlist the favours of the Castle Ward electorate. All day, from early morning until late at night, he was cultivating the acquaintance of the burgesses. He had little time for any other business than this—there were but ten days before the election. But now and then he visited the police station and interviewed Hawthwaite; and at each visit he found the superintendent becoming increasingly reserved and mysterious in manner. Hawthwaite would say nothing definite, but he dropped queer hints about certain things that he had up his sleeve,to be duly produced at the adjourned inquest. As to what they were, he remained resolutely silent, even to Brent.

CHAPTER X

THE CAT IN THE BAG

But as the day of the adjourned inquest drew near Brent became aware that there were rumours in the air—rumours of some sensational development, the particulars of which were either non-obtainable or utterly vague. He heard of them from Peppermore, whose journalistic itching for news had so far gone unrelieved; Peppermore himself knew no more than that rumour was busy, and secret.

"Can't make out for the life of me what it is, Mr. Brent!" said Peppermore, calling upon Brent at the *Chancellor* on the eve of the inquiry. "But there's something, sir, something! You know that boy of mine—young Pryder?"

"Smart youth!" replied Brent.

"As they make 'em, sir," agreed Peppermore. "That boy, Mr. Brent, will go far in the profession of which you're a shining and I'm a dim light!—he's got what the French, I believe, sir, call a *flair* for news. Took to our line like a duck to water, Mr. Brent! Well, now, young Pryder's father is a policeman—sergeant in the Borough Constabulary, and naturally he's opportunities of knowing. And when he knows he talks—in the home circle, Mr. Brent."

"Been talking?" asked Brent.

"Guardedly, sir, guardedly!" replied Peppermore. "Young Pryder, he told me this afternoon that his father, when he came home to dinner to-day, said to him and his mother that when the inquest's reopened to-morrow there's be something to talk about—somebody, said Sergeant Pryder, would have something to talk of before the day was over. So—there you are!"

"I suppose old Pryder didn't tell young Pryder any more than that?" suggested Brent.

"He did not, sir," said Peppermore. "Had he done so, Jimmy Pryder would have made half a column, big type, leaded, out of it. No; nothing more. There are men in this world,

Mr. Brent, as you have doubtless observed, who are given to throwing out mere hints—sort of men who always look at you as much as to say, 'Ah, I could tell a lot if I would!' I guess Sergeant Pryder's one of 'em."

"Whatever Sergeant Pryder knows he's got from Hawthwaite, of course," remarked Brent.

"To be sure, sir!" agreed Peppermore. "Hawthwaite's been up to something—I've felt that for some days. I imagine there'll be new witnesses to-morrow, but who they'll be I can't think."

Brent could not think, either, nor did he understand Hawthwaite's reserve. But he wasted no time in speculation: he had already made up his mind that unless something definite arose at the resumed inquiry he would employ professional detective assistance and get to work on lines of his own. He had already seen enough of Hathelsborough ways and Hathelsborough folk to feel convinced that if this affair of his cousin's murder could be hushed up it would be hushed up—the Simon Crood gang, he was persuaded, would move heaven and earth to smooth things over and consign the entire episode to oblivion. Against that process he meant to labour: in his opinion the stirring up of strong public interest was the line to take, and he was fully determined that if the Coroner and his twelve good men and true could not sift the problem of this inquiry to the bottom he would.

That public feeling and curiosity—mainly curiosity—were still strong enough, and were lasting well over the proverbial nine days, Brent saw as soon as he quitted the hall door of the *Chancellor* next morning. The open space between High Cross and the Moot Hall was packed with people, eager to enter the big court room as soon as the doors were thrown open. Conscious that he himself would get a seat whoever else did not, Brent remained standing on the steps of the hotel, lazily watching the gossiping crowd And suddenly Mrs. Saumarez, once more attired in the semi-mourning which she had affected at the earlier proceedings, and attended by the same companion, came along the market-place in his direction. Brent went down and joined her.

"Pretty stiff crowd!" he remarked laconically. "I'm afraid you'll find it a bit of a crush this time. I suppose you'll not let that stop you, though?"

He noticed then that Mrs. Saumarez was looking anxious, perhaps a little distressed, and certainly not too well pleased. She gave him a glance which began at himself and ended at a folded paper which she carried in her well-gloved hand.

"I've got to go!" she murmured. "Got to—whether I like it or not! They've served me with a summons, as a witness. Ridiculous! What do I know about it? All that I do know is—private."

Brent stared at the bit of paper. He, too, was wondering what the Coroner wanted with Mrs. Saumarez.

"I'm afraid they haven't much respect for privacy in these affairs," he remarked. "Odd, though, that if they want you now they didn't want you at the first sitting!"

"Do you think they'll ask questions that are—private?" she suggested half-timidly.

"Can't say," replied Brent. "You'd better be prepared for anything. You know best, after all, what they can ask you. I reckon the best thing, in these affairs, is just to answer plainly, and be done with it."

"There are certain things one doesn't want raking up," she murmured. "For instance—do you think you'll have to give evidence again?"

"Maybe," said Brent.

She gave him a meaning look and lowered her voice.

In the Mayor's Parlour

"Well," she whispered, "if you have to, don't let anything come out about—about those letters. You know what I mean—the letters you got for me from his rooms? I—I don't want it to be known, in the town, that he and I corresponded as much as all that. After all, there are some things——"

Just then, and while Brent was beginning to speculate on this suddenly-revealed desire for secrecy, a movement in the crowd ahead of them showed that the doors of the Moot Hall had been thrown open; he, too, moved forward, drawing his companion with him.

"You'll not forget that?" said Mrs. Saumarez insistently. "It's—those letters, I mean—they're nothing to do with this, of course—nothing! Don't let it out that——"

"I shan't volunteer any evidence of any sort," responded Brent. "If I'm confronted with a direct question which necessitates a direct answer, that's another matter. But I don't think you've anything to worry about—I should say that what they want you for is to ask a question or two as to my cousin's movements that night, didn't he call at your house on his way to the Mayor's Parlour? Yes, why that'll be about it!"

"I hope so!" said Mrs. Saumarez, with a sigh of relief. "But—that witness-box, and before all these people—I don't like it."

"Got to be done," observed Brent. "Soon over, though. Now let's get in."

He piloted Mrs. Saumarez and her companion into the borough Court, handed over to the Coroner for the special purposes of his inquest, found them seats in a reserved part, and leaving them went over to the solicitor's table, where he took a place by the side of Tansley, already settled there with his notes and papers. Tansley gave him a significant glance, nodding his head sideways at other men near them.

"Going to be a more serious affair, this, than the first was, Brent," he whispered. "These police chaps have either got something up their sleeves or Hawthwaite's got some bee in his bonnet! Anyway, there's a barrister in the case on their behalf—that little, keen-eyed chap at the far end of the table on your left; that's Meeking, one of the sharpest criminal barristers going—and I hear they're meaning to call a lot of new witnesses. But what it's all about, I don't know."

Brent looked up and down the table at which they were sitting. There were men there—legal-looking men—whom he had not seen at the opening day's proceedings.

"Who are these other fellows?" he asked.

"Oh, well, Crood's got a man representing his interests," replied Tansley. "And there's another solicitor watching the case on behalf of the Corporation. And I rather fancy that that chap at the extreme end of the table is representing the Treasury—which may mean that this affair is going to be taken up at Head-quarters. But we know nothing till the cards are on the board! Hawthwaite looks important enough this morning to hold all the aces!"

Brent glanced at the superintendent, who was exchanging whispers with the Coroner's officer, and from him to the crowded seats that ran round three sides of the court. All the notabilities of Hathelsborough were there again, in full force: Simon Crood, in a seat of honour, as befitted his new dignity of Mayor; Mallett; Coppinger, anybody and everybody of consequence. And there, too, was Krevin Crood, and Queenie, and, just behind Mrs. Saumarez, Dr. Wellesley, looking distinctly bored, and his assistant, Dr. Carstairs, a young Scotsman, and near them another medical man, Dr. Barber; and near the witness-box were several men whom Brent knew by sight as townsmen and who were obviously expecting to be called for testimony. He turned away wondering what was to come out of all this.

Once more the Coroner, precise and formal as ever, took his seat; once more the twelve jurymen settled in their places. And while Brent was speculating on the first order of procedure he was startled by the sharp, official voice of the Coroner's officer.

"Mrs. Anita Saumarez!"

Brent heard Tansley smother an exclamation of surprise; a murmur that was not smothered ran round the crowded benches behind him. There was something dramatic in the sudden calling of the pretty young widow, whose personality was still more or less of a mystery to Hathelsborough folk, and something curiosity-raising in the mere fact that she was called. All eyes were on her as, showing traces of confusion and dislike, she made her way to the witness-box. There was delay then; Mrs. Saumarez had to be instructed to lift her veil and remove her right-hand glove; this gave the crowd abundant opportunity for observing that her usually bright complexion had paled and that she was obviously ill at ease. It was with much embarrassment and in a very low voice that she replied to the preliminary questions. Anita Saumarez. Widow of the late Captain Roderick Francis Saumarez. Has been resident at the Abbey House, Hathelsborough, for about two years. "Doesn't like this job!" whispered Tansley to Brent. "Queer! From what bit I've seen of her, I should have said she'd make a very good and self-possessed witness. But she's nervous! Old Seagrave'll have to tackle her gently."

The Coroner evidently realized this as much as Tansley did. He leaned forward confidentially from his desk, toying with his spectacles, and regarded the witness with an encouraging and paternal smile.

"Mrs. Saumarez," he began, "we want to ask you a few questions—questions your replies to which may perhaps give us a little light on this very sad matter. I believe I am right in thinking that you and the late Mr. Wallingford were personal friends?"

Mrs. Saumarez's answer came in low tones—and in one word:

"Yes."

"Very close friends, I believe?"

"Yes."

"He used to visit at your house a great deal?"

"Yes."

"Dine with you, I think, once or twice a week?"

"At one time—yes."

"You say at one time? When was that period, now?"

Mrs. Saumarez, who up to this had kept her eyes on the ledge of the witness-box, began to take courage. She lifted them towards the Coroner and, encountering his placidly benevolent gaze, let them remain there.

"Well," she replied, "from about the time he became Mayor until the time of his death."

"Regularly?"

"Yes—regularly."

"We may take it, then, that you were fond of each other's society?"

Mrs. Saumarez hesitated.

"He was a very interesting man," she said at last. "I liked to talk to him."

The Coroner bent a little nearer.

"Well, now, a more personal question," he said suavely. "You will see the importance of it. Mr. Wallingford was constantly visiting you. I want a plain answer to what I am going to ask you. Was he a suitor for your hand?"

Mrs. Saumarez's cheeks flushed, and she looked down at the ungloved hand which rested, pressed on its gloved fellow, on the ledge before her.

"He certainly asked me to marry him," she murmured.

"When was that?"

"Not—not long before his death."

"And—I'm afraid I must ask you—what was your answer?"

"I refused his offer."

"Did that make any difference to your friendship?"

"It hadn't done up to the time of his death."

"He still visited you?"

"Yes, just as often."

The Coroner remained silent for a moment, glancing at his notes. When he looked towards the witness again he was blander than ever.

"Now I shall have to ask you still more personal questions," he said. "It is, as you must be aware, Mrs. Saumarez, well known in the town that on your first coming here as a resident you became on terms of great friendship with Dr. Wellesley. Do you agree to that?"

"Yes, I suppose so."

"You used to go out a great deal with Dr. Wellesley—driving, and so on?"

"Yes."

"In fact, Dr. Wellesley at that time paid you great attention?"

"Yes."

"Did those attentions cease about the time that you became so friendly with Mr. Wallingford?"

"Well, they didn't altogether cease."

"But, shall we say, fell off?"

Mrs. Saumarez hesitated, obviously disliking the question.

"I have always been friends with Dr. Wellesley," she said eventually.

"All the same, has your friendship with him been quite what it was originally, since you became so very friendly with the late Mayor?"

"Well, perhaps not."

"Will you give me a plain answer to this question? Was there any jealousy aroused between Dr. Wellesley and Mr. Wallingford because of you?"

This time Mrs. Saumarez took a long time to answer. She seemed to be thinking, reflecting. And when she replied it was only to question the Coroner:

"Am I obliged to answer that?" she asked.

"I am afraid I must press for an answer," said the Coroner, "it is important."

"I think there was jealousy," she replied in a low voice.

"On whose part?"

"Dr. Wellesley thought I had thrown him over for Mr. Wallingford."

"Had Dr. Wellesley ever asked you to marry him?"

Mrs. Saumarez's answer came with unexpected swiftness.

"Oh, yes! two or three times!"

"Had you refused him also, then?"

Mrs Saumarez paused. Her cheeks flushed a deeper red.

"The fact was—I didn't want to marry anybody—just then anyway," she answered. "They—both asked me—several times. I—if you please, will you not ask me any more about my private affairs?—they've nothing to do with this! It wasn't my fault that those two were jealous of each other, and——"

"She's let the cat out of the bag now!" whispered Tansley to Brent. "Gad! I see how this thing's going to develop! Whew! Well, there she goes!"

For the Coroner had politely motioned Mrs. Saumarez away from the box, and the next instant the official voice rapped out another name:

"Dr. Rutherford Carstairs!"

CHAPTER XI

THE NINETEEN MINUTES' INTERVAL

Carstairs, a red-haired, blue-eyed, stolid-faced young Scotsman, stepped into the witness-box with the air of a man who is being forced against his will to the performance of some distasteful obligation. Everybody looked wonderingly at him; he was a comparative stranger in the town, and the unimaginative folk amongst the spectators were already cudgelling their brains for an explanation of his presence. But Brent, after a glance at Carstairs, transferred his attention to Carstairs's principal, at whom he had already looked once or twice during Mrs. Saumarez's brief occupancy of the witness-box. Wellesley, sitting in a corner seat a little to the rear of the solicitor's table, had manifested some signs of surprise and annoyance while Mrs. Saumarez was being questioned; now he showed blank wonder at hearing his assistant called. He looked from Carstairs to the Coroner, and from the Coroner to Hawthwaite, and suddenly, while Carstairs was taking the oath, he slipped from his seat, approached Cotman, a local solicitor, who sat listening, close by Tansley, and began to talk to him in hurried undertones. Tansley nudged Brent's elbow.

"Wellesley's tumbled to it!" he whispered. "The police suspect—him!"

"Good heavens!" muttered Brent, utterly unprepared for this suggestion. "You really think—that?"

"Dead sure!" asserted Tansley. "That's the theory! What's this red-headed chap called for, else? You listen!"

Brent was listening, keenly enough. The witness was giving an account of himself. Robert Carstairs, qualified medical practitioner—qualifications specified—at present assistant to Dr. Wellesley; been with him three months.

"Dr. Carstairs," began the Coroner, "do you remember the evening on which the late Mayor, Mr. Wallingford, was found dead in the Mayor's Parlour?"

"I do!" replied Carstairs bluntly.

"Where were you on that evening?"

"In the surgery."

In the Mayor's Parlour

"What are your surgery hours at Dr. Wellesley's?"

"Nine to ten of a morning; seven to nine of an evening."

"Was Dr. Wellesley with you in the surgery on that particular evening?"

"He was—some of the time."

"Not all the time?"

"No."

"What part of the time was he there, with you?"

"He was there, with me, from seven o'clock until half-past seven."

"Attending to patients, I suppose?"

"There were patients—three or four."

"Do you remember who they were?"

"Not particularly. Their names will be in the book."

"Just ordinary callers?"

"Just that."

"You say Dr. Wellesley was there until half-past seven. What happened then?"

"He went out of the surgery."

"Do you mean out of the house?"

"I mean what I say. Out of the surgery."

"Where is the surgery situated?"

"At the back of the house; behind the dining-room. There's a way into it from St. Lawrence Lane. That's the way the patients come in."

"Did Dr. Wellesley go out that way, or did he go into the house?"

"I don't know where he went. All I know is—he went, leaving me there."

"Didn't say where he was going?"

"He didn't say anything."

"Was he dressed for going out?"

"No—he was wearing a white linen jacket. Such as we always wear at surgery hours."

"And that was at half-past seven?"

"Half-past seven precisely."

"How do you fix the time?"

"There's a big, old-fashioned clock in the surgery. Just as Dr. Wellesley went out I heard the Moot Hall clock chime half-past seven, and then the chimes of St. Hathelswide's Church. I noticed that our clock was a couple of minutes slow, and I put it right."

"When did you next see Dr. Wellesley?"

"At just eleven minutes to eight."

"Where?"

"In the surgery."

"He came back there?"

"Yes."

"How do you fix that precise time—eleven minutes to eight?"

"Because he'd arranged to see a patient in Meadow Gate at ten minutes to eight. I glanced at the clock as he came in, saw what time it was, and reminded him of the appointment."

"Did he go to keep it?"

"He did."

"Was he still wearing the white linen jacket when he came back to you?"

"Yes. He took it off, then put on his coat and hat and went out again."

"According to what you say he was out of the surgery, wearing that white linen jacket, exactly nineteen minutes. Did he say anything to you when he came back at eleven minutes to eight of where he had been or what he had been doing during the interval between 7.30 and 7.49?"

"He said nothing."

"You concluded that he had been in the house?"

"I concluded nothing. I never even thought about it. But I certainly shouldn't have thought that he would go out into the street in his surgery jacket."

"Well, Dr. Wellesley went out at 7.50 to see this patient in Meadow Gate. Did anything unusual happen after that—in the surgery, I mean?"

"Nothing, until a little after eight. Then a policeman came for Dr. Wellesley, saying that the Mayor had been found dead in his Parlour, and that it looked like murder. I sent him to find Dr. Wellesley in Meadow Gate, told him where he was."

"You didn't go to the Moot Hall yourself?"

"No; there were patients in the surgery."

The Coroner paused in his questioning, glanced at his papers, and then nodded to the witness as an intimation that he had nothing further to ask him. And Carstairs was about to step down from the box, when Cotman, the solicitor to whom Wellesley had been whispering, rose quickly from his seat and turned towards the Coroner.

"Before this witness leaves the box, sir," he said, "I should like to ask him two or three questions. I am instructed by Dr. Wellesley to appear for him. Dr. Wellesley, since you resumed this inquest, sir, learns with surprise and—yes, I will say disgust—for strong word though it is, it is strictly applicable!—that all unknown to him the police hold him suspect, and are endeavouring to fasten the crime of murder on him. In fact, sir, I cannot sufficiently express my condemnation of the methods which have evidently been resorted to, in underhand fashion——"

The Coroner waved a deprecating hand.

"Yes, yes!" he said. "But we are here, Mr. Cotman, to hold a full inquiry into the circumstances of the death of the late Mayor, and the police, or anybody else, as you know very well, are fully entitled to pursue any course they choose in the effort to get at the truth. Just as you are entitled to ask any questions of any witness, to be sure. You wish to question the present witness?"

"I shall exercise my right to question this and any other witness, sir," replied Cotman. He turned to Carstairs, who had lingered in the witness-box during this exchange between coroner and solicitor. "Dr. Carstairs," he continued, "you say that after being away from his surgery for nineteen minutes on the evening of Mr. Wallingford's death, Dr. Wellesley came back to you there?"

"Yes," answered Carstairs. "That's so."

"Was anyone with you in the surgery when he returned?"

"No, no one."

"You were alone with him, until he went out again to the appointment in Meadow Gate?"

"Yes, quite alone."

"So you had abundant opportunity of observing him. Did he seem at all excited, flurried, did you notice anything unusual in his manner?"

"I didn't. He was just himself."

"Quite calm and normal?"

"Oh, quite!"

"Didn't give you the impression that he'd just been going through any particularly moving or trying episode—such as murdering a fellow-creature?"

"He didn't," replied Carstairs, without the ghost of a smile. "He was—just as usual."

"When did you see him next, after he went out to keep the appointment in Meadow Gate?"

"About half-past eight, or a little later."

"Where?"

"At the mortuary. He sent for me. I went to the mortuary, and found him there with Dr. Barber. They were making an examination of the dead man and wanted my help."

"Was Dr. Wellesley excited or upset then?"

"He was not. He seemed to me—I'm speaking professionally, mind you—remarkably cool."

Cotman suddenly sat down, and turned to his client with a smile on his lips. Evidently he made some cynical remark to Wellesley, for Wellesley smiled too.

"Smart chap, Cotman!" whispered Tansley to Brent. "That bit of cross-exam'll tell with the jury. And now, what next?"

Bunning, recalled from the previous sitting, came next—merely to repeat that the Mayor went up to his parlour at twenty-five minutes past seven, and that he and Mr. Brent found his Worship dead just after eight o'clock. Following him came Dr. Barber, who testified that when he first saw Wallingford's dead body, just about a quarter-past eight, he came to the conclusion that death had taken place about forty-five minutes previously, perhaps a little less. And from him Cotman drew evidence that Wellesley, in the examination at the mortuary, was normal, calm, collected, and, added Dr. Barber, of his own will, greatly annoyed and horrified at the murder.

Brent was beginning to get sick of this new development: to him it seemed idle and purposeless. He whispered as much to Tansley. But Tansley shook his head.

"Can't say that," he replied. "Where was Wellesley during that nineteen minutes' absence from the surgery? He'll have to explain that anyway. But they'll have more evidence than what we've heard. Hello! here's Walkershaw, the Borough Surveyor! What are they going to get out of him, I wonder?"

Brent watched an official-looking person make his way to the witness-box. He was armed with a quantity of rolls of drawing-paper, and a clerk accompanied him whose duty, it presently appeared, was to act as a living easel and hold up these things, diagrams and outlines, while his principal explained them. Presently the eager audience found itself listening to what was neither more nor less than a lecture on the architecture of Hathelsborough Moot Hall and its immediately adjacent buildings—and then Brent began to see the drift of the Borough Surveyor's evidence.

The whole block of masonry between Copper Alley and Piper's Passage, testified Walkershaw, illustrating his observations by pointing to the large diagram held on high by his clerk, was extremely ancient. In it there were three separate buildings—separate, that was, in their use, but all joining on to each other. First, next to Copper Alley, which ran out of Meadow Gate, came the big house long used as a bank. Then came the Moot Hall itself. Next, between the Moot Hall and Piper's Passage, which was a narrow entry between River Gate and St. Lawrence Lane, stood Dr. Wellesley's house. Until comparatively recent times Dr. Wellesley's house had been the official residence of the Mayor of Hathelsborough. And between it and the Moot Hall there was a definite means of communication: in short, a private door.

There was a general pricking of ears upon this announcement, and Tansley indulged in a low whistle: he saw the significance of Walkershaw's statement.

"Another link in the chain, Brent!" he muttered. "'Pon my word, they're putting it together rather cleverly: nineteen minutes' absence? door between his house and the Moot Hall? Come!"

Brent made no comment. He was closely following the Borough Surveyor as that worthy pointed out on his plans and diagrams the means of communication between the Moot Hall and the old dwelling-place at its side. In former days, said Walkershaw, some Mayor of Hathelsborough had caused a door to be made in a certain small room in the house; that door opened on a passage in the Moot Hall which led to the corridor wherein the Mayor's Parlour was situated. It had no doubt been used by many occupants of the Mayoral chair during their term of office. Of late, however, nobody seemed to have known of it; but he himself having examined it, for the purposes of this inquiry, during the last day or two, had found that it showed unmistakable signs of recent usage. In fact, the lock and bolts had quite recently been oiled.

The evidence of this witness came to a dramatic end in the shape of a question from the Coroner:

"How long would it take, then, for any person to pass from Dr. Wellesley's house to the Mayor's Parlour in the Moot Hall?"

"One minute," replied Walkershaw promptly. "If anything—less."

Cotman, who had been whispering with his client during the Borough Surveyor's evidence, asked no questions, and presently the interest of the court shifted to a little shrewd-faced, self-possessed woman who tripped into the witness-box and admitted cheerfully that she was Mrs. Marriner, proprietor of Marriner's Laundry, and that she washed for several of the best families in Hathelsborough. The fragment of handkerchief which had been found in the Mayor's Parlour was handed to her for inspection, and the Coroner asked her if she could say definitely if she knew whose it was. There was considerable doubt and scepticism in his voice as he put the question; but Mrs. Marriner showed herself the incarnation of sure and positive conviction.

"Yes, sir," she answered. "It's Dr. Wellesley's."

"You must wash a great many handkerchiefs at your laundry, Mrs. Marriner," observed the Coroner. "How can you be sure about one—about that one?"

"I'm sure enough about that one, sir, because it's one of a dozen that's gone through my hands many a time!" asserted Mrs. Marriner. "There's nobody in the town, sir, leastways not amongst my customers—and I wash for all the very best people, sir—that has any handkerchiefs like them, except Dr. Wellesley. They're the very finest French cambric. That there is a piece of one of the doctor's best handkerchiefs, sir, as sure as I'm in this here box—which I wish I wasn't!"

The Coroner asked nothing further; he was still plainly impatient about the handkerchief evidence, if not wholly sceptical, and he waved Mrs. Marriner away. But Cotman stopped her.

"I suppose, Mrs. Marriner, that mistakes are sometimes made when you and your assistants send home the clean clothes?" he suggested. "Things get in the wrong baskets, eh?"

"Well, not often—at my place, sir," replied Mrs. Marriner. "We're very particular."

"Still—sometimes, you know?"

"Oh, I'll not say that they don't, sometimes, sir," admitted Mrs. Marriner. "We're all of us human creatures, as you're very well aware, sir."

"This particular handkerchief may have got into a wrong basket?" urged Cotman. "It's—possible?"

"Oh, it's possible, sir," said Mrs. Marriner. "Mistakes will happen, sir."

Mrs. Marriner disappeared amongst the crowd, and a new witness took her place. She, too, was a woman, and a young and pretty one—and in a tearful and nervous condition. Tansley glanced at her and turned, with a significant glance, to Brent.

"Great Scott!" he whispered. "Wellesley's housemaid!"

CHAPTER XII

CIRCUMSTANTIAL EVIDENCE

Interest was beginning to thicken: the people in court, from Simon Crood, pompous and aloof in his new grandeur of chief magistrate, to Spizey the bellman, equally pompous in his ancient livery, were already open-mouthed with wonder at the new and startling development. But the sudden advent of the young and pretty domestic, whose tears betrayed her unwillingness to come forward, deepened the interest still further; everybody leaned forward towards the centre of the court, intent on hearing what the girl had to tell. She, however, paid no attention to these manifestations of inquisitiveness; standing in the witness-box, a tear-soaked handkerchief in her hands, half-sullen, half-resentful of mouth and eye, she looked at nobody but the Coroner; her whole expression was that of a defenceless animal, pinned in a corner and watchful of its captor.

But this time it was not the Coroner who put questions to the witness. There had been some whispering between him, Hawthwaite and Meeking, the barrister who represented the police authorities, and it was Meeking who turned to the girl and began to get her information from her by means of bland, suavely-expressed, half-suggesting interrogatories. Winifred Wilson; twenty years of age; housemaid at Dr. Wellesley's—been in the doctor's employ about fourteen months.

"Did you give certain information to the police recently?" inquired Meeking, going straight to his point as soon as these preliminaries were over. "Information bearing on the matter now being inquired into?"

"Yes, sir," replied the witness in a low voice.

"Was it relating to something that you saw, in Dr. Wellesley's house, on the evening on which Mr. Wallingford was found dead in the Mayor's Parlour?"

"Yes, sir."

"What was it that you saw?"

The girl hesitated. Evidently on the verge of a fresh outburst of tears, she compressed her nether lip, looking fixedly at the ledge of the witness-box.

"Don't be afraid," said Meeking. "We only want the truth—tell that, and you've nothing to be afraid of, nor to reproach yourself with. Now what did you see?"

The girl's answer came in a whisper.

"I saw Dr. Wellesley!"

"You saw your master, Dr. Wellesley. Where did you see Dr. Wellesley?"

"On the hall staircase, sir."

"On the hall staircase. That, I suppose, is the main staircase of the house? Very well. Now where were you?"

"Up on the top landing, sir."

"What were you doing there?"

"I'd just come out of my room, sir—I'd been getting dressed to go out."

"And how came you to see your master?"

"I heard a door open on the landing below, sir, and I just looked over the banister to see who it was."

"Who was it?"

"Dr. Wellesley, sir."

"Dr. Wellesley. What was he doing?"

"He'd just come out of the drawing-room door, sir."

"Are you sure he'd come out of that particular door?"

"Well, sir, I saw him close it behind him."

"What happened then?"

"He stood for a minute, sir, on the landing."

"Doing anything?"

"No, sir—just standing."

"And what then?"

"He went downstairs, sir."

"And disappeared?"

"He went towards the surgery, sir."

"How was the staircase lighted when you saw all this?"

"Well, sir, there was a light in the hall, at the foot of the staircase, and there was another on the drawing-room floor landing."

"Then you could see Dr. Wellesley quite clearly?"

"Yes, sir."

"How was he dressed?"

"He'd his surgery jacket on, sir—a white linen jacket."

"You saw Dr. Wellesley quite clearly, wearing a white linen jacket, and coming out of the drawing-room door. Now I want to ask you about the drawing-room. Is there another room, a small room, opening out of Dr. Wellesley's drawing-room?"

"Yes, sir."

"How big is it?"

"Well, sir, it's a little room. Not very big, sir."

"What is it used for? What is there in it now?"

"Nothing much, sir. Some book-cases and a desk and a chair or two."

"Is there a door on its farther side—the next side to the Moot Hall?"

"Yes, sir."

"Have you ever seen it open?"

"No, sir, never."

"You don't know where it gives access to?"

"No, sir."

"Might be a cupboard door, eh?"

"I always thought it was a cupboard door, sir."

"Very good. Now I want you to be very particular about answering my next question. What time was it when you saw Dr. Wellesley come out of his drawing-room?"

"It would be just about a quarter to eight, sir."

"Are you quite sure about that?"

"Quite sure, sir!"

"Did anything fix the time on your mind?"

"Yes, sir—at least, I heard the clocks strike the quarter just after. The Moot Hall clock, sir, and the parish church."

"You're sure it was a quarter to eight o'clock that you heard?"

"Yes, sir, quite sure."

"Why are you quite sure?"

The witness reddened a little and looked shyly aside.

"Well, sir, I'd got to meet somebody, outside the house, at a quarter to eight o'clock," she murmured.

"I see! Did you meet him?"

"Yes, sir."

"Punctually?"

"I might have been a minute late, sir. The clocks had done striking."

"Very good. And just before they began to strike you saw Dr. Wellesley come out of his drawing-room door?"

"Yes, sir."

Meeking suddenly dropped back into his seat and began to shuffle his papers. The Coroner glanced at Cotman—and Cotman, with a cynical smile, got to his feet and confronted the witness.

"Was it your young man that you went out to meet at a quarter to eight o'clock that evening?" he asked.

"Yes, sir," admitted the girl.

"What's his name?"

"Joe Green, sir."

"Did you tell Joe Green that you'd just seen Dr. Wellesley come out of his drawing-room?"

"No, sir!"
"Why not?"
"Because I didn't think anything of it, sir."
"You didn't think anything of it? And pray when did you begin to think something of it?"

"Well, sir, it was—it was when the police began asking questions."
"And of whom did they ask questions?"
"Me and the other servants, sir."
"Dr. Wellesley's servants?"
"Yes, sir."
"How many servants has Dr. Wellesley?"
"Four, sir—and a boy."
"So the police came asking questions, did they? About Dr. Wellesley? What about him?"
"Well, sir, it was about what we knew of Dr. Wellesley's movements on that evening, sir—where he was from half-past seven to eight o'clock. Then I remembered, sir."
"And told the police?"
"No, sir—not then. I said nothing to anybody—at first."
"But you did later on. Now, to whom?"
The witness here began to show more signs of tearfulness.
"Don't cry!" said Cotman. "Whom did you first mention this to?"
"Well, sir, it was to Mrs. Lane. I got so upset about it that I told her."
"Who is Mrs. Lane?"
"She's the lady that looks after the Girls' Friendly Society, sir."
"Are you a member of that?"
"Yes, sir."
"So you went and told Mrs. Lane all about it?"
"Yes, sir."
"What did Mrs. Lane say?"

"She said I must tell Mr. Hawthwaite, sir."
"Did she take you to Mr. Hawthwaite?"
"Yes, sir."
"And you told him all that you have told us now?"
"Yes, sir—Mrs. Lane said I must."
"You didn't want to, eh?"
Here the girl burst into tears, and Cotman turned to the Coroner.
"I have no further questions to put to this witness, sir," he said, "but I would make a respectful suggestion to yourself. That is, that my client, Dr. Wellesley, should be called at once. We know now that the police have been secretly working up a case against Dr. Wellesley—in fact, I am very much surprised that, ignoring these proceedings altogether, they have not gone to the length of arresting him! Perhaps that's a card which Superintendent Hawthwaite still keeps up his sleeve. I may tell him, on behalf of my client, that he's quite welcome to arrest Dr. Wellesley and bring him before the

In the Mayor's Parlour

magistrates whenever he likes! But as Dr. Wellesley's name has been very freely mentioned this morning I think it will be only fair, sir, that he should be allowed to go into that box at once, where he will give evidence on oath——"

"If Dr. Wellesley elects to go into the box," interrupted the Coroner, "I shall, of course, warn him in the usual way, Mr. Cotman. He is not bound to give any evidence that might incriminate himself, but no doubt you have already made him aware of that."

"Dr. Wellesley is very well aware of it, sir," replied Cotman. "I ask that he should be allowed to give evidence at once."

"Let Dr. Wellesley be called, then," said the Coroner. "That course, perhaps, will be best."

Brent inspected Wellesley closely as he stepped into the witness-box. He was a well set-up, handsome man, noted in the town for his correct and fashionable attire, and he made a distinguished figure as the centre-point of these somewhat sordid surroundings. That he was indignant was very obvious; he answered the preliminary questions impatiently; there was impatience, too, in his manner as after taking the oath he turned to the Coroner; it seemed to Brent that Wellesley's notion was that the point-blank denial of a man of honour was enough to dispose of any charge.

This time the Coroner went to work himself, quietly and confidentially.

"Dr. Wellesley," he began, leaning over his desk, "I need not warn you in the way I mentioned just now: I'm sure you quite understand the position. Now, as you have been in Court all the morning, you have heard the evidence that has already offered itself. As regards the evidence given by your assistant, Dr. Carstairs, as to your movements and absence from the surgery between 7.30 and 7.49—is that correct?"

Wellesley drew himself to his full height, and spoke with emphasis:

"Absolutely!"

"And the evidence of the young woman, your housemaid? Is she correct in what she told us?"

"Quite!"

The Coroner looked down at his papers, his spectacled eyes wandering about them as if in search of something. Suddenly he looked up.

"There's this matter of the handkerchief, or portion of a handkerchief," he said. "Picked up, we are told, from the hearth in the Mayor's Parlour, where the rest of it had been burned. Did you hear Mrs. Marriner's evidence about that, Dr. Wellesley?"

"I did!"

"Is what she said, or suggested, correct? Is the handkerchief yours?"

"I have never seen the handkerchief, or, rather, the remains of it. I heard that some portion of a handkerchief, charred and blood-stained, was found on the hearth in the Mayor's Parlour, and that it had been handed over to Superintendent Hawthwaite, but I have not had it shown to me."

The Coroner glanced at Hawthwaite, who since the opening of the Court had sat near Meeking, occasionally exchanging whispered remarks.

"Let Dr. Wellesley see that fragment," he said.

All eyes were fixed on the witness as he took the piece of charred and faintly stained stuff in his hands and examined it. Everybody knew that the stain was from the blood of the murdered man; the same thought was in everybody's mind—was that stain now being critically inspected by the actual murderer?

In the Mayor's Parlour

Wellesley suddenly looked up; at the same time he handed back the fragment to the policeman who had passed it to him.

"To the best of my belief," he said, turning to the Coroner, "that is certainly part of a handkerchief of mine. The handkerchief is one of a dozen which I bought in Paris about a year ago."

A murmur ran round the crowded court at this candid avowal; as it died away the Coroner again spoke:

"Had you missed this handkerchief?"

"I had not. I have a drawer in my dressing-room full of handkerchiefs—several dozens of them. But—from the texture—I am positive that that is mine."

"Very well," said the Coroner. "Now about the evidence of Mr. Walkershaw. Did you know of the door between your house and the Moot Hall?"

"Yes! So did the late Mayor. As a matter of fact, he and I, some time ago, had it put to rights. We both used it; I, to go into the Moot Hall; he, to come and see me."

"There was no secrecy about it, then?"

"Not between Wallingford and myself at any rate."

The Coroner took off his spectacles and leaned back in his chair—sure sign that he had done. And Meeking rose, cool, level-voiced.

"Dr. Wellesley, I think you heard the evidence of Mrs. Saumarez?"

But before Dr. Wellesley could make answer, the other doctors present in the Court-room were suddenly called into action. As the barrister pronounced her name, Mrs. Saumarez collapsed in her seat, fainting.

CHAPTER XIII

A WOMAN INTERVENES

I n the midst of the commotion that followed and while Mrs. Saumarez, attended by the doctors, was being carried out of the Court-room, Tansley, at Brent's elbow, drew in his breath with a sharp sibilant sound that came near being a whistle. Brent turned from the withdrawing figures to look at him questioningly.

"Well?" he said.

"Queer!" muttered Tansley. "Why should she faint? I wonder——"

"What?" demanded Brent as the solicitor paused.

"I'm wondering if she and Wellesley know anything that they're keeping to themselves," said Tansley. "She was obviously nervous and frightened when she was in that box just now."

"She's a nervous, highly-strung woman—so I should say, from what bit I've seen of her," remarked Brent. "Excitable!"

"Well, he's cool enough," said Tansley, nodding towards the witness-box. "Hasn't turned a hair! Meeking'll get nothing out of him!"

The barrister was again addressing himself to Wellesley, who, after one glance at Mrs. Saumarez as she fainted, had continued, erect and defiant, facing the Court.

"You heard Mrs. Saumarez's evidence just now, Dr. Wellesley?" asked Meeking quietly.

"I did!"

"Was it correct?"

"I am not going to discuss it!"

"Nor answer any questions arising out of it?"

"I am not!"

"Perhaps you will answer some questions of mine. Was there any jealousy existing between you and the late John Wallingford, of which Mrs. Saumarez was the cause?"

Wellesley hesitated, taking a full minute for evident consideration.

"I will answer that to a certain extent," he replied at last. "At the time of his death, no! None!"

"Had there been previously?"

"At one time—yes. It was over."

"You and he were good friends?"

"Absolutely! Both in private and public—I mean in public affairs. I was in complete touch and sympathy with him as regards his public work."

"Now, Dr. Wellesley, I think that for your own sake you ought to give us some information on one or two points. Mrs. Saumarez said on oath that you asked her to marry you, two or three times. She also said that the late Mayor asked her too. Now——"

Wellesley suddenly brought down his hand on the ledge of the witness-box.

"I have already told you, sir, that I am not going to discuss my affairs with Mrs. Saumarez nor with the late Mayor in relation to Mrs. Saumarez!" he exclaimed with some show of anger. "They are private and have nothing to do with this inquiry. I shall not answer any question relating to them."

"In that case, Dr. Wellesley, you will lay yourself open to whatever conclusions the jury chooses to make," said Meeking. "We have already heard Mrs. Saumarez say—what she did say. But, as you won't answer, I will pass to another matter. You have already told us that the evidence of your assistant, Dr. Carstairs, is correct as to your movements between half-past seven and eleven minutes to eight, or, rather, as to your absence from the surgery during those nineteen minutes. You adhere to that?"

"Certainly! Carstairs is quite correct."

"Very well. Where were you during that time—nineteen minutes?"

"For the most part of the time, in my drawing-room."

"What do you mean by most part of the time?"

"Well, I should say three parts of it."

"And the other part?"

"Spent in letting a caller in and letting the caller out."

"By your front door?"

"No; by a side door—a private door."

"You took this caller to your drawing-room?"

"Yes."

"For a private interview?"

"Precisely."

Meeking allowed a minute to elapse, during which he affected to look at his papers. Suddenly he turned full on his witness.

"Who was the caller?"

Wellesley drew his tall figure still more erect.

"I refuse to say!"

"Why?"

"Because I am not going to drag in the name of my caller! The business my caller came upon was of a very private and confidential nature, and I am not going to break my rule of professional silence. I shall not give the name."

Meeking again paused. Finally, with a glance at the Coroner, he turned to his witness and began to speak more earnestly.

"Let me put this to you," he said. "Consider calmly, if you please, what we have heard already, from previous witnesses, and what you yourself have admitted. Mrs. Saumarez has sworn that you and the late Mayor were rivals for her hand and that there was jealousy between you. You admit that Mrs. Marriner is correct in identifying the burnt and blood-stained fragment of handkerchief found in the Mayor's Parlour after the murder as your property; you also acknowledge the existence of a door communicating between your house and the Moot Hall. You further admit that you were away from your surgery for nineteen minutes at the very time the murder was committed—according to the medical evidence—and that you were in your drawing-room from an inner room of which the door I have just referred to opens. Now I suggest to you, Dr. Wellesley, that you should give us the name of the person who was with you in your drawing-room?"

Wellesley, who, during this exordium, had steadily watched his questioner, shook his head more decidedly than before.

"No!" he answered promptly. "I shall not say who my caller was."

Meeking spread out his hands in a gesture of helplessness. He turned to the Coroner who, for the last few minutes, had shown signs of being ill at ease, and had frequently shaken his head at Wellesley's point-blank refusals.

"I don't know if it is any use appealing to you, sir," said Meeking. "The witness——"

The Coroner leaned towards Wellesley, his whole attitude conciliatory and inviting.

"I really think that it would be better, doctor, if you could find it in your way to answer Mr. Meeking's question——"

"I have answered it, sir," interrupted Wellesley. "My answer is—no!"

"Yes, yes, but I don't want the jury to get any false impressions—to draw any wrong conclusions," said the Coroner a little testily. "I feel sure that in your own interest——"

"I am not thinking of my own interest," declared Wellesley. "Once again—I shall not give the name of my caller."

There was a further pause, during which Meeking and the Coroner exchanged glances. Then Meeking suddenly turned again to the witness-box.

"Was your caller a man or a woman?" he asked.

"That I shan't say!" answered Wellesley steadily.

"Who admitted him—or her?"

"I did."

"How—by what door of your house?"

"By the side-door in Piper's Passage."

"Did any of your servants see the caller?"

"No."

"How came that about? You have several servants."

"My caller came to that door by arrangement with myself at a certain time—7.30—was admitted by me, and taken straight up to my drawing-room by a side staircase. My caller left, when the interview was over, by the same way."

"The interview, then, was a secret one?"

"Precisely! Secret; private; confidential."

"And you flatly refuse to give us the caller's name?"

"Flatly!"

Meeking hesitated a moment. Then, with a sudden gesture, as though he washed his hands of the whole episode, he dropped back into his seat, bundled his papers together, and made some evidently cynical remark to Hawthwaite who sat near to him. But Hawthwaite made no response: he was watching the Coroner, and in answer to a questioning glance he shook his head.

"No more evidence," whispered Tansley to Brent, as Wellesley, dismissed, stepped down from the witness-box. "Whew! this is a queer business, and our non-responsive medical friend may come to rue his obstinacy. I wonder what old Seagrave will make of it? He'll have to sum it all up now."

The Coroner was already turning to the jury. He began with his notes of the first day's proceedings and spent some time over them, but eventually he told his listeners that all that had transpired in the opening stages of the inquiry faded into comparative insignificance when viewed in the light of the evidence they had heard that morning. He analysed that evidence with the acumen of the cute old lawyer that everybody knew him to be, and at last got to what the sharper intellects amongst his hearers felt, with him, to be the crux of the situation—was there jealousy of an appreciable nature between Wallingford and Wellesley in respect of Mrs. Saumarez? If there was—and he brushed aside, rather cavalierly, Wellesley's denial that it existed at the time of Wallingford's death, estimating lightly that denial in face of the fact that the cause was still there, and that Wellesley had admitted that it had existed, at one time—then the evidence as they had it clearly showed that between 7.30 and 7.49 on the evening of the late Mayor's death, Wellesley had ready and easy means of access to the Mayor's Parlour. Something might have occurred which had revivified the old jealousy—there might have been a sudden scene, a quarrel, high words: it was a pity, a thousand pities, that Dr. Wellesley refused to give the name of the person who, according to his story, was with him during the nineteen minutes' interval which——

"Going dead against him!" whispered Tansley to Brent. "The old chap's taken Meeking's job out of his hands. Good thing this is a coroner's court—if a judge said as much as Seagrave's saying to an assize jury, Gad! Wellesley would hang! Look at these jurymen! They're half dead-certain that Wellesley's guilty already!"

"Well?" muttered Brent. "I'm not so far off that stage myself. Why didn't he speak out, and be done with it. There's been more in that love affair than I guessed at, Tansley—that's where it is! The woman's anxious enough anyway—look at her!"

Mrs. Saumarez had come back into court. She was pale enough and eager enough—and it seemed to Brent that she was almost holding her breath as the old Coroner, in his slow, carefully-measured accents and phrases, went on piling up the damning conclusions that might be drawn against Wellesley.

"You must not allow yourselves to forget, gentlemen," he was saying, "that Dr. Wellesley's assertion that he was busy with a caller during the fateful nineteen minutes is wholly uncorroborated. There are several—four or five, I think—domestic servants in his establishment, and there was also his assistant in the house, and there were patients going in and out of the surgery, but no one has been brought forward to prove that he was engaged with a visitor in his drawing-room. Now you are only concerned with the evidence that has been put before you, and I am bound to tell you that there is no evidence that Dr. Wellesley had any caller——"

A woman's voice suddenly rang out, clear and sharp, from a point of the audience immediately facing the Coroner.

"He had! I was the caller!"

In the excitement of the moment Tansley sprang to his feet, stared, sank back again.

"Good God!" he exclaimed. "Mrs. Mallett! Who'd have thought it!"

Brent, too, got up and looked. He saw a handsome, determined-looking woman standing amidst the closely-packed spectators. Mallett sat by her side; he was evidently struck dumb with sudden amazement and was staring open-mouthed at her; on the other side, two or three men and women, evidently friends, were expostulating with the interrupter. But Mrs. Mallett was oblivious of her husband's wonder and her friends' entreaties; confronting the Coroner she spoke again.

"Mr. Seagrave, I am the person who called on Dr. Wellesley!" she said in a loud, clear voice. "I was there all the time you're discussing, and if you'll let me give evidence you shall have it on my oath. I am not going to sit here and hear an innocent man traduced for lack of a word of mine."

The Coroner, who looked none too well pleased at this interruption, motioned Mrs. Mallett to come forward. He waved aside impatiently a protest from Wellesley, who seemed to be begging this voluntary witness to go back to her seat and say nothing, and, as Mrs. Mallett entered the witness-box, turned to Meeking.

"Perhaps you'll be good enough to examine this witness," he said a little irritably. "These irregular interruptions! But let her say what she has to say."

Mrs. Mallett, in Brent's opinion, looked precisely the sort of lady to have her say, and to have it right out. She was calm enough now, and when she had taken the oath and told her questioner formally who she was, she faced him with equanimity. Meeking, somewhat uncertain of his ground, took his cue from the witness's dramatic intervention.

"Mrs. Mallett, did you call on Dr. Wellesley at 7.30 on the evening in question—the evening on which Mr. Wallingford met his death?"

"I did."

"By arrangement?"

"Certainly—by arrangement."

"When was the arrangement made?"

"That afternoon. Dr. Wellesley and I met, in the market-place, about four o'clock. We made it then."

"Was it to be a strictly private interview?"

"Yes, it was. That was why I went to the side door in Piper's Passage."

"Did Dr. Wellesley admit you himself?"

"Yes, he did, and he took me straight up to his drawing-room by a side staircase."

"No one saw you going in?"

"No; nor leaving, either!"

"Why all this privacy, Mrs. Mallett?"

"My business was of a private sort, sir!"

"Will you tell us what it was?"

"I will tell you that I had reasons of my own—my particular own—for seeing Dr. Wellesley and the Mayor."

"The Mayor! Did you see the Mayor—there?"

"No. I meant to see him, but I didn't."

"Do you mean that you expected to meet him there—in Dr. Wellesley's drawing-room?"

"No. Dr. Wellesley had told me of the door between his house and the Moot Hall, and he said that after he and I had had our talk I could go through that door to the Mayor's Parlour, where I should be sure to find Mr. Wallingford at that time."

"I see. Then, did you go to see Mr. Wallingford?"

"I did."

"After talking with Dr. Wellesley?"

"Yes. He showed me the way—opened the door for me——"

"Stay, what time would that be?"

"About 7.35 or so. I went along the passage to the Mayor's Parlour, but I never entered."

"Never entered? Why, now, Mrs. Mallett?"

"Because, as I reached the door, I heard people talking inside the Parlour. So I went back."

CHAPTER XIV

WHOSE VOICES?

Meeking, who by long experience knew the value of dramatic effect in the examination of witnesses, took full advantage of Mrs. Mallett's strange and unexpected announcement. He paused, staring at her—he knew well enough that when he stared other folk would stare too. So for a full moment the situation rested—there stood Mrs. Mallett, resolute and unmoved, in the box, with every eye in the crowded court fixed full upon her, and Meeking still gazing at her intently—and, of set purpose, half-incredulously. There was something intentionally sceptical, cynical, in his tone when, at last, he spoke:

"Do you say—on oath—that you went, through the door between Dr. Wellesley's house and the Moot Hall, to the Mayor's Parlour—that evening?"

"To the door of the Mayor's Parlour," corrected Mrs. Mallett. "Yes. I do. I did!"

"Was the door closed?"

"The door was closed."

"But you say you heard voices?"

"I heard voices—within."

In the Mayor's Parlour

"Whose voices?"

"That I can't say. I couldn't distinguish them."

"Well, did you hear the Mayor's voice?"

"I tell you I couldn't distinguish any voice. There were two people talking inside the Mayor's Parlour, anyway, in loud voices. It seemed to me that they were both talking at the same time—in fact, I thought——"

"What did you think?" demanded Meeking, as Mrs. Mallett paused.

"Well, I thought that, whoever they were, the two people were quarrelling—the voices were loud, lifted, angry, I thought."

"And yet you couldn't distinguish them?"

"No, I couldn't. I might have recognized the Mayor's voice perhaps, if I'd gone closer to the door and listened, but I didn't stay. As soon as I heard—what I have told you of—I went straight back."

"By the same way? To Dr. Wellesley's drawing-room?"

"Yes."

"What happened then?"

"I told Dr. Wellesley that the Mayor had somebody with him and that they appeared to be having high words, and as I didn't want to stop he suggested that I should come again next evening. Then I went home."

"In the same way—by the private door into Piper's Passage?"

"Exactly."

"Did Dr. Wellesley go downstairs with you and let you out?"

"He did."

"See anybody about on that occasion?"

"No—no one."

Meeking paused, and after a glance round the table at which he was standing looked at his notes.

"Now, Mrs. Mallett," he said presently, "what time was this—I mean, when you left Dr. Wellesley's?"

"A little before a quarter to eight. The clock struck a quarter to eight just after I got into my own house."

"And—where is your house?"

"Next door to the Moot Hall. Dr. Wellesley's house is on one side of the Moot Hall; ours is on the other."

"It would take you a very short time, then, to go home?"

"A minute or two."

"Very well. And you went to Dr. Wellesley's at 7.30?"

"Just about that."

"Then you were with him most of the time you were there—in his drawing-room?"

"Certainly! All the time except for the two or three minutes spent in going to the Mayor's Parlour."

"Talking to Dr. Wellesley?"

"Of course! What do you suppose I went for?"

"That's just what I want to find out!" retorted Meeking, with a glance that took in the audience, now all agog with excitement. "Will you tell us, Mrs. Mallett?"

Mrs. Mallett's handsome face became rigid, and her well-cut lips fixed themselves in a straight line. But she relaxed them to rap out one word.

"No!"

"Come, now, Mrs. Mallett! This is a serious, a very serious inquiry. It is becoming more serious the more it becomes mysterious, and it is becoming increasingly mysterious. You have already told us that you went secretly to Dr. Wellesley's house in order that you might see him and, afterwards, the Mayor, Mr. Wallingford. Now, you must have had some very special reason, or cause, for these interviews. Tell me what it was. What was it, Mrs. Mallett?"

"No! That's my business! Nobody else's. I shall not say."

"Does Dr. Wellesley know what it was?"

"Of course!"

"Would the Mayor have known if you'd seen him?"

"Considering that that was the object I had in wanting to see him, of course he would!" retorted Mrs. Mallett. "I should think that's obvious."

"But you didn't see him, eh?"

"You know very well I didn't!"

"Pardon me, madam," said Meeking with lightning-like promptitude. "I don't know anything of the sort! However, does anyone else know of this—business?"

"That, too, is my concern," declared Mrs. Mallett, who had bridled indignantly at the barrister's swift reply. "I shan't say."

"Does your husband know of it?"

"I'm not going to say that, either!"

"Did your husband—who, I believe, is one of the Town Trustees—did he know of your visit to Dr. Wellesley's house on this particular occasion?"

"I'll answer that! He did not."

"Where was he, while you were at Dr. Wellesley's? Had you left him at home?"

"No, he had gone out before I went out myself. As to where he was, I should say he was either at the Conservative Club or at Mr. Simon Crood's. Is it relevant?"

Amidst a ripple of laughter Meeking made a gesture which signified that he had done with Mrs. Mallett, and she presently stepped down from the witness-box. Meeking turned to the Coroner.

"I want to have Dr. Wellesley in that box again, sir," he said.

"Let Dr. Wellesley be recalled," commanded the Coroner.

Wellesley, once more in the full gaze of the court, looked vexed and impatient. Those who had occasionally glanced at him while Mrs. Mallett was giving her evidence had observed that he showed signs of being by no means pleased at the turn things had taken since her sudden intervention—sometimes he had frowned; once or twice he had muttered to himself. And he now looked blackly at Meeking as the barrister once more confronted him.

"You have heard the evidence of the last witness?" asked Meeking abruptly.

"All of it," replied Wellesley.

"Is it correct as to details of time?"

"So far as I recollect, quite!"

"When Mrs. Mallett went by the private door between your drawing-room and the Moot Hall to see the Mayor, what did you do?"

"Waited for her in my drawing-room."

"How long was she away?"

"Five minutes perhaps."

"Had you made any appointment with the Mayor on her behalf?"

"No. I had not."

"You sent her to see him on the chance of her finding him there—in the Mayor's Parlour?"

"There was no chance about it. I knew—as a good many other people did—that just then Wallingford spent almost every evening in the Mayor's Parlour."

"Had you ever visited him in the Mayor's Parlour during these evening attendances of his?"

"Oh, yes—several times!"

"By this communicating door?"

"Certainly. And he had made use of it in coming to see me."

"Do you know what the Mayor was doing on these occasions—I mean, do you know why he spent so much time at the Mayor's Parlour of an evening?"

"Yes. He was going as thoroughly as he could into the financial affairs of the Corporation."

"Now I want to put a very particular question to you—with the object of getting at some solution of this mystery. What was Mrs. Mallett's business with you and the Mayor?"

"I cannot reply to that."

"You won't give me an answer?"

"I won't!"

"Do you base your refusal on professional privilege, doctor?"

"No! Not at all. Mrs. Mallett's business was of an absolutely private nature. It had nothing whatever to do with the subject of this inquiry—I tell you that on my honour, on my oath. Nothing whatever!"

"You mean—directly?"

Meeking threw a good deal of significance into this question, which he put slowly, and with a peculiarly meaning glance at his witness. But Wellesley either did not see or affected not to see any significance, and his answer came promptly:

"I mean precisely what I say—as I always do."

Meeking leaned across the table, eyeing Wellesley still more closely.

"Do you think, knowing all that you do now, that it had anything to do with it indirectly? Indirectly!"

Self-controlled though he was, Wellesley could not repress a start of surprise at this question. It was obviously unexpected—and it seemed to those who, like Brent and Tansley, were watching him narrowly, that he was considerably taken aback by it. He hesitated.

"I want an answer to that," said Meeking, after a pause.

"Well," replied Wellesley at last, "I can't say. What I mean by that is that I am not in a position to say. I am not sufficiently acquainted with—let me call them facts to be able to say. What I do say is that Mrs. Mallett's business with me and with Wallingford that evening was of an essentially private nature and had nothing whatever to do with what happened in the Mayor's Parlour just about the time she was in my drawing-room."

"That is, as far as you are aware?"

"As far as I am aware—yes! But I am quite sure it hadn't."

"You can't give this court any information that would help to solve this problem?"

"I cannot!"

"Well, a question or two more. When Mrs. Mallett left you at your door in Piper's Passage—I mean, when you let her out, just before a quarter to eight, what did you next do?"

"I went upstairs again to my drawing-room."

"May I ask why?"

"Yes. I thought of going to see Wallingford, in the Mayor's Parlour."

"Did you go?"

"No. I should have gone, but I suddenly remembered that I had an appointment with a patient in Meadow Gate at ten minutes to eight o'clock. So I went back to the surgery, exchanged my jacket for a coat and went out."

"On your oath, have you the slightest idea as to who killed John Wallingford?"

"I have not the least idea! I never have had."

Meeking nodded, as much as to imply that he had no further questions to ask; when his witness had stepped down, he turned to the Coroner.

"I should like to have Bunning, the caretaker, recalled, sir," he said. "I want to ask him certain questions which have just occurred to me. Bunning," he continued, when the ex-sergeant had been summoned to the witness-box, "I want you to give me some information about the relation of your rooms to the upper portion of the Moot Hall. You live in rooms on the ground floor, don't you? Yes? Very well, now, is there any entrance to your rooms other than that at the front of the building—the entrance from the market-place?"

"Yes, sir. There's an entrance from St. Lawrence Lane, at the back."

"Is there any way from your rooms to the upper floors of the Moot Hall?"

"Yes, sir. There's a back stair, from our back door."

"Could anybody reach the Mayor's Parlour by that stair?"

"They could, sir, certainly; but either me or my wife would see them."

"Just so, if you were in your rooms. But you told us in your first evidence that from about 7.20 or so until eight o'clock you were smoking your pipe at the market-place entrance to the Moot Hall, where, of course, you couldn't see your back door. That correct? Very well. Now, while you were at the front, was your wife in your rooms at the back?"

"Yes, sir."

"Do you know what she was doing?"

"I do, sir. She was getting our supper ready."

"Are you sure she never left the house—your rooms, you know?"

Bunning started. Obviously, a new idea had occurred.

"Ay!" said Meeking, with a smile. "Just so, Bunning. You're not sure?"

"Well, sir," replied Bunning slowly, "now that I come to think of it, I'm not! It never occurred to me before, but during that time my missis may have been out of the place for a few minutes or so, to fetch the supper beer, sir."

"To be sure! Now where does Mrs. Bunning get your supper beer?"

"At the *Chancellor* Vaults, sir—round the corner."

Meeking turned quietly to the Coroner.

"I think we ought to have Mrs. Bunning's evidence," he remarked.

It took ten minutes to fetch Mrs. Bunning from her rooms in the lower regions of the old Moot Hall. She came at last, breathlessly, and in her working attire, and turned a wondering, good-natured face on the barrister.

"Just a little question or two, Mrs. Bunning," he said half-indifferently. "On the evening of the late Mayor's death, did you go out to the *Chancellor* Vaults to fetch your supper beer?"

"I did, sir—just as usual."

"What time?"

"A bit earlier than usual, sir—half-past seven."

"How long were you away?"

"Why, sir, to tell you the truth, nigh on to half an hour. I met a neighbour at the corner and——"

"Exactly! And stopped chatting a bit. So you were out of your rooms in the Moot Hall that evening from 7.30 to nearly eight o'clock?"

"Yes, sir."

Meeking gave the Coroner a glance, thrust his hands into his pockets, and dropped back into his seat—silent and apparently satisfied.

CHAPTER XV

THE SPECIAL EDITION

But if the barrister was satisfied with the possibilities suggested by this new evidence, the gist of which had apparently altered the whole aspect of the case, the Coroner obviously was not. Ever since Mrs. Mallett had interrupted his summing-up to the jury, he had shown signs of fidgetiness. He had continually put on and taken off his spectacles; he had moved restlessly in his chair; now and then he had seemed on the point of interrupting counsel or witnesses: it was evident that things were not at all to his liking. And now as Meeking sat down the Coroner turned to Mrs. Bunning, who stood, looking wonderingly about her, and still fingering the apron in which she had been found at her work.

"Mrs. Bunning," he said, "I want to ask you some questions about this back entrance of yours. What is it—a door opening out of the rear of the Moot Hall?"

"Yes, sir; that's it, sir."

"Does it open on St. Lawrence Lane?"

"Yes, sir."

"What does it open into—a hall, lobby, passage, or what?"

"A lobby, sir, next to our living-room."

"Is there a staircase, then, in that lobby—I mean, by which you can get to the upper rooms in the Moot Hall?"

"Oh, yes, sir; that's the staircase we use, me and my husband, when we go up for cleaning and dusting, sir."

"Then, if anybody went in by that door while you were out that evening, whoever it was could go up that staircase to the upper rooms?"

"Oh, yes, sir, they could."

"And get to the Mayor's Parlour?"

"Yes, sir. The staircase opens on to the big landing, sir, and the door of the Mayor's Parlour is at the far end of it."

"And you were out of your rooms for half an hour that evening?"

"Just about that, sir. It would be a bit after half-past seven when I went out, and it was just before eight when I went in again."

"Did you notice anything that made you think somebody had been in?"

"Oh, no, sir, nothing!"

"Had you left your door open—your outer door?"

"Yes, sir—a bit ajar. Of course I never thought to be away many minutes, sir."

"Very good. That's all, thank you, Mrs. Bunning," said the Coroner. He looked round the court. "Is the Borough Surveyor still there?" he asked. "Mr. Walkershaw? Let him come into the witness-box again."

But the Borough Surveyor had gone—nor was he to be found in his office in another part of the building. Once more the Coroner looked round.

"I dare say we are all quite familiar with what I may call the geography of St. Lawrence Lane," he remarked. "But I want some formal evidence about it that can be put on the record. I see Mr. Krevin Crood there—I believe Mr. Crood is as big an authority on Hathelsborough as anybody living—perhaps he'll oblige me by coming forward."

Krevin Crood, sitting at the front of the densely-packed mass of spectators, rose and walked into the witness-box. The Coroner leaned confidentially in his direction.

"Mr. Crood," he said, "I think you're perfectly familiar with St. Lawrence Lane—in its relation to the immediately surrounding property?"

"I am, sir," replied Krevin. "Every inch of it!"

"Just describe it to us, as if we knew nothing about it," continued the Coroner. "You know what I want, and what I mean."

"Certainly, sir," assented Krevin. "St. Lawrence Lane is a narrow thoroughfare, about eighty to ninety yards in length which lies at the back of Mr. Mallett's house—I mean the bank premises—the Moot Hall, and Dr. Wellesley's house. It's north entrance, at the corner of the bank, is in Woolmarket; its south in Strand Lane. On its west side there is a back door to the bank house; another into Bunning's rooms on the basement of the Moot Hall; a third into the Police Office, also in that basement; a fourth into the rear of Dr. Wellesley's house. On the opposite side of the lane—the east—there is nothing but St. Lawrence's Church and churchyard. St. Lawrence's church tower and west end faces the back of the Moot Hall; there is a part of the churchyard opposite the bank premises—the rear premises; the rest of the churchyard faces Dr. Wellesley's house—the back of it, of course."

"Is the lane much frequented?"

"No, sir; it is very little used. Except by tradesmen going to Mr. Mallett's or to Dr. Wellesley's back doors, and by people going to the Police Office, it is scarcely used at all. There is no traffic along it. On Sundays, of course, it is used by people going to the services at St. Lawrence."

"Would it be likely to be quiet, unfrequented, of an evening?"

"Emphatically—yes."

"Do you think it likely that any person wishing to enter the Moot Hall unobserved and seeing Mrs. Bunning go away from her rooms and round the corner to the *Chancellor* Vaults—as we've just heard she did—could slip in unseen?"

"Oh, to be sure!" affirmed Krevin. "The easiest thing in the world! If I may suggest something——?"

"Go on, go on!" said the Coroner, waving his spectacles. "Anything that helps—suggest whatever you like."

"Well," said Krevin, slowly and thoughtfully, "if I may put it in my own way. Suppose that there is somebody in the town who is desirous of finding the late Mayor alone in the Mayor's Parlour, being also cognizant of the fact—well known to many people—that the late Mr. Wallingford was to be found there every evening? Suppose, too, that that person was well acquainted with the geography of St. Lawrence Lane and the Moot Hall? Suppose further that he or she was also familiar with the fact that Mrs. Bunning invariably went out every evening to fetch the supper beer from the *Chancellor* Vaults? Such a person could easily enter the Bunnings' back door with an absolutely minimum risk of detection. The churchyard of St. Lawrence is edged with thick shrubs and trees, anybody could easily hide amongst the shrub—laurel, myrtle, ivy—watch for Mrs. Bunning's going out, and, when she had gone, slip across the lane—a very narrow one!—and enter the door which, as she says, she left open. It would not take two minutes for any person who knew the place to pass from St. Lawrence Churchyard to the Mayor's Parlour, or from the Mayor's Parlour to St. Lawrence Churchyard."

A murmur of comprehension and understanding ran round the court: most of the people present knew St. Lawrence Lane and the Moot Hall as well as Krevin Crood knew them; his suggestion appealed to their common sense. And Tansley, with a sudden start, turned to Brent.

"That's done it!" he whispered. "Everybody tumbles to that! We've been going off on all sorts of side-tracks all the morning, now Wellesley, now Mrs. Mallett, and now—here's another! Access to the Mayor's Parlour—there you are! Easy as winking, on Krevin Crood's theory. Lay you a fiver to a shilling old Seagrave won't go on any farther."

Herein Tansley was quickly proved to be right. The Coroner was showing unmistakable symptoms of his satiety for the time being. He thanked Krevin Crood punctiliously for his assistance, and once again toying restlessly with his spectacles, turned to the jury, who, on their part, looked blank and doubtful.

"Well, gentlemen," he said, "it seems to me that the entire complexion of this matter is changed by the evidence we have heard since Mrs. Mallett broke in so unexpectedly upon what I was saying to you. I don't propose now to say any more as regards the evidence of either Dr. Wellesley or Mrs. Mallett: since we heard what they had to say we have learnt a good deal which I think will be found to have more importance than we attach to it at present. As matters stand, the evidence of Mrs. Bunning is of supreme importance—there is no doubt whatever that there was easy means of access to the Mayor's Parlour during that half hour wherein the Mayor met his death. The mystery of the whole affair has deepened considerably during to-day's proceedings, and instead of bringing this inquiry to a definite conclusion I feel that I must wait for more evidence. I adjourn this inquest for a month from to-day."

The court cleared; the spectators filtered out into the market-place in various moods, and under different degrees of excitement. Some were openly disappointed that the jury had not been allowed to return a verdict; some were vehement in declaring that the jury never would return a verdict; here and there were men who wagged their heads sagely and remarked with sinister smiles that they knew what they thought about it. But, within the rapidly emptying court Brent, Tansley and Hawthwaite were grouped around Meeking—the barrister was indulging in some private remarks upon the morning's proceedings, chiefly addressed to the police superintendent.

"There's no doubt about it, you know," he was saying. "The evidence of the Bunning woman, supplemented by what Krevin Crood said—which was a mere, formal, crystallizing of common knowledge—has altered the whole thing. Here's the back entrance to the Moot Hall left absolutely unprotected, unguarded, unwatched—whatever you like to call it—for half an hour, the critical half hour. Of course the murderer got up to the Mayor's Parlour that way and got away by the same means. You're as far off as ever, Hawthwaite, and it's a pity you wasted time on that jealousy business. I watched Wellesley closely, and I believe that he spoke the truth when he said that whatever there might have been there was no jealousy about Mrs. Saumarez between him and Wallingford at the end. My own impression is that Wellesley was clear off with Mrs. Saumarez."

Hawthwaite, essentially a man of fixed ideas, looked sullen.

"Well, it isn't mine, then," he growled. "From all I've learnt—and I've chances and opportunities that most folks haven't—my impression is that both men were after her, right up to the time Wallingford was murdered. I can tell you this—and I could have put it in evidence if I'd thought it worth while—Wellesley used to go and see her, of an evening, constantly, up to a very recent date, though she was supposed to have broken off with him and to be on with the Mayor. Now then!"

"Do you know that for a fact, Hawthwaite?" asked Tansley.

"I know it for a fact! He used to go there late at night, and stop late. If you want to know where I got it from, it was from a young woman that used to be housemaid at the Abbey House, Mrs. Saumarez's place. She's told me a lot; both Wallingford and Wellesley used to visit there a good deal, but as I say, Wellesley used to go there very late of an evening. This young woman says that she knows for a fact that he was often with her mistress till close on midnight. I don't care twopence what Wellesley said; I believe he was, and is, after her, and of course he'd be jealous enough about her being so friendly with Wallingford. There's a deal more in all this than's come out yet—let me tell you that!"

"I don't think anybody will contradict you, Hawthwaite," observed the barrister dryly. "But the pertinent fact is what I tell you—the fact of access! Somebody got to the Mayor's Parlour by way of the back staircase, through Bunning's rooms, that evening. Who was it? That's what you've got to find out. If you'd only found out, before now, that Mrs. Bunning took half an hour to fetch the supper beer that night we should have been spared a lot of talk this morning. As things are, we're as wise as ever."

Then Meeking, with a cynical laugh, picked up his papers and went off, and Brent, leaving Tansley talking to the superintendent, who was inclined to be huffy, strolled out of the Moot Hall, and went round to the back, with the idea of seeing for himself the narrow street which Krevin Crood had formally described. He saw at once that Krevin was an admirable exponent of the art of description: everything in St. Lawrence Lane was as the ex-official had said: there was the door into the Bunnings' rooms, and there, facing it, the ancient church and its equally ancient churchyard. It was to the churchyard that Brent gave most attention; he immediately realized that Krevin Crood was quite right in speaking of it as a place wherein anybody could conveniently hide—a dark, gloomy, sheltered, high-walled place, filled with thick shrubbery, out of which, here and there, grew sombre yew-trees, some of them of an antiquity as venerable as that of the church itself. It would be a very easy thing indeed, Brent decided, for any designing person to hide amongst these trees and shrubs, watch the Bunnings' door until Mrs. Bunning left it, jug in hand, and then to slip across the grass-grown, cobble-paved lane, silent and lonely enough, and up to the Mayor's Parlour. But all that presupposed knowledge of the place and of its people and their movements.

He went back to the market-place and towards the *Chancellor*. Peppermore came hurrying out of the hotel as Brent turned into it. He carried a folded paper in his hand, and he waved it at Brent as, at sight of him, he came to a sudden halt.

"Just been looking for you, Mr. Brent!" he said mysteriously. "Come into some quiet spot, sir, and glance at this. Here we are, sir, corner of the hall."

He drew Brent into an alcove that opened close by them, and affecting a mysterious air began to unfold his paper, a sheet of news-print which, Brent's professional eye was quick to see, had just been pulled as a proof.

"All that affair to-day, Mr. Brent," he whispered, "most unsatisfactory, sir, most unsatisfactory—unconvincing, inconclusive, Mr. Brent! The thing's getting no farther, sir, no farther, except, of course, for the very pertinent fact about Mrs. Bunning's absence from her quarters that fateful evening. My own impression, sir, is that Hawthwaite and all the rest of 'em don't know the right way of going about this business. But the *Monitor's* going to wade in, sir—the *Monitor* is coming to the rescue! Look here, sir, we're going to publish a special edition to-night, with a full account of to-day's proceedings at the inquest, and with it we're going to give away, as a gratis supplement—what do you think, sir? This, produced at great cost, sir, in the interest of Justice! Look at it!"

Therewith Peppermore, first convincing himself that he and his companion were secure from observation, spread out before Brent a square sheet of very damp paper, strongly redolent of printers' ink, at the head of which appeared, in big, bold, black characters, the question:

WHO TYPED THIS LETTER?

Beneath it, excellently reproduced, was a facsimile of the typewritten letter which Wallingford had shown to Epplewhite and afterwards left in his keeping. And beneath that was a note in large italics inviting anyone who could give any information as to the origin of the document to communicate with the Editor of the *Monitor*, at once.

"What d'ye think of that for a *coup*, Mr. Brent?" demanded Peppermore proudly. "Up to Fleet Street form that, sir, ain't it? I borrowed the original, sir, had it carefully reproduced in facsimile, and persuaded my proprietor to go to the expense of having sufficient copies struck off on this specially prepared paper to give one away with every copy of the *Monitor* that we shall print to-night. Five thousand copies, Mr. Brent! That facsimile, sir, will be all over Hathelsborough by supper time!"

"Smart!" observed Brent. "Top-hole idea, Peppermore. And you hope——?"

"There aren't so many typewriters in Hathelsborough as all that," replied Peppermore. "I hope that somebody'll come forward who can tell something. Do you notice, sir, that this has been done—the original, I mean—on an old-fashioned machine, and that the lettering is considerably worn, sir? I hope the *Monitor's* efforts will solve the mystery!"

"Much obliged to you," said Brent. "There's a lot of spade-work to do—yet."

He was thinking over the best methods of further attempts on that spade-work, when, late that evening, he received a note from Queenie Crood. It was confined to one line:

To-morrow usual place three urgent—Q.

CHAPTER XVI

THE CASTLE WALL

Brent went to bed that night wondering what it was that Queenie Crood wanted. Since their first meeting in the Castle grounds they had met frequently. He was getting interested in Queenie: she developed on acquaintance. Instead of being the meek and mild mouse of Simon Crood's domestic hearth that Brent had fancied her to be on his visit to the Tannery, he was discovering possibilities in her that he had not suspected. She had spirit and imagination and a continually rebellious desire to get out of Simon Crood's cage and spread her wings in flight—anywhere, so long as Hathelsborough was left behind. She had told Brent plainly that she thought him foolish for buying property in the town; what was there in that rotten old borough, said Queenie, to keep any man of spirit and enterprise there? Brent argued the point in his downright way: it was his job, he conceived, to take up his cousin's work where it had been laid down; he was going to regenerate Hathelsborough.

"And that you'll never do!" affirmed Queenie. "You might as well try to blow up the Castle keep with a halfpenny cracker! Hathelsborough people are like the man in the Bible—they're joined to their idols. You can try and try, and you'll only break your heart, or your back, in the effort, just as Wallingford would have done. If Wallingford had been a wise man he'd have let Hathelsborough go to the devil in its own way; then he'd have been alive now."

"Well, I'm going to try," declared Brent. "I said I would, and I will! You wait till I'm elected to that Town Council! Then we'll see."

"It's fighting a den of wild beasts," said Queenie. "You won't have a rag left on you when they're through with you."

She used to tell him at these meetings of the machinations of Simon Crood and Coppinger and Mallett against his chances of success in the Castle Ward election: according to her they were moving heaven and earth to prevent him from succeeding Wallingford. Evidently believing Queenie to be a tame bird that carried no tales, they were given to talking freely before her during their nightly conclaves. Brent heard a good deal about the underhand methods in which municipal elections are carried on in small country towns, and was almost as much amused as amazed at the unblushing corruption and chicanery of which Queenie told him. And now he fancied that she had some special news of a similar sort to give him: the election was close at hand, and he knew that Simon and his gang were desperately anxious to defeat him. Although Simon had been elected to the Mayoralty, his party in the Town Council was in a parlous position—at present it had a majority of one; if Brent were elected, that majority would disappear, and there were signs that at the annual elections in the coming November it would be transformed into a minority. Moreover, the opponent whom Brent had to face in this by-election was a strong man, a well-known, highly respected ratepayer, who, though an adherent of the Old Party, was a fair-minded and moderate politician, and likely to secure the suffrages of the non-party electors. It was going to be a stiff fight, and Brent was thankful for the occasional insights into the opposition's plans of campaign which Queenie was able to give him.

But there were other things than this to think about, and he thought much as he lay wakeful in bed that night and as he dressed next morning. The proceedings at the adjourned inquest had puzzled him; left him doubtful and uncertain. He was not sure about the jealousy theory. He was not sure about Mrs. Saumarez, from what he had seen of her personally and from what he had heard of her. He was inclined to believe that she was not only a dabbler in politics with a liking for influencing men who were concerned in them but that she was also the sort of woman who likes to have more than one man in leash. He was now disposed to think that there had been love-passages between her and Wallingford, and not only between her and Wallingford but between her and Wellesley—there might, after all, be something in the jealousy idea. But then came in the curious episode of Mrs. Mallett, and the mystery attaching to it—as things presented themselves at present there seemed to be no chance whatever that either Mrs. Mallett or Wellesley would lift the veil on what was evidently a secret between them. The only satisfactory and straightforward feature about yesterday's proceedings, he thought, was the testimony of Mrs. Bunning as to her unguarded door. Now, at any rate, it was a sure thing that there had been ready means of access to the Mayor's Parlour that evening; what was necessary was to discover who it was that had taken advantage of them.

After breakfast Brent went round to see Hawthwaite. Hawthwaite gave him a chair and eyed him expectantly.

"We don't seem to be going very fast ahead," remarked Brent.

"Mr. Brent," exclaimed Hawthwaite, "I assure you we're doing all we can! But did you ever know a more puzzling case? Between you and me, I'm not at all convinced about either Dr. Wellesley or Mrs. Mallett—there's a mystery there which I can't make out. They may have said truth, and they mayn't, and——"

"Cut them out," interrupted Brent. "For the time being anyway. We got some direct evidence yesterday—for the first time."

"As—how?" questioned Hawthwaite.

"That door into Bunning's room," replied Brent. "That's where the murderer slipped in."

"Ay; but did he?" said Hawthwaite. "If one could be certain——"

"Look here!" asserted Brent. "There is one thing that is certain—dead certain. That handkerchief!"

"Well?" asked Hawthwaite.

"That should be followed up, more," continued Brent. "There's no doubt whatever that that handkerchief, which Wellesley admits is his, got sent by mistake to one or other of Mrs. Marriner's other customers. That's flat! Now, you can trace it."

"How?" exclaimed Hawthwaite. "A small article like that!"

"It can be done, with patience," said Brent. "It's got to be done. That handkerchief got into somebody's hands. That somebody is probably the murderer. As to how it can be traced—well, I suggest this. As far as I'm conversant with laundry matters, families, such as Mrs. Marriner says she works for, have laundry books. These books are checked, I believe, when the washing's sent home. If there's an article missing, the person who does the checking notes it; if a wrong article's enclosed, that, too, is noted, and returned to the laundry."

"If Wellesley's handkerchief got to the wrong place, why wasn't it returned?" demanded Hawthwaite.

"To be sure; but that's just what you've got to find out," retorted Brent. "You ought to go to Mrs. Marriner's laundry and make an exhaustive search of her books, lists, and so on till you get some light—see?"

"Mrs. Marriner has, I should say, a hundred customers," remarked Hawthwaite.

"Don't matter if Mrs. Marriner's got five hundred customers," said Brent. "That's got to be seen into. If you aren't going to do it, I will. Whoever it was that was in that Mayor's Parlour tried to burn a blood-stained handkerchief there. That handkerchief was Wellesley's. Wellesley swears he was never near the Mayor's Parlour. I believe him! So that handkerchief got by error into the box or basket of some other customer of Mrs. Marriner. Trace it!"

He rose and moved towards the door, and Hawthwaite nodded.

"We'll make a try at it, Mr. Brent," he said. "But, as I say, to work on a slight clue like that——"

"I've known of far slighter clues," replied Brent.

Yet, as he went away, he reflected on the extreme thinness of this clue—it was possible that the handkerchief had passed through more hands than one before settling in those of the person who had thrown it on the hearth, stained with Wallingford's blood, in the Mayor's Parlour. But it was a clue, and, in Brent's opinion, *the* clue. One fact in relation to it had always struck him forcibly—the murderer of his cousin was either a very careless and thoughtless person or had been obliged to quit the Mayor's Parlour very hurriedly. Anyone meticulously particular about destroying clues or covering up traces would have seen to it that the handkerchief was completely burnt up before leaving the room. As it was, it seemed to Brent that the murderer had either thrown the handkerchief on the hearth, seen it catch fire and paid no more attention to it—which would denote carelessness—or had quitted the place immediately after flinging it aside, which would imply that some sound from without had startled him—or her. And, was it him—or was it her? There were certain features of the case which had inclined Brent of late to speculating on the possibility that his cousin had been murdered by a woman. And, to be sure, a woman was now in the case—Mrs. Mallett. If only he knew why Mrs. Mallett went to see the doctor and the Mayor....

But that, after all, was mere speculation, and he had a busy morning before him, in relation to his election business. He had been continuously engaged all the time when at three o'clock he hurried to the Castle Grounds to meet Queenie. He found her in her usual haunt, a quiet spot in the angle of a wall, where she was accustomed to sit and read.

"Well, and why 'urgent'?" asked Brent as he dropped on the seat at her side.

"To make sure that you'd come," retorted Queenie. "Didn't want to leave it to chance."

"I'm here!" said Brent. "Go ahead with the business."

"Did you see the *Monitor* last night and that facsimile they gave away with it?" inquired Queenie.

"I did! Saw the facsimile before it was published. Peppermore showed it to me."

"Very well—that's the urgent business. I know whose machine that letter—the original, I mean—was typed on!"

"You do? Great Scott! Whose, then?"

"Uncle Simon Crood's! Fact!"

"Whew! So the old fossil's got such a modern invention as a typewriter, has he? And you think——"

"Don't think—I know! He's had a typewriter for years; it's an old-fashioned thing, a good deal worn out. He rarely uses it, but now and then he operates, with one finger, slowly. And that letter originated from him—his machine."

"Proof!" said Brent.

Queenie took up a book that lay on the seat between them and from it extracted a folded copy of the *Monitor's* facsimile. She leaned nearer to Brent.

"Now look!" she said. "Do you notice that two or three of the letters are broken? That *M*—part of it's gone. That *O*—half made. The top of that *A* is missing. More noticeable still—do you see that the small *t* there is slanting the wrong way? Well, all that's on Uncle Simon's machine! I knew where that letter had originated as soon as ever I saw this facsimile last night."

She laid aside the supplement and once more opening her book produced a sheet of paper.

"Look at this!" she continued. "When Uncle Simon went out to the tannery this morning, I just took advantage of his absence to type out the alphabet on his machine. Now then, you glance over that and compare the faulty letters with those in the facsimile! What do you say now?"

"You're a smart girl, Queenie!" said Brent. "You're just the sort of girl I've been wanting to meet—the sort that can see things when they're right in front of her eyes. Oh, my! that's sure, positive proof that old Simon——"

"Oh!" broke in Queenie sharply. "Oh, I say!"

Before Brent could look up, he was conscious that a big and bulky shadow had fallen across the gravelled path at their feet. He lifted his eyes. There, in his usual raiment of funereal black, his top-hat at the back of his head, his hands behind him under the ample skirts of his frock-coat, his broad, fat face heavy with righteous and affectedly sorrowful indignation, stood Simon Crood. His small, pig-like eyes were fixed on the papers which the two young people were comparing.

"Hello!" exclaimed Brent. He was quick to see that he and Queenie were in for a row, probably for a row of a decisive sort which would affect both their lives, and he purposely threw as much hearty insolence into his tone as he could summon. "Eavesdropping, eh, Mr. Crood?"

Simon withdrew a hand from the sable folds behind him, and waved it in lordly fashion.

"I've no words to waste on impudent young fellers as comes from nobody knows where," he said loftily. "My words is addressed to my niece, as I see sitting there, a-deceiving of her lawful rellytive and guardian. Go you home at once, miss!"

"Rot!" exclaimed Brent. "She'll go home when she likes—and not at all, if she doesn't like! You stick where you are, Queenie! I'm here."

And as if to prove the truth of his words he slipped his right arm round Queenie's waist, clasped it tightly, and turned a defiant eye on Simon.

"See that?" he said. "Well! that's just where Queenie stops, as long as ever Queenie likes! Eh, Queenie?"

The girl, reddening as Brent's arm slipped round her, instinctively laid her free hand on his wrist. And as he appealed to her he felt her fingers tighten there with a firm, understanding pressure.

"That's all right!" he whispered to her. "We've done it, girlie—it's for good!" He looked up at Simon, whose mouth was opening with astonishment. "Queenie's my girl, old bird!" he went on. "She isn't going anywhere—not anywhere at all—at anybody's bidding, unless she likes. And why shouldn't she be here?"

It seemed, from the pause that followed, as if Simon would never find his tongue again. But at last he spoke.

"So this here is what's been going on behind my back, is it, miss?" he demanded, pointedly ignoring Brent and fixing his gaze on Queenie. "A-carrying on with strangers at my very gates, as you might say, and in public places in a town of which I'm chief magistrate! What sort o' return do you call this, miss, I should like to know, for all that I've done for you? me that's lodged and boarded and clothed you, ever since——"

"What have I done for you in return?" demanded Queenie with a flash of spirit. "Saved you the wages of a couple of servants for all these years! But this is the end, if you're going to throw that in my teeth——"

Brent drew Queenie to her feet and turned her away from Simon. He gave the big man a look over his shoulder.

"That's it, my friend!" he said. "That's the right term—the end! Find somebody else to do your household drudgery—this young lady's done her last stroke for you. And now don't begin to bluster," he added, as Simon, purpling with wrath, shook his fist. "We'll just leave you to yourself."

He led Queenie away down a side-path, and once within its shelter, put a finger under her chin, and lifting her face, looked steadily at her.

"Look here, girlie," he said. "You heard what I whispered to you just now? 'It's for good!' Didn't I say that? Well, is it?"

Queenie managed to get her eyes to turn on him at last.

"Do you mean it?" she murmured.

"I just do!" answered Brent fervently. "Say the word!"

"Yes, then!" whispered Queenie.

She looked at him wonderingly when he had bent and kissed her.

"You're an extraordinary man!" she said. "Whatever am I going to do—now? Homeless!"

"Not much!" exclaimed Brent. "You come along with me, Queenie. I'm a good hand at thinking fast. I'll put you up, warm and comfortable, at Mother Appleyard's; and as quick as the thing can be done we'll be married. Got that into your little head? Come on, then!"

That night Brent told Tansley of what had happened and what he was going to do. Tansley listened, laughed, and shook his head.

"All right, my lad!" he said. "I've no doubt you and Queenie'll suit each other excellently. But you've settled your chances of winning that election, Brent! Simon Crood'll bring up every bit of his heavy artillery against you, now—and will smash you!"

CHAPTER XVII

IMPREGNABLE

B rent received this plain-spoken declaration with a curious tightening of lips and setting of jaw which Tansley, during their brief acquaintance, had come to know well enough. They were accompanied by a fixed stare—the solicitor knew that too. These things meant that Brent's fighting spirit was roused and that his temper became ugly. Tansley laughed.

"You're the sort of chap for a scrap, Brent," he continued, "and a go-ahead customer too! But—you don't know this lot, nor their resources. Whatever anybody may say, and whatever men like your late cousin, and Epplewhite, and any of the so-called Progressives—I'm not one, myself; it pays me to belong to neither party!—whatever these folks may think or say, Simon Crood and his lot are top-dogs in this little old town! Vested interests, my boy!—ancient tree, with roots firmly fixed in the piled-up soil, strata upon strata, of a thousand years! You're not going to pull up these roots, my lad!"

"How'll Simon Crood smash me?" demanded Brent quietly.

"As to the exact how," answered Tansley, "can't say! Mole work—but he'll set the majority of the electors in that Castle Ward against you."

"I've enough promises of support now to give me a majority," retorted Brent.

"That for promises!" exclaimed Tansley, snapping his fingers. "You don't know Hathelsborough people! They'll promise you their support to your face—just to get rid of your presence on their door-steps—and vote against you when they reach the ballot-box. I'll lay anything most of the folk you've been to see have promised their support to both candidates."

"Why should these people support Crood and his crew?" demanded Brent.

"Because Crood and his crew represent the only god they worship!" said Tansley, with a cynical laugh. "Brass!—as they call it. All that a Hathelsborough man thinks about is brass—money. Get money where you can—never mind how, as long as you get it, and keep just within the law. Simon Crood represents the Hathelsborough principle of graft, and whatever you may think, he's the paramount influence in the town to-day."

"He and his lot have only got the barest majority on the Council," remarked Brent.

"Maybe; but they've got all the really influential men behind 'em, the moneyed men," said Tansley. "And they've distributed all the various official posts, sinecures most of 'em, amongst their friends. That Town Trustee business is the nut to crack here, Brent, and a nut that's been hardening for centuries isn't going to be cracked with an ordinary implement. Come now, are you an extraordinary one?"

"I'll make a try at things anyway," replied Brent. "And I don't believe I shall lose that election, either."

"You might have scraped in if you hadn't carried Simon Crood's niece away from under his very nose," said Tansley. "But now that you've brought personal matters into the quarrel, the old chap'll move every piece he has on the board to checkmate you. It won't do to have you on the Council, Brent, you're too much of an innovator. Now this town—the real town!—doesn't want innovation. Innovation in an ancient borough like this is—unsettling and uncomfortable. See?"

"This world doesn't stand still," retorted Brent. "I'm going ahead!"

But he reflected, as he left the solicitor's office, that much of what Tansley had said was true. There was something baffling in the very atmosphere of Hathelsborough—he felt like a man who fights the wind. Everything was elusive, ungraspable, evasive—he seemed to get no further forward. And, if Tansley was right in affirming that Hathelsborough people made promises which they had no intention of redeeming, his chances of getting a seat on the Town Council and setting to work to rebuild his late cousin's schemes of reformation were small indeed. But once more he set his jaw and nerved himself to endeavour, and, as the day of election was now close at hand, plunged into the task of canvassing and persuading—wondering all the time, now that he had heard Tansley's cynical remarks, if the people to whom he talked and who were mostly plausible and ingratiating in their reception of him were in reality laughing at him for his pains. He saw little of the efforts of the other side; but Peppermore agreed with Tansley that the opposition would leave no stone unturned in the task of beating him.

The *Monitor* was all for Brent—Peppermore's proprietor was a Progressive; a tradesman who had bought up the *Monitor* for a mere song, and ran it as a business speculation which had so far turned out very satisfactorily. Consequently, Brent at this period went much to the *Monitor* office, and did things in concert with Peppermore, inspiring articles which, to say the least of them, were severely critical of the methods of the Crood regime. On one of these visits Peppermore, in the middle of a discussion about one of these effusions, abruptly switched off the trend of his thought in another direction.

"I'd a visit from Mrs. Saumarez this morning, Mr. Brent," he said, eyeing his companion with a knowing look. "Pretty and accomplished woman, that, sir; but queer, Mr. Brent, queer!"

"What do you mean?" asked Brent.

"Odd ideas, sir, very odd!" replied Peppermore. "Wanted to find out from me, Mr. Brent, if, in case she's called up again at this inquest business, or if circumstances arise which necessitate police proceedings at which she might be a witness, her name couldn't be suppressed? Ever hear such a proposal, sir, to make to a journalist? 'Impossible, my dear madam!' says I. 'Publicity, ma'am,' I says, 'is—well, it's the very salt of life, as you might term it,' I says. 'When gentlemen of our profession report public affairs we keep nothing back,' I says; firmly, sir. 'I very much object to my name figuring in these proceedings,' she says. 'I object very strongly indeed!' 'Can't help it, ma'am,' says I. 'If the highest in the land was called into a witness-box, and I reported the case,' I says, 'I should have to give the name! It's the glory of our profession, Mrs. Saumarez.' I says, 'just as it's that of the law, that we don't countenance hole-and-corner business. The light of day, ma'am, the light of day! that's the idea, Mrs. Saumarez!' I says. 'Let the clear, unclouded radiance of high noon, ma'am, shine on'—but you know what I mean, Mr. Brent. As I said to her, the publicity that's attendant on all this sort of thing in England is one of the very finest of our national institutions.

"Odd, sir, but, for a woman that's supposed to be modern and progressive, she didn't agree. 'I don't want to see my name in the papers in connection with this affair, Mr. Peppermore,' she declared again. 'I thought, perhaps,' she says, rather coaxingly, 'that you could suggest some way of keeping it out if there are any further proceedings.' 'Can't, ma'am!' says I. 'If such an eventuality comes to be, it'll be my duty to record faithfully and fully in the *Monitor* whatever takes place.' 'Oh,' says she. 'But it's not the *Monitor* that I so much object to—it's the London papers. I understand that you supply the reports to them, Mr. Peppermore.' Well, of course, as you know, Mr. Brent, I am district correspondent for two of the big London agencies, but I had to explain to her that in a sensational case like this the London papers generally sent down men of their own: there were, for instance, two or three London reporters present the other day.

"Yes, she said; so she'd heard, and she'd got all the London papers to see if her name was mentioned, and had been relieved to find that it hadn't: there were nothing but summarized reports: her name hadn't appeared anywhere but in the *Monitor*. 'And what I wanted, Mr. Peppermore,' she says, more wheedlingly than ever, 'was that, if it lay in your power, and if occasion arises, you would do what you could to keep my name out of it—I don't want publicity!' Um!" concluded Peppermore. "Pretty woman, Mr. Brent, and with taking ways, but of course I had to be adamant, sir—firm, Mr. Brent, firm as St. Hathelswide's tower. 'The Press, Mrs. Saumarez,' I says, as I dismissed the matter—politely, of course—'has its Duties. It can make no exception, Mrs. Saumarez, to wealth, or rank, or—beauty.' I made her a nice bow, Mr. Brent, as I spoke the last word. But she wasn't impressed. As I say—queer woman! What's publicity matter to her as long as she's no more than a witness?"

Brent was not particularly impressed by Peppermore's story. He saw nothing in it beyond the natural desire of a sensitive, highly-strung woman to keep herself aloof from an unpleasant episode, and he said so.

"I don't see what good Hawthwaite hoped to get by ever calling Mrs. Saumarez before the Coroner," he added. "She told nothing that everybody didn't know. What did it all amount to?"

"Ay, but that's just it, in a town like this, Mr. Brent," answered Peppermore with a wink. "I can tell you why the police put the Coroner up to calling Mrs. Saumarez as a witness. They'd got a theory—that Wellesley killed your cousin in a fit of jealousy, of which she was the cause, and they hoped to substantiate it through her evidence. There's no doubt, sir, that there were love-passages between Dr. Wellesley and this attractive lady and between her and your cousin, but—shall I tell you, sir, something that's in my mind?"

"Ay. Why not?" answered Brent. He was thinking of the thick pile of letters which he had returned to Mrs. Saumarez and of the unmistakable love-tokens which he had seen deposited with them in the casket wherein Wallingford had kept them. "What is it you're thinking of?"

Peppermore edged his chair closer to his visitor's, and lowered his voice.

"I am not unobservant, Mr. Brent," he said. "Our profession, as you know, sir, leads us to the cultivation of that faculty. Now, I've thought a good deal about this matter, and I'll tell you a conclusion I've come to. Do you remember that when Dr. Wellesley was being questioned the other day he was asked if there was jealousy between him and Mr. Wallingford about Mrs. Saumarez? To be sure! Now what did he answer? He answered frankly that *there had been but it no longer existed*! Do you know what I deduced from that, Mr. Brent? This—that the little lady had had both those men as strings to her bow at the same time, indecisive as to which of 'em she'd finally choose, but that, not so long since, she'd given up both, in favour of a third man!"

Brent started, and laughed.

"Ingenious, Peppermore, very ingenious!" he said. "Given 'em both the mitten as they say? But the third man?"

"Mrs. Saumarez was away on the Continent most of the winter," answered Peppermore. "The Riviera, Nice, Monte Carlo—that sort of thing. She may have met somebody there that she preferred to either Wellesley or Wallingford. Anyway, Mr. Brent, what did the doctor mean when he frankly admitted that there had been jealousy between him and Wallingford, but that it *no longer existed*? He meant, I take it, that there was no reason for its further existence. That implies that another man had come into the arena!"

"Ay, but does it?" said Brent. "It might mean something else—that she'd finally accepted Wellesley. Eh?"

"No," declared Peppermore. "She's not engaged to Wellesley: I'll lay anything she isn't, Mr. Brent. There's a third man, somewhere in the background, and it's my opinion that that's the reason why she doesn't want the publicity she came to me about."

Brent fell into a new train of thought, more or less confused. Mrs. Saumarez's talk to him about Wallingford, and the letters, and the things in the casket, were all mixed up in it.

"Had you any opportunity of seeing Wellesley and my cousin together during the last week or two before my cousin's death?" he asked presently.

"Several, Mr. Brent, several opportunities," answered Peppermore. "I went to report the proceedings of two or three committees of the Town Council during the fortnight preceding that lamentable occurrence, sir, and saw them at close quarters. I saw them frequently at the Club, of which I am a member. I should say, sir, from what I observed, that they were on very good terms with each other—more friendly than ever, Mr. Brent."

"Um," said Brent. "Well, there's a lot of queer stuff about this business, Peppermore. But let's get back to that of the moment. Look here, I've got a fine notion for your *Monitor*—you'll just have time to get it out before my election day. Let's make a real, vigorous, uncompromising attack on the *principle* of the Town Trustee business. We'll not say one word about the present Trustees, old Crood, Mallett and Coppinger—we'll have no personalities, and make no charges; we'll avoid all stuff of that sort. We'll just attack the thing on its principle, taking up the line that it's a bad principle that the finances of a borough should be entrusted to the sole control of three men responsible to nobody and with the power, if one dies, to elect his successor. Let's argue it out *on* the principle; then, later, we'll have another article on the argument that the finances of a town should be wholly controlled by the elected representatives of the people—see?"

"Your late cousin's theories, Mr. Brent," said Peppermore. "Excellent notions, both, sir. You write the articles; I'll find the space. All on principle—no personalities. Plain and practical, Mr. Brent, let them be, so that everybody can understand. Though to be sure," he added regretfully, "what our readers most like is personalities! If we dared to slate old Crood with all the abuse we could lay our pens to, the readers of the *Monitor*, sir, would hug themselves with pleasure. But libel, Mr. Brent, libel! Do you know, sir, that ever since I occupied the editorial chair of state I have always felt that the wet blanket of the law of libel sat at my banquet like the ghost in Macbeth, letting its sword hang by a thread an inch from my cranium! Bit mixed in my metaphors, sir, but you know what I mean. Mustn't involve my respected proprietor in a libel suit, Mr. Brent, so stick to abstract principles, sir, and eschew those saucy personal touches which I regret—deeply—I can't print."

Brent had no intention of indulging in personalities in his warfare with Simon Crood and the reactionaries, but as the day of the election approached he discovered that his adversaries were not at all particular about putting forth highly personal references to himself. Hathelsborough suddenly became flooded with handbills and posters, each bearing a few pithy words in enormous type. These effusions were for the most part in the form of questions, addressed to the recipients; there was a cynical and sinister sneer in all of them. "Who *is* Mr. Brent?" "Why Support a Stranger?" "Who Wants a Carpet-Bagger?" "Vote for the Home-Made Article." "Hathelsborough Men for Hathelsborough Matters." "Stand by the True and Tried!" These appeals to the free and enlightened burgesses whose suffrages he solicited met Brent on every side, and especially on the day of the election. He had gone in for nothing of this sort himself: his original election address, it seemed to him, contained everything that he had to say, and beyond posting it all over the town in great placards and distributing it in the form of handbills to the electors of the Castle Ward he had issued nothing in the shape of literature. But he had stumped his desired constituency thoroughly, making speeches at every street corner and at every public meeting-place, and he had a personal conviction from his usual reception on these occasions that the people were with him. He was still sure of victory when, at noon on the polling-day, he chanced to meet Tansley.

"Going strong, as far as I can make out," he answered, in response to the solicitor's inquiry. "I've been about all the morning, and from what I've seen and what my Committee tell me, I'm in!"

Tansley shook his head.

"Look here, my lad," he said, drawing Brent aside as they stood together in the marketplace, "don't you build too high! They're working against you to-day, the Crood gang, as they never worked in their lives! They're bringing every influence they can get hold of against you. And—you haven't been over wise."

"What have I done now?" demanded Brent.

"Those articles that are appearing in the *Monitor*," replied Tansley. "Everybody knows they're yours. Do you think there's a soul in Hathelsborough who believes that Peppermore could write them? Now, they're a mistake! They may be true——"

"They are true!" growled Brent.

"Granted! But, however true they are, they're an attack on Hathelsborough," said Tansley. "Now, of whatever political colour they are, Hathelsborough folk are Hathelsborough folk, and they're prouder of this old town than you know. Look round you, my lad; there isn't a stone that you can see that wasn't just where it is now hundreds of years before you were born. Do you think these people like to hear you, a stranger, criticizing their old customs, old privileges, as you are doing in those articles? Not a bit of it! They're asking who you are to come judging them. You'd have done a lot better, Brent, if you'd been a bit diplomatic. You should have left all politics and reforms out of it, and tried to win the seat simply on your relationship to Wallingford. You could have shown your cards when you'd got in—you've shown 'em too soon!"

"That be damned!" said Brent. "I've played the game straightforwardly anyhow. I don't want any underhand business—there's enough of that in this rotten place now. And I still think I shall be in!"

But before the summer evening had progressed far, Brent learnt that the vested interests of an ancient English borough are stronger than he thought. He was hopelessly defeated—only rather more than a hundred voters marked their papers for him. His opponent was returned by a big majority. He got a new idea when he heard the result, and went straight off to Peppermore and the *Monitor* with it. They would go on with the articles, and make them of such a nature that the Local Government Board in London would find it absolutely necessary to give prompt and searching attention to Hathelsborough and its affairs.

CHAPTER XVIII

LOOSE STRANDS

By business time next morning Brent had cast aside all thought of the previous day's proceedings and of his defeat at the hands of the Old Gang, and had turned to affairs which were now of far more importance. He had three separate enterprises in hand; to be sure, they were all related, but each had a distinctive character of its own. He specified all three as he ate his breakfast at the *Chancellor*, where he was still located. First, now that he had done with his electioneering—for the time being—he was going to work harder than ever at the task of discovering Wallingford's murderer. Secondly, he was going to marry Queenie, and that speedily. Queenie and he had settled matters to their mutual satisfaction as soon as the row with Uncle Simon Crood was over, and they had already begun furnishing the house which Brent had bought in order to constitute himself a full-fledged burgess of Hathelsborough. Thirdly, he was going to put all he knew into the articles which he was writing for the *Monitor*—two had already appeared; he was going on writing them until public opinion, gradually educated, became too strong for the reactionary forces that had beaten him yesterday but which he would infallibly defeat to-morrow, or, if not to-morrow, the day after.

And first the murderer. He fetched Queenie from Mrs. Appleyard's that morning, and, utterly careless of the sly looks that were cast on him and her, marched her through the market-place to Hawthwaite's office at the police station. To Hawthwaite, keenly interested, he detailed particulars of Queenie's discovery about the typewritten letter and produced her proofs. Hawthwaite took it all in silently.

"You'll have to go into that, you know," concluded Brent. "Now that I've got through with that election I'm going to give more time to this business. We've got to find out who killed my cousin, Hawthwaite, somehow—it's not going to rest. I won't leave a stone unturned! And there," he added, pointing to the sheet of paper on which Queenie had made specimens of the broken type of Simon's antiquated machine, "is a stone which needs examining on all four sides!"

Hawthwaite picked up the sheet of paper, twisted it in his big fingers, and looked over it at the two young people with a quizzical smile.

"I understand that you and Miss Queenie there are contemplating matrimony, Mr. Brent?" he remarked. "That so, sir?"

"That's so," replied Brent promptly. "As soon as we've got our house furnished we'll be married."

"Then I can speak freely and in confidence before Mrs. Brent that's to be," responded Hawthwaite, with another smile. "Well, now, what you've just told me isn't exactly fresh news to me! I'll show you something." He turned, drew out a drawer from a chest behind his chair, and finding a paper in it took it out and handed it to his visitors. "Look at that, now!" he said. "You see what it is?"

Brent saw at once. It was a half-sheet of notepaper, on which were examples of faulty type, precisely similar to those on Queenie's bit of evidence.

"Hello!" exclaimed Brent. "Somebody else been at the same game, eh?"

"I'll tell you," answered Hawthwaite, settling himself in his chair. "It's a bit since—let us think, now—yes, it would be a day or two after that facsimile appeared in the *Monitor* that a young man came to me here one evening: respectable artisan sort of chap. He told me that he was in the employ of a typewriter company at Clothford, which, Mr. Brent, as Miss Queenie there knows, is our big town, only a few miles away. He said that he'd come to tell me something in confidence. The previous day, he said, Mr. Crood, of Hathelsborough, had come to their place in Clothford and had brought with him an old-fashioned typewriter which, he told them, he had bought when such things first came out. He wanted to know the thing being, he said, an old favourite—if they couldn't do it up for him, go through its mechanism thoroughly, supply new letters, and so on. They said they could. He left it to be done, and it was handed over to this young man. Now then, this young man, my informant, has some relations here in Hathelsborough; a day or so before Simon Crood called with his machine, they sent him—the young man—a copy of the *Monitor* with this facsimile letter enclosed. Being concerned with such things in his trade, he was naturally interested in the facsimile, and of course, as an expert, he noticed the broken letters. However, he didn't connect the facsimile with Crood's machine at first. But, happening to look at that machine more narrowly, to see exactly what had to be done to it, he—as he phrased it—ran off the keys on a sheet of paper, and he then saw at once that he had before him the identical machine on which the threatening letter to our late Mayor had been typed! And so he came to me!"

"What have you done about it?" asked Brent.

Hawthwaite gave him a knowing look.

"Well, I'll tell you that too," he answered. "I've got the machine! It's there—in that box in the corner. The Clothford firm will make an excuse to Mr. Crood that they've had to send this machine away for repairs—eh? Of course I'm not going to let it out of my possession until—well, until we know more."

"There's no doubt he wrote that threatening letter," observed Brent.

"Oh, no doubt, no doubt whatever," agreed Hawthwaite.

"What about that handkerchief and the inquiry at the laundry?" asked Brent.

Hawthwaite accompanied his reply with a nod and a wink.

"That's being followed up," he said. "Don't ask me any more now; we're progressing, and, I believe, in the right direction this time. Do you leave it to us, Mr. Brent; you'll be surprised before long and so will some other folks. You go on with those articles you've started in the *Monitor*. It doesn't do for me to say much, being an official," he added, with another wink, "but you'll do some good in that way—there's a lot under the surface in this old town, sir, that only needs exposing to the light of day to ensure destruction! Public opinion, Mr. Brent, public opinion! You stir it up, and leave this matter to me; I may be slow, Mr. Brent, but I'll surely get there in the end!"

"Good! It's all I ask," said Brent. "Only get there!"

He took Queenie away, but before they had gone many steps from the superintendent's office Hawthwaite called Brent back, and leading him inside the room closed the door on him.

"Your young lady'll not mind waiting a minute or two," he said, with a significant glance. "As she already knew about old Simon's typewriter, I didn't mind telling that I knew, d'ye see? But there's another little matter that I'd like to tell you about—between ourselves, and to go no further, you understand?"

"Just so," agreed Brent.

"Well," continued Hawthwaite, "there may be nothing in it. But I've always had a suspicion that there was nothing definite got out of either Dr. Wellesley or Mrs. Saumarez about their—well, I won't say love affairs, but relations. Anyway, that there was something mysterious about the sort of three-cornered relations between her and Wellesley and your cousin I'm as dead certain as that I see you! I've an idea too that somehow or other those relations have something to do with your cousin's murder. But now, this is it—you know, I dare say, that at the back of Mrs. Saumarez's garden at the Abbey House, there's a quiet, narrow lane, little used?"

"I know it," replied Brent. "Farthing Lane."

"Just so, and why so called none of our local antiquaries know," said Hawthwaite. "Well, not so many nights ago I had some business in that lane, at a late hour—I was watching for somebody, as a matter of fact, though it came to nothing. I was in a secret place, just as it was getting nicely dark. Now then, who should come along that lane but Krevin Crood!"

"Krevin Crood!" exclaimed Brent. "Ay?"

"Krevin Crood," repeated Hawthwaite. "And thinks I to myself, 'What may you be doing here, my lad, at this hour of the night?' For as you know that lane, Mr. Brent, you'll know that on one side of it there's nothing but the long wall of Mrs. Saumarez's garden and grounds, and on the other a belt of trees that shuts off Robinson's market-garden and orchards. I was safe hidden amongst those trees. Well, Krevin came along—I recognized him well enough. He sort of loitered about, evidently waiting for somebody. And just as the parish church clock struck ten I heard the click of a latch, and the door in Mrs. Saumarez's back garden opened, and a woman came out! I knew her too."

"Not Mrs. Saumarez?" suggested Brent.

"No," replied Hawthwaite. "Not Mrs. Saumarez. But that companion of hers, Mrs. Elstrick. Tall, thin, very reserved woman; you may have noticed that she goes about the town very quietly—never talks to anybody."

"I've scarcely noticed her except when she was here in court with Mrs. Saumarez," replied Brent. "But I know the woman you mean. So it was she?"

"Just so—Mrs. Elstrick," said Hawthwaite. "And I saw, of course, that this was a put-up job, an arranged meeting between her and Krevin. They met, turned, walked up and down the lane together for a good ten minutes, talking in whispers. They passed and repassed me several times, and I'd have given a good deal to hear what they were talking about. But I couldn't catch a word—they were on the opposite side of the lane, you see, close to the garden wall."

"And eventually?" asked Brent.

"Oh, eventually they parted of course," replied Hawthwaite. "She slipped back into the garden, and he went off down the lane. Now——"

"They're both tending to elderliness, I think," interrupted Brent, with a cynical laugh, "but one's never surprised at anything nowadays. So, did you see any love-making?"

"Oh, Lord save us, no!" exclaimed Hawthwaite. "Nothing of that sort! They never even shook hands. Just talked—and very earnestly too."

Brent reflected for a while.

"Queer!" he said at last. "What did they want with each other?"

"Ay!" said Hawthwaite. "As I said just now, I'd have given a good deal to know. But Krevin Crood is a deep, designing, secret sort of man, and that woman, whoever she may be, looks just the same."

"Has she been with Mrs. Saumarez long?" asked Brent.

"Came with her, when Mrs. Saumarez first came and took the Abbey House," replied Hawthwaite. "Always been with her; went away with her when Mrs. S. was in the South of France all last winter. Odd couple I call the two of 'em, Mr. Brent; between you and myself."

"Why, exactly?" inquired Brent. "I've seen nothing particularly odd about Mrs. Saumarez, except that she's evidently a highly-strung, perhaps a bit excitable sort of woman, all nerves, I should say, and possibly a bit emotional. Clever woman, I think, and pretty."

"Pretty enough—and clever enough," assented Hawthwaite dryly. "And I dare say you're right about the rest. But I'll tell you why I used that term; at least, in regard to her. When Mrs. Saumarez first came here, it was understood that she was the widow of a naval officer of high rank. Well, naturally, the big folk of the neighbourhood called on her when she'd settled down—she furnished and fitted her house from local shops, and it took her some time to get fixed up—expecting, of course, that she'd return their calls. She never returned a single one! Not one, sir!"

"That certainly sounds odd," admitted Brent.

"Ay, doesn't it?" said Hawthwaite. "You'd have thought that a young and stylish woman, coming to live here as she did, would have been glad of society. But, though some dozen or so ladies of the place called on her, she never, as I say, returned a single call; in fact, it very soon became evident that she didn't want any society of that sort. She used to go out bicycling a good deal by herself in those early days—that, I fancy, was how she got to know both Wellesley and your cousin. She was fond enough of their society anyway!"

"Always?" asked Brent. He was learning things that he had never heard of, and was already thinking deeply about them. "From the beginning?"

"Well, practically," replied Hawthwaite. "First it was the doctor; then it was Wallingford. And," he added, with a wink, "there are folk in the town who declare that she carried on with both, playing one off against the other, till the very end! I don't know how that may be, but I do know that at one time she and Wellesley were very thick, and that afterwards your cousin was always running after her. Naturally, there was talk, especially amongst the folk who'd called on her and whose calls she didn't return. And, to tell you the plain truth, they said things."

"What sort of things?" inquired Brent.

"Oh, well!" said Hawthwaite, with a laugh. "If you'd lived as long in this town as I have, and been in my position, you'd know that it—like all little places—is a hotbed of scandal and gossip. The women, of course, seeing her partiality for men friends, said things and hinted more. Then the Vicar's wife—parsons' ladies are great ones for talk—found something out and made the most of it. I told you that when Mrs. Saumarez first came here it was understood that she was the widow of an officer of some high position in the Royal Navy. Well, our Vicar's wife has a brother who's a big man in that profession, and she was a bit curious to know about the new-comer's relation to it. She persisted in calling on Mrs. Saumarez though her calls weren't returned—she could make excuses, you see, about parish matters and charities and what not. And one day she asked Mrs. Saumarez point-blank what ship her late husband had last served on? Now *she* says that Mrs. Saumarez snapped her up short—anyway, Mrs. S. gave her an answer. 'My late husband,' said Mrs. S., 'was not in the British service!' And of course that wasn't in her favour with the people whom she'd already snubbed."

"Um!" said Brent. There were many things in this retailing of gossip that he wanted to think about at leisure. "Well," he added, after a pause, "I dare say all sorts of small items help towards a solution, Hawthwaite. But you're already busy about it."

"I'm not only busy, but actively so," replied the superintendent. "And—again between you and me and nobody else—I'm expecting some very special professional and expert assistance within the next few days. Oh, you leave this to me, Mr. Brent, I'll run down your cousin's murderer or murderess yet! Go you on with your articles—they're helpful, for they're rousing public interest."

Brent went away and followed Hawthwaite's advice. His articles came out in the *Monitor* twice a week. Peppermore printed them in big type, leaded, and gave them the most prominent place in the paper. He himself was as proud of these uncompromising attacks on the municipal government of Hathelsborough as if he had written them himself; the proprietor of the *Monitor* was placidly agreeable about them, for the simple reason that after the first two had appeared the circulation of his journal doubled, and after the next three was at least four times what it had ever been before. Everybody in their immediate neighbourhood read and discussed the articles; extracts from them were given in the county papers; some of the London dailies began to lift them. Eventually a local Member of Parliament asked a question about them in the House of Commons. And one day Peppermore came rushing to Brent in a state of high excitement.

"The pen *is* mightier than the sword, Mr. Brent, sir, that's a fact," he gasped, tumbling headlong into Brent's room. "Heard the news, sir? All through your articles!"

"Heard nothing," replied Brent. "What is it?"

"I had it from the Town Clerk just now, so it's gospel truth," replied Peppermore. "The Local Government Board, sir, is, at last, moved to action! It's going to send down an inspector—a real full-fledged inspector! The Town Clerk is in a worse state of righteous indignation than I ever saw a man, and as for Mayor Simon Crood, I understand his anger is beyond belief. Mr. Brent, you've done it!"

But Brent was not so sure. He had some experience of Government officials, and of official methods, and knew more of red tape than Peppermore did. As for Tansley, who came in soon after, he was cynically scornful.

"Local Government Board Inspector!" he exclaimed scoffingly. "Pooh! some old fossil who'll come here—I'll tell you how! He'll ask for the responsible authorities. That's Simon Crood and Company. He'll hear all they've got to say. They'll say what they like. He'll examine their documents. The documents will be all ready for him. Everything will be nice and proper and in strict order, and every man will say precisely what he's been ordered to say—and there you are! The Inspector will issue his report that he's carefully examined everything and found all correct, and the comedy will conclude with the farce of votes of thanks all round! That's the line, Brent."

"Maybe!" said Brent. "And only maybe!"

"You're in a pessimistic vein, Mr. Tansley, sir," declared Peppermore. "Sir, we're going to clean out the Augean stable!"

"Or perish in the attempt, eh, Peppermore?" retorted Tansley good-humouredly. "All right, my lad! But it'll take a lot more than *Monitor* articles and Local Government Board inquiries to uproot the ancient and time-honoured customs of Hathelsborough. *Semper eadem*, Peppermore, *semper eadem*, that's the motto of this high-principled, respectably ruled borough. Always the same—and no change."

"Except from bad to worse!" said Peppermore. "All right, sir; but something's going to happen, this time."

Something did happen immediately following on the official announcement of the Local Government Board inquiry, and it was Tansley who told Brent of it.

"I say," he said, coming up to Brent in the street, "here's a queer business—I don't know if you've heard of it. Mrs. Mallett's run away from her husband! Fact! She's cleared clean out, and let it be known too. Odd—mysteries seem to be increasing, Brent. What do you make of it?"

Brent could make nothing of it. There might be many reasons why Mrs. Mallett should leave her husband. But had this sudden retreat anything to do with Mrs. Mallett's evidence at the inquest. He was speculating on this when he got a request from Hawthwaite to go round at once to his office. He responded immediately, to find the superintendent closeted with Dr. Wellesley.

CHAPTER XIX

BLACK SECRETS AND RED TAPE

Before ever Brent dropped into the chair to which Hawthwaite silently pointed him, he knew that he was about to hear revelations. He was conscious of an atmosphere in that drab, sombre little room. Hawthwaite's glance at him as he entered was that of a man who bids another to prepare himself for news; Wellesley looked unusually stern and perplexed.

"Dr. Wellesley got me to send for you, Mr. Brent," said the superintendent. "He's got something to tell which he thinks you, as next-of-kin to our late Mayor, ought to know."

Brent nodded, and turned, in silence, to Wellesley. Wellesley, who had been staring moodily at the fireless grate, looked up, glancing from one man to the other.

"You understand, Mr. Brent, and you, Hawthwaite, that whatever I tell you is told in the very strictest confidence?" he said. "As you say, Hawthwaite, I think it's something that you ought to know, both of you; but, at present, I don't know if there's anything in it—I mean anything that has real, practical relation to Wallingford's death, or not. I am to speak in confidence?"

"To me—yes," answered Brent promptly.

"It'll not go beyond me, doctor," said Hawthwaite with a smile. "I'm used to this job! Heard more secrets and private communications in my time than I can remember; I've clean forgotten most of 'em."

"Very well," agreed Wellesley. "This is strictly private, then, at present. Now, to begin with, I suppose you have both heard—it's pretty well known through the town, I understand—that Mrs. Mallett has left her husband?"

"Ay!" replied Hawthwaite. "I've heard that."

"Yes," said Brent. "I too."

"I dare say you both gathered from that evidence, of mine and of Mrs. Mallett's, at the adjourned inquest, that there was some mystery underlying her visit to me?" continued Wellesley. "Some secret, eh?"

"Couldn't very well gather anything else, doctor!" replied Hawthwaite. "Evident!"

"The fact of the case is," said Wellesley suddenly, "that wasn't the first visit Mrs. Mallett had paid to me—and to Wallingford—in that way. She'd been twice before, during that week. On the first occasion she only saw me; on the second she and I saw Wallingford together, in the Mayor's Parlour; on the third—the one we gave evidence about—she went to see Wallingford alone, but, as she told you, she found he was engaged, so she came away."

The three men looked at each other. Hawthwaite voiced what two of the three were wondering.

"Some business which concerned all three of you, then, doctor?" he suggested.

"Business which deeply concerned her, and on which she came to consult me and Wallingford," replied Wellesley. "Now I'll tell you straight out what it was. Mrs. Mallett had found out that there was some sort of an intrigue between her husband and Mrs. Saumarez!"

For a moment a deep silence fell over the room. Brent felt his brows drawing together in a frown—the sort of frown that spreads over a man's face when he tries to think quickly and clearly over a problem unexpectedly presented to him. Hawthwaite folded his arms across his braided tunic, stared at the ceiling, and whistled softly. He was the first to speak.

"Oh, oh!" he said. "Um! So that's—But she'd have some proof, doctor, for an assertion of that sort? Not mere guess-work?"

"I'm afraid there's no guess-work about it," said Wellesley. "It's not a pleasant matter to discuss, but that's unavoidable now. This is what Mrs. Mallett told Wallingford and myself; Mrs. Mallett, as you know, is a downright, plain-spoken woman, with strong views of her own, and she's just the sort to go through with a thing. Some little time ago she found, evidently through Mallett's carelessness, a receipt for a very valuable diamond ring from a London jeweller, a lady's ring. This, of course, aroused her suspicions, and without saying anything to her husband she determined to have his movements watched. She knew that Mallett was frequently going away for a day at a time, ostensibly on business connected with the bank, and she employed a private inquiry agent to watch him. This man followed Mallett from Hathelsborough to Clothford one morning, and from Clothford station to the Royal County Hotel, where, in the lounge, he was joined by Mrs. Saumarez, who had been previously pointed out to the agent here in Hathelsborough, and who had evidently cycled over to Clothford. She and Mallett lunched at the Royal County in a private room and spent the greater part of the afternoon there; the same thing occurred on two other occasions. So then Mrs. Mallett came to me and to Wallingford."

"Why to you?" demanded Brent.

"I think," replied Wellesley, with a forced smile, "she may have had a womanish feeling of revenge, knowing that Wallingford and myself had—well, both paid a good deal of attention to Mrs. Saumarez. But there were other reasons—Mrs. Mallett has few friends in the town; I was her medical attendant, and she and Wallingford frequently met each other on one or two committees—Mrs. Mallett took a good deal of interest in social affairs. Anyway, she came and confided in us about this."

"I suppose you and Wallingford discussed it?" suggested Brent.

"Yes," replied Wellesley. "Briefly, on the night before his death."

"Was that the reason of your saying at the inquest that there was no jealousy between you, at the time of his death, as regards Mrs. Saumarez?"

"Just so! There couldn't be any jealousy, could there, after what we'd heard?"

"You believed this, then?"

"We couldn't do anything else! The man whom Mrs. Mallett employed is a thoroughly dependable man. There's not the slightest doubt that Mrs. Saumarez secretly met Mallett and spent most of the afternoon with him, under the circumstances I mentioned, on three separate occasions."

"And that's the reason of Mrs. Mallett's sudden flight—if you call it so; is it, doctor?" asked Hawthwaite, who had been listening intently.

"That's the reason—yes," replied Wellesley.

"What's she going to do?" inquired Hawthwaite. "Divorce?"

"She said something about a legal separation," answered Wellesley. "I suppose it will come to the other thing."

"And how do you think this is related to Wallingford's murder?" asked Hawthwaite with sudden directness. "Let's be plain, doctor—do you suspect Mallett?"

Wellesley showed signs of indecision.

"I don't like to say that I do," he replied at last. "And yet, I don't know. I've rather wondered if there'd been any meeting between Mallett and Wallingford after Wallingford knew about this: I believe they did meet, on business, during the day. Now, to tell you the truth, Wallingford was much more—shall we say upset?—about this affair than I was: he was very much gone on Mrs. Saumarez. It's struck me that he may have threatened Mallett with exposure; and exposure, of course, would mean a great deal to a man in Mallett's position—a bank-manager, and Town Trustee, and so on. And——But I really don't know what to think."

"There's a thing I'd like to know," said Brent. "What do you think about the woman in the case? You've had chances of knowing her."

Wellesley gave his questioner a searching look.

"I would rather not say, Mr. Brent," he replied. "Discoveries of this sort, substantiated, are—well, disconcerting. Besides, they tend to a revision of opinion; they're sidelights—unfortunate ones."

"Look here," said Brent, "were you greatly surprised?"

"Well, looking back," responded Wellesley thoughtfully, "perhaps not greatly. I think she's a bit of a mystery."

Brent turned to Hawthwaite. Hawthwaite, however, looked at the doctor.

"Well, doctor," he said, "I think you've done right to tell this. There's something in the suggestion that there may have been a fatal quarrel between Mallett and Wallingford. But I don't want to go into this at present—I'm full up otherwise. Leave it until this Local Government Board inspection is over."

"Why until then?" asked Wellesley.

"Why, because, for anything we know to the contrary, something may come out at that which will dovetail into this," replied Hawthwaite. "The Inspector is coming down at once—we'll leave this over till he's been. Look here, has Mrs. Mallett let this out to anybody but you?"

"No, I'm sure of that," answered Wellesley. "It's been known in the town for some time—common knowledge—that she and Mallett weren't on good terms, but she assured me just before leaving that she hasn't mentioned the episodes I've detailed to any other person here than myself. And, of course, Wallingford."

"And he's gone, poor fellow!" said Hawthwaite. "And Mr. Brent and myself'll be secret as the grave he lies in! All right, doctor—just leave it to me."

When Wellesley had gone away, Hawthwaite turned to Brent.

"I don't believe for one moment that Mallett murdered your cousin!" he said. "I'm not surprised about this other affair, but I don't think it's anything to do with what we're after. No; that's on a side-track. But I'll tell you what, Mr. Brent—I shouldn't be astonished if I found out that Mallett knows who the murderer is!"

"I wish you'd tell me if you've any idea yourself who the murderer is!" exclaimed Brent. "I'm wearying to get at something concrete!"

"Well, if you must have it, I have an idea," answered the superintendent. "It's a strong idea too. I'm working at it. To tell you the truth, though nobody knows it but one or two of my trusted men, I've had a very clever man down from New Scotland Yard for the past fortnight—he went away yesterday—and he was of great assistance in unearthing certain facts. And I'm only waiting now for some expert evidence on a very important point, which I can't get until next week, in order to make a move. As soon as ever this Local Government Board inspection's over, I'll make that move. And how do you think that inspection'll turn out, Mr. Brent?"

"Don't know, can't say, no idea," replied Brent.

"Nor have I!" remarked Hawthwaite. "Candidly, I never expect much from so-called public inquiries. There's too much officialism about 'em. Still, every little helps."

These conversations, and the revelations which had transpired during their course led Brent into a new train of thought. He had been well aware ever since his coming to Hathelsborough of an atmosphere of intrigue and mystery; every development that occurred seemed to thicken it. Here again was more intrigue centring in a domestic imbroglio. There was nothing much to be wondered at in it, he thought; Mallett was the sort of man to attract a certain type of woman, and, from all Brent had heard in the town, a man given to adventure; Mrs. Saumarez was clearly a woman fond of men's society; Mrs. Mallett, on the other hand, was a strait-laced, hard sort, given to social work and the furtherance of movements in which her husband took no interest. The sequence of events seemed probable to Brent. First there had been Wellesley; then Wallingford; perhaps a cleverly-contrived double affair with both. But during a recent period there had been this affair with Mallett—that, from Wellesley's showing, had come to Wallingford's ears. Brent knew his cousin sufficiently well to know that Wallingford would develop an ugly frame of mind on finding that he had been deceived—all sorts of things might well develop out of a sudden discovery. But had all this anything to do with Wallingford's murder? That, after all, was, to him, the main point. And so far he saw no obvious connection. He felt like a man who is presented with a mass of tangled cord, from which protrude a dozen loose ends—which end to seize upon that, on being drawn out, would not reveal more knots and tangles he did not know, for the very life of him. Perhaps, as Hawthwaite had remarked, it all helped, but as far as Brent could see it was still difficult to lay hold of a continuous and unbroken line.

It puzzled him, being still a stranger to the habits and customs of these people, to see that life in Hathelsborough went on, amidst all these alarums and excursions, very much as usual. He had already cultivated a habit of frequenting places of public resort, such as the smoking-room of his hotel, the big bar-room at Bull's, the rooms of the Town Club, to which he had without difficulty been duly elected a member on Tansley's nomination; at all these places he heard a great deal of gossip, but found no surprise shown at its subjects. Within a day or two, everybody who frequented these places knew that there had been a domestic upheaval at Mallett's and had at least some idea of the true reason of it. But nobody showed any astonishment; everybody, indeed, seemed to take it as a matter of course. Evidently it made no difference to Mallett himself, who was seen about the town just as usual, in his accustomed haunts. And when Brent remarked on this seeming indifference to Epplewhite, whom he sometimes conversed with at the Club, Epplewhite only laughed.

"If you knew this town and its people as well as I do, Mr. Brent," he said, "you'd know that things of this sort are viewed in a light that outsiders, perhaps, wouldn't view them in. The underhand affairs, the intrigues, the secret goings-on that exist here are multitudinous. Hathelsborough folk have a fixed standard—do what you like, as long as you don't get found out! Understand, sir?"

"But in this case the thing seems to have been found out," remarked Brent.

"That, in the Hathelsborough mental economy, is the only mistake in it," replied Epplewhite dryly. "It's the only thing that Mallett'll get blamed for! Lord bless you, do you think he's the only man in the place that's had such an affair? But Hathelsborough folk, men and women, are past masters and mistresses at secrecy and deception! If you could take the top off this town, and look deep down under it—ah! there would be something to see. But, as I dare say you're beginning to find out, that's no easy job."

"Will the top be lifted at this Local Government Board inspection?" asked Brent.

Epplewhite shook his head.

"I doubt it, sir!" he answered. "I doubt it very much. I've seen a bit too much of officialism, Mr. Brent, to cherish any hopes of it. I'll tell you what'll probably happen when this inspector comes. To start with, he's bound to be more or less in the hands of the officials. We know who they are—the three Town Trustees and the staff under them. Do you think they won't prepare their books and documents in such a fashion as to ensure getting a report in their favour? Of course! And what's to stop it? Who's to interfere?"

"I suppose he will hear both sides of the question?" suggested Brent.

"Who is there to put the other side of the question, except on broad lines, such as you've taken up in your *Monitor* articles?" asked Epplewhite. "True, the inspector can ask for information and for criticism, and for any facts bearing on the subject. But who'll come forward to give it? Can I? Can Wellesley? Can any of our party? Not one, in any satisfactory fashion. We've nothing but impressions and suspicions to go on—we haven't access to the books and papers. The only man who could have done something was your cousin, our late Mayor; and he's gone! And talking about that, Mr. Brent, there's a matter that I've been thinking a good deal about lately, and I think it should be put to Hawthwaite. You know, of course, that your cousin and I were very friendly—that came out in my evidence when the inquest was first opened. Well, he used to tell me things about his investigation of these Corporation finances, and I happen to know that he kept his notes and figures about them in a certain memorandum book—a thickish one, with a stout red leather cover—which he always carried about with him. He'd have it on him, or on his desk in the Mayor's Parlour, when he met his death, I'm certain! Now then—where is that book?"

"That's highly important!" said Brent. "I never heard of it. It certainly wasn't on him, and it wasn't on the desk, for I examined that myself, in company with the police."

"Well, he had such a book, and search should be made for it," remarked Epplewhite. "If it could have been produced at this inquiry, some good might have come of it. But, as things are, I see little hope of any change. Vested interests and old customs aren't upset in a day, Mr. Brent."

And Brent was soon to discover that both Tansley and Epplewhite were correct in their prophecies about the investigation which he himself had so strenuously advocated in his articles. The Local Government Board inspector came. He sat in the Moot Hall for two days, in public. He examined the ancient charters and deeds. He questioned the Town Trustees. He went through the books. He invited criticism and objections—and got nothing but a general statement of the policy of the reforming party from Epplewhite, as its leader: that party, said Epplewhite, objected to the old constitution as being outworn and wished for a more modern arrangement. Finally, the inspector, referring to the articles in the *Monitor* which had led to the holding of the inquiry, expressed a wish to see and question their writer.

Brent stood up, in the midst of a crowded court, and confessed himself sole author of the articles in question.

"Why did you write them?" inquired the inspector.

"From a sense of public duty," replied Brent.

"But I understand that you are a stranger, or a comparative stranger, to the town?" suggested the inspector.

"I am a burgess, a resident, and a property-owner in the town. I took up this work—which I mean to see right through!—in succession to my cousin, John Wallingford, late Mayor of this borough, who was murdered in this very hall," said Brent. "There are men here who know that he was working day and night to bring about the financial reforms which I advocate."

The inspector moved uneasily in his seat at the sound of the word which Brent emphasized in his reference to his cousin.

"I am sure I sympathize with you, Mr. Brent," he said. "I have been much grieved to hear of the late Mayor's sad fate. But you say you have voluntarily taken up his work? Did he leave you any facts, figures, statistics, particulars, to work on?"

"If he had known that I was going to take up his work he would doubtless have left me plenty," replied Brent. "But he was murdered! He had such things—a certain note-book, filled with his discoveries."

"Where is that book?" inquired the inspector. "Can it be produced?"

"It cannot," said Brent. "It was stolen when my cousin was killed."

The inspector hesitated, shuffling his papers.

"Then you have no figures, facts, anything, Mr. Brent?" he said presently. "Nothing to support your newspaper articles?"

"Nothing of that sort," answered Brent. "My articles refer wholly to the general principle of the thing."

The inspector smiled.

"I'm afraid governments—national or municipal—aren't run on general principles, Mr. Brent," he remarked.

"No!" said Brent. "They seem to be run on the lack of them."

The official inquiry came to an end on that—amidst good-humoured laughter at Brent's apparently ingenuous retort. The inspector announced that he would issue his report in due course, and everybody knew what it would be. The good old ways, the time-honoured customs would have another lease of life. Once more, Simon Crood had come out on top.

But as he was leaving the Moot Hall, Brent felt his arm touched and turned to see Hawthwaite. The superintendent gave him a knowing look.

"To-morrow!" he whispered. "Be prepared! All's done; all's ready!"

CHAPTER XX

THE FELL HAND

Brent heard what the superintendent said, nodded a silent reply, and five minutes later had put that particular thing clean out of his mind. During the progress of the Local Government Board inquiry he had learned something: that men like Tansley and Epplewhite knew a lot more about Hathelsborough and Hathelsborough folk than he did, or than Wallingford had known, despite the murdered man's longer experience of town and people. Reform was not going to be carried out in a day in that time-worn borough, nor were its ancient customs, rotten and corrupt as they were, to be uprooted by newspaper articles. So far, Simon Crood and his gang had won all along the line, and Brent realized that most men in his position would have given up the contest and retired from the field in weariness and disgust. But he was not going to give up, nor to retire. He had a feeling, amounting to something near akin to a superstition, that it was his sacred duty to carry on his dead cousin's work, especially as Wallingford, by leaving him all his money, had provided him with the means of doing it. There in Hathelsborough he was, and in Hathelsborough he would stick, holding on like a bulldog to the enemy.

"I'm not counted out!" he said that evening, talking the proceedings of the day over with Queenie. "I'm up again and ready for the next round. Here I am, and here I stop! But new tactics! Permeation! that's the ticket. Reckon I'll nitrate and percolate the waters of pure truth into these people in such a fashion that they'll come to see that what that old uncle of yours and his precious satellites have been giving 'em was nothing but a very muddy mixture. Permeation! that's the game in future."

Queenie scarcely knew what he meant. But she gathered a sense of it from the set of his square jaw and the flash of his grey eyes; being increasingly in love with him, it was incomprehensible to her that anybody could beat Brent at any game he took a hand in.

"The inquiry was all cut-and-dried business," remarked Queenie. "Arranged! Of course the accounts and things would be cooked. Uncle Simon and Mallett and Coppinger would see to that. They'll have an extra bottle to-night over this victory. And if they could only hear to-morrow that you're going to clear out their joy would be full."

"Well, I'm not!" declared Brent. "Instead of clearing out, I'm going to dig in. I guess they'll find me entrenched harder than ever before long. We'll get on at that to-morrow, now that this all-hollow inquiry's over."

Queenie understood him perfectly that time. He and she were furnishing the house which Brent had purchased in order to get a properly legal footing in Hathelsborough. It was serious and occasionally deeply fascinating work, necessitating much searching of the shops wherein antique furniture was stored, much consultation with upholsterers and decorators, much consideration of style and effect. Brent quickly discovered that Queenie was a young woman of artistic taste with a natural knowledge and appreciation of colour schemes and values; Queenie found out that Brent had a positive horror of the merely modern. Consequently, this furnishing and decorating business took up all their spare time: Queenie eventually spent all hers at the house, superintending and arranging; Brent was there when he was not writing his *Monitor* articles or interviewing Hawthwaite. The unproductive inquiry had broken into this domestic adventure; Brent now proposed to go ahead with it until it was finished; then he and Queenie would quietly get married and settle down. Hathelsborough, he remarked, might not want him, but there in Hathelsborough he had set up his tent, and the pegs were firmly driven in.

On the day succeeding the Local Government Board inquiry Brent and Queenie had spent morning, afternoon, and the first part of the evening at the house, at the head of a small gang of workmen, and had reduced at least half of the chaos to order. As dusk grew near Brent put on his coat and gave Queenie one of his looks which signified that there was no answer needed to what he was about to say.

"That's enough!" said Brent. "Dog tired! Now we'll go round to the *Chancellor* and get the best dinner they can give us. Put on your hat!"

Queenie obeyed, readily enough: she was in that stage whereat a young woman finds obedience the most delightful thing in the world. Brent locked up the house, and they went away together towards the hotel. In the old market square the lamps were just being lighted; as usual there were groups of townsfolk gathered about High Cross and Low Cross, and the pavements were thronged with strolling pedestrians. Something suggested to Brent that all these folk were discussing some news of moment; he heard excited voices; once or twice men glanced inquisitively at Queenie and himself as they walked towards the *Chancellor*; on the steps outside the hotel a knot of men, amongst them the landlord, were plainly in deep debate. They became silent as Queenie and Brent passed in, and Brent, ushering Queenie into the inner hall, turned back to them.

"Something going?" he asked laconically.

The men looked at each other; the landlord, with a glance in Queenie's direction, replied, lowering his voice:

"Then you haven't heard, Mr. Brent?" he said. "I thought you'd have known. Hawthwaite's arrested Krevin Crood for the murder."

In spite of his usual self-possession, Brent started.

"What!" he exclaimed. "Krevin!"

"Krevin," answered the landlord. "And Simon! Both of 'em. Got 'em at seven o'clock. They're in the police station—cells of course. Nice business—Mayor of a town arrested for the murder of his predecessor!"

"As far as I can make out, Simon's charged with being accessory," remarked one of the other men. "Krevin's the culprit-in-chief."

"Well, there they both are anyway," said the landlord. "And, if I know anything about the law, it's as serious a thing to be accessory to a murder as to be the principal in one. What do you say, Mr. Brent?"

Brent made no reply. He was thinking. So this was what Hawthwaite had meant when he said, the day before, that all was ready? He wished that Hawthwaite had given him a hint, or been perfectly explicit with him. For there was Queenie to consider.

And now, without further remark to the group of gossipers, he turned on his heel and went back to her and took her into the coffee-room and to the table which was always specially reserved for him. Not until Queenie had eaten her dinner did he tell her of what he had learned.

"So now there's going to be hell for a time, girlie," he said in conclusion. "No end of unpleasantness for me—and for you, considering that these men are your folk. And so all the more reason why you and I stick together like leeches—not all the Simons and the Krevins in the world are going to make any difference between you and me, and we'll just go forward as if they didn't exist, whatever comes out. And now, come along and I'll see you home to Mother Appleyard's, and then I'll drop in on Hawthwaite and learn all about it."

"Do—do you think they did it?" asked Queenie in a fearful whisper. "Actually?"

"God knows!" muttered Brent. "Damned if I do, or if I know what to think. But Hawthwaite must have good grounds for this!"

He saw Queenie safely home to Mrs. Appleyard's and hurried off to the police station, where he found the superintendent alone in his office.

"You've heard?" said Hawthwaite.

"I've heard," replied Brent. "I wish you'd given me an idea—a hint."

Hawthwaite shook his head. There was something peculiarly emphatic in the gesture.

"Mr. Brent," he said solemnly. "I wouldn't have given the King himself a hint! I'd reasons—good reasons—for keeping the thing a profound secret until I could strike. As it is, I've been foiled. I've got Krevin Crood, and I've got Simon Crood—safely under lock and key. But I haven't got the other two!"

"What other two?" exclaimed Brent.

Hawthwaite smiled sourly.

"What other two?" he repeated. "Why, Mallett and Coppinger! They're off, though how the devil they got wind of what was going on I can't think. Leaked out, somehow."

"You suspect them too?" asked Brent.

"Suspect!" sneered Hawthwaite. "Lord! You wait till Simon and Krevin are brought up before the magistrates to-morrow morning! We've got the whole evidence so absolutely full and clear that we can go right full steam ahead with the case to-morrow. Meeking'll prosecute, and I hope to get 'em committed before the afternoon's over."

"Look here," said Brent, "tell me—what's the line? How does the thing stand?"

"Thus," replied Hawthwaite. "We shall charge Krevin with the murder of your cousin, and Simon with being accessory to the fact."

"Before or after?" asked Brent.

"Before!"

"And those other two—Mallett and Coppinger?"

"Same charge as Simon."

Brent took a turn or two about the room.

"That," he remarked, pausing at last in front of Hawthwaite's desk, "means that there was a conspiracy?"

"To be sure!" assented Hawthwaite. "Got proof of it!"

"Then I wish you'd laid hands on Mallett and Coppinger," said Brent. "You've no idea of their whereabouts, I suppose?"

"None, so far," replied Hawthwaite. "Nor can I make out how or precisely when they slipped off. But they are off. Oddly enough, Mrs. Mallett's back in the town—I saw and spoke to her an hour ago. Of course she knows nothing about Mallett. She didn't come back to him. I don't know what she came back for. She's staying with friends, down Waterdale."

"What time will these men be brought up to-morrow morning?" asked Brent.

"Ten o'clock sharp," answered Hawthwaite. "And I hope that before the end of the afternoon they'll have been fully committed to take their trial! As I said just now, we can go straight on. Careful preparation makes speedy achievement, Mr. Brent! And by the Lord Harry, we've done some preparing!"

"If only the whole thing is cleared ... at last," said Brent quietly. "You think ... now ... it will be?"

Hawthwaite smacked his hand on his blotting-pad.

"Haven't the shadow of a doubt, Mr. Brent, that Krevin Crood murdered your cousin!" he asserted. "But you'll hear for yourself to-morrow. Come early. And a word of advice——"

"Yes?" Brent inquired.

"Leave your young lady at home," said Hawthwaite. "No need for her feelings to be upset. They're her uncles, these two, after all, you know. Don't bring her."

"No; of course," assented Brent. "Never intended to."

He went away to his hotel, sorely puzzled. Hawthwaite seemed positively confident that he had solved the problem at last; but was Hawthwaite right? Somehow, Brent could scarcely think of Krevin Crood as a cold-blooded murderer, nor did it seem probable to him that calculating, scheming men like Simon Crood, Mallett, and Coppinger would calmly plot assassination and thereby endanger their own safety. One thing, anyway, seemed certain—if Wallingford's knowledge of the financial iniquities of the Town Trustees was so deep as to lead them to commit murder as the only way of compelling his silence, then those iniquities must have been formidable indeed and the great and extraordinary wonder was that they had just been able to cloak them so thoroughly and successfully.

He was early in attendance at the court-room of the Moot Hall next morning, and for a particular reason of his own selected a seat in close proximity to the door. Long before the magistrates had filed on to the bench, the whole place was packed, and Hawthwaite, passing him, whispered that there were hundreds of people in the market square who could not get in. Everybody of any note in Hathelsborough was present; Brent particularly observed the presence of Mrs. Mallett who, heavily veiled, sat just beneath him. He looked in vain, however, for Mrs. Saumarez; she was not there. But in a corner near one of the exits he saw her companion, Mrs. Elstrick, the woman whom Hawthwaite had seen in secret conversation with Krevin Crood in Farthing Lane.

Tansley caught sight of Brent, and leaving the solicitors' table in the well of the court went over to him.

"What're you doing perched out there?" he asked. "Come down with me—I'll find room for you."

"No," said Brent. "I'm all right here; I may have to leave. And I'm not on in this affair. It's Hawthwaite's show. And is he right, this time?"

"God knows!" exclaimed Tansley. "He's something up his sleeve anyway. Queerest business ever I knew! Simon! If it had been Krevin alone, now. Here, I'll sit by you—I'm not on, either—nobody's instructed me. I say, you'll not notice it, but there's never been such a show of magistrates on that bench for many a year, if ever. Crowded! every magistrate in the place present. And the chief magistrate to be in the dock presently! That's dramatic effect, if you like!"

Brent was watching the dock: prisoners came into it by a staircase at the back. Krevin came first: cool, collected, calmly defiant—outwardly, he was less concerned than any spectator. But Simon shambled heavily forward, his big, flabby face coloured with angry resentment and shame. He beckoned to his solicitor and began to talk eagerly to him over the separating partition; he, it was evident, was all nerves and eagerness. But Krevin, after a careful look round the court, during which he exchanged nods with several of his acquaintance, stood staring reflectively at Meeking, as if speculating on what the famous barrister was going to say in opening the case.

Meeking said little. The prisoners, he observed, addressing the bench in quiet, conversational tones, were charged, Krevin Crood with the actual murder of the late Mayor, John Wallingford; Simon, with being accessory to the fact, and, if they had not absconded during the previous twenty-four hours, two other well-known residents of the borough, Stephen Mallett and James Coppinger, would have stood in the dock with Simon Crood, similarly charged. He should show their worships by the evidence which he would produce that patient and exhaustive investigation by the local police had brought to light as wicked a conspiracy as could well be imagined. There could be no doubt in the mind of any reasonable person after hearing that evidence, that Simon Crood, Mallett and Coppinger entered into a plot to rid themselves of a man who, had his investigations continued, would infallibly have exposed their nefarious practices to the community, nor that they employed Krevin Crood to carry out their designs. He would show that the murder of Wallingford was deliberately plotted at Mallett's house, between the four men, on a certain particular date, and that Krevin Crood committed the actual murder on the following evening. Thanks to the particularly able and careful fashion in which Superintendent Hawthwaite had marshalled the utterly damning body of evidence against these men, their Worships would have no difficulty in deciding that there was a *prima facie* case against them and that they must be committed to take their trial at the next Assizes.

Hawthwaite, called first, gave evidence as to the arrest of the two prisoners. He arrested Krevin Crood in the passage leading from Bull's Snug about 6.30 the previous evening, and Simon at his own home, half an hour later. Krevin took the matter calmly, and merely remarked that he, Hawthwaite, was making the biggest mistake he had ever made in his life; Simon manifested great anger and indignation, and threatened an action for false imprisonment. When actually charged neither of the accused made any answer at all.

The superintendent stood down, and Meeking looked towards an inner door of the court. An attendant came forward at his nod, bearing a heavy package done up in Crown canvas and sealed. At the same moment a smart-looking young man answered to the name of Samuel Owthwaite and stepped alertly into the witness-box.

CHAPTER XXI

CORRUPTION

T he tightly-wedged mass of spectators watched, open-mouthed and quivering with anticipation, while the attendant, at Meeking's whispered bidding, broke the seals and cut the strings of the package which he had just carried in. Clearly, this was some piece of material evidence—but what? A faint murmur of interest rose as the last wrappings fell aside and revealed a somewhat-the-worse-for-wear typewriter. People glanced from it to the witness: some of those present recognized him as a young mechanic, a native of Hathelsborough, who had gone, a few years previously, to work in the neighbouring manufacturing city of Clothford—such began to ask themselves what he could have to do with this case and waited eagerly for his evidence.

But Meeking, the battered typewriter before him, kept the witness waiting. Turning to the bench, he put in the depositions taken at the Coroner's inquest with respect to the typewritten threatening letter sent to Wallingford and by him entrusted to Epplewhite; the letter itself, and the facsimile of the letter published as a supplement by the *Monitor*, with a brief explanation of his reasons for bringing them into evidence. Then he addressed himself to his witness and got the first facts from him—Samuel Owthwaite. Mechanic. Employed by Green & Polford, Limited, of Clothford, agents for all the leading firms of typewriter manufacturers.

"I believe you're a native of Hathelsborough, aren't you, Owthwaite?" began Meeking.

"I am, sir."

"Keep up your interest in the old place, eh?"

"I do, sir."

"Have you any relations in the town?"

"Yes, sir, several."

In the Mayor's Parlour

"Do they send you the Hathelsborough paper, the *Monitor*, every week?"

"Yes, sir, regularly."

"Did they send you a copy of the *Monitor* in which there was a facsimile of the threatening letter addressed to the late Mayor by some anonymous correspondent?"

"Yes, sir."

"Did you look at the facsimile?"

"I did, sir."

"Notice anything peculiar, or strange, or remarkable about it?"

"Yes, sir, I notice that some of the letters were broken and some defective."

"You noticed that as an expert mechanic, working at these things?"

"It was obvious to anybody, sir. The letters—some of them—were badly broken."

"Look at the dock, Owthwaite. Do you know the prisoner, Simon Crood?"

"Well enough, sir!"

"How long have you known him?"

"Ever since I was a youngster, sir—always!"

"Have you ever seen Simon Crood at Green & Polford's, your employers?"

"I have, sir."

"When was that?"

"He came in two days after I'd seen the facsimile, sir."

"Bring anything with him?"

"Yes, sir, that typewriter before you."

"Sure it was this particular machine?"

"Positive, sir; it's an old Semmingford machine, number 32,587."

"Did you hear him say anything about it?"

"I did, sir. He told our Mr. Jeaveson—manager he is—that this was a machine he'd bought in London, many years ago; that the lettering seemed to be getting worn out, and that he wanted to know if we could supply new letters and do the machine up generally."

"Yes; what then?"

"Mr. Jeaveson said we could, and the machine was handed over to me for repair."

"Did you make any discovery about it?"

"Yes, sir. That afternoon I just ran the lettering off, to see what defects there were. I found then that the broken and defective letters were identical with those in the facsimile letter that I'd seen in the *Monitor* two days before."

"Just come down here, Owthwaite; take this sheet of paper, and run the letters off again so that their Worships can compare the broken and defective letters with those in the threatening letter. Now," continued Meeking, when the mechanic had complied with this suggestion and gone back to the witness-box, "what did you do on making this discovery?"

"I told Mr. Jeaveson about it, sir, and showed him what I meant. He discussed the matter with Mr. Polford afterwards, and it was decided that I should go over to Hathelsborough and see Mr. Hawthwaite, taking the machine with me."

"Did you do that?"

"Yes, sir, next day, in the evening."

"Did you tell Superintendent Hawthwaite of your discovery and hand the machine to him?"

"Yes, sir; both."

"Did he have the machine wrapped and sealed up in your presence?"

"He did, sir."

"This machine, now on the table?"

"That machine, sir."

"And this is the machine that the prisoner, Simon Crood, brought himself to Green & Polford's?"

"That's the machine, sir."

Meeking nodded to his witness, signifying that he had no more to ask, but before Owthwaite could leave the box, Stedman, the local solicitor with whom Simon Crood had held a whispered conversation on coming into court, rose and began to cross-examine him.

"Did you happen to be in Green & Polford's shop—the front shop, I mean—when Alderman Crood brought in that machine?" he asked.

"I was there at the time, sir," replied Owthwaite.

"Did he come quite openly?"

"Yes, sir. In a cab, as a matter of fact. The cabman carried in the machine."

"Did Alderman Crood say who he was?"

"Well, sir, to be exact, he saw me as soon as he came in, and recognized me. He said, 'Oh, a Hathelsborough lad, I see? You'll know me, young man.' Then he told Mr. Jeaveson and myself what he wanted."

"The whole business was quite open and above-board, then?"

"Quite so, sir."

"He drew your attention himself to the defects of the machine?"

"He did, sir."

"And this was after—not before—that facsimile appeared in the *Monitor*?"

"After, sir."

"Now I want a particularly careful answer, Owthwaite, to my next question. Did Alderman Crood ask you to get these repairs made immediately?"

"No, sir, he did not. He said he was in no hurry."

"You were to take your own time about them, the machine remaining with you?"

"Just that, sir."

Stedman sat down, as if satisfied, and Owthwaite left the witness-box. At the calling of the next witness's name Tansley nudged Brent.

"Now we may hear something lively!" he whispered. "This chap's been the Borough Accountant for some years, and I've often wondered if he doesn't know a good deal that he's kept to himself. But, if he does, will he let it out? Old Crood doesn't look over pleased to see him anyway!"

Brent glanced from the new witness, a quiet, reserved-looking man of middle age, to Simon Crood. There was a dark scowl on the heavy features, and, Brent fancied, a look of apprehension. Once more Simon beckoned to his solicitor and exchanged a few whispered words with him across the front of the dock before turning to the witness. And to him Brent also turned, with an instinctive feeling that he possibly held a key to those mysteries which had not yet been produced.

Matthew James Nettleton, Member of the Society of Incorporated Accountants and Auditors. Borough Accountant of Hathelsborough during the last seven years. During that period in close touch with all the persons concerned in the present matter.

"Mr. Nettleton," said Meeking, "you are Borough Accountant of Hathelsborough?"

The witness folded his hands on the ledge of the box and shook his head.

"No," he answered. "Was."

"Was? What do you mean?"

"I have resigned my appointment."

"When?"

"Yesterday—at six o'clock last evening, to be precise."

"May I ask why?"

"You may, sir. Because I knew the inquiry just held by the Inspector of the Local Government Board to be an absolute farce! Because I know that the financial affairs of the borough are rotten-ripe! Because I utterly refuse to be a cat's paw in the hands of the Town Trustees any longer! Those are my reasons."

Tansley dug his elbow into Brent's ribs as an irrepressible murmur of surprise broke out all round the court. But Brent was watching the men in the dock. Krevin Crood smiled cynically; the smile developed into a short, sharp laugh. But Simon's flabby face turned a dull red, and presently he lifted his big silk handkerchief and wiped his forehead. Meeking waited a moment, letting the witness's outburst have its full effect. Then, amidst a dead silence, he leaned towards the box.

"Why didn't you say all that at the recent inquiry?" he asked.

"Because it wouldn't have been a scrap of good!" retorted the witness. "Those affairs are all cut-and-dried. My only course was to do what I did last night—resign. And to give evidence now."

Meeking twisted his gown together and looked at the magistrates. He ran his eye carefully along the row of faces, and finally let it settle again on his witness.

"Tell their Worships, in your own fashion, your considered opinion as to the state of the borough finances," he said. "Your opinion based on your experience."

"They are, as I said just now, absolutely rotten!" declared Nettleton. "It is now seven years since I came to this place as Borough Accountant. I found that under an ancient charter the whole of the financial business of the borough was in the hands of a small body known as the Town Trustees, three only in number. It is marvellous that such a body should be allowed to exist in these days! The Town Trustees are responsible to nobody. They elect themselves. That is to say, if one dies, the surviving two elect his successor. They are not bound to render accounts to anyone; the Corporation, of which they are a permanent committee, only know what they choose to tell. This has gone on for at least three centuries. It may have served some good purpose at some period, under men of strict probity, but, in my opinion, based on such experience as I have been able to command, it has of late years led to nothing but secret peculation, jobbery and knavery. As regards my own position, it has simply been that I have never at any time been permitted to see any accounts other than those placed before me by the Town Trustees. My belief is that no one but themselves actually knows what the financial condition of the town really is. I am of impression that this Corporation, as a Corporation, is bankrupt!"

There now arose a murmur in court which the Chairman and officials found it difficult to suppress. But curiosity prevailed over excitement, and the silence was deep enough when Meeking got in his next question.

"You affirm all this in face of the recent inquiry?"

"I do—and strongly! The accounts shown at the recent inquiry were all carefully manipulated, arranged, cooked by the Town Trustees. I had nothing to do with them. They were prepared by the Town Trustees, chiefly, I imagine, by Mallett and Coppinger, with Crood's approval and consent. They were never shown to me. In short, my position has been this, simply, I have had certain accounts placed before me by the Town Trustees with the curt intimation that my sole duty was to see that the merely arithmetical features were correct and to sign them as accountant."

"Could you not have made a statement to this effect at the inquiry?"

"I could not!"

"Why, now?"

"Because I could not have produced the books and papers. All the books and papers to which I have ever had access are merely such things as rate books and so on—the sort of things that can't be concealed. But the really important books and papers, showing the real state of things, are in the possession of Mallett and Coppinger, who, with Crood, have never allowed anybody to see them. If I could have had those things brought before the inspector, I could have proved something. But I couldn't bring them before a court of inquiry like that. You can bring them before this!"

"How?" demanded Meeking.

"Because, I take it, they bear a very sinister relation to the murder of the late Mayor," replied the witness. "He was as well aware as I am that things were all wrong."

"You know that?"

"I know that he did his best, from such material as he could get at, to find out what the true state of things was. He worked hard at examining such accounts as were available. To my knowledge he did his best to get at the secret accounts kept by the Town Trustees. He failed utterly—they defied him. Yet, just before his murder, he was getting at facts in a fashion which was not only unpleasant but highly dangerous to them, and they were aware of it."

"Can you give us an example of any of these facts—these discoveries?"

"Yes, I can give you one in particular. Wallingford was slowly but surely getting at the knowledge of the system of secret payment which has gone on in this place for a long time under the rule of the Town Trustees. He had found out the truth, for instance, as regards Krevin Crood. Krevin Crood was supposed to be paid a pension of £150 a year; in reality he was paid £300 a year. Wallingford ascertained this beyond all doubt, and that it had gone on ever since Krevin Crood's retirement from his official position. There are other men in the borough, hangers-on and supporters of the Town Trustees, who benefit by public money in the shape of pensions, grants, doles—in every case the actual amount paid is much more than the amount set down in such accounts as are shown. Wallingford meant to sweep all this jobbery clean away!"

"How?"

"By getting the financial affairs of the town into the full and absolute control of the Corporation. He wanted to abolish the Town Trustees as a body. If he had succeeded in his aims, he would have done away with all the abuses which they not only kept up but encouraged."

"Then, if Wallingford's reforms had been carried out, Krevin Crood would have lost £150 a year?"

"He would have lost £300 a year. Wallingford's scheme included the utter abolition of all these Town Trustee-created pensions and doles. Lock, stock and barrel, they were all to go."

"And the Town Trustees—Crood, Mallett, Coppinger—were fully acquainted with his intentions and those of his party?"

The witness shrugged his shoulders.

"That's well known!" he answered. "They were frightened of him and his schemes to the last degree. They knew what it meant."

"What did it mean?"

Nettleton glanced at Simon Crood and smiled.

"Just what it's come to, at last," he said. "Exposure—and disgrace!"

"Well," said Meeking, when a murmur of excited feeling had once more run round the court, "a more particular question, Mr. Nettleton. Did the late Mayor ever come to your office in the course of his investigations?"

"He did, frequently. Not that I had much to show him. But he carefully examined all the books and papers of which I was in possession."

"Did he make notes?"

"Notes and memoranda—yes. At considerable length, sometimes."

"What in?"

"In a thickish memorandum book, with a stout cover of red leather, which he always carried in his pocket."

"Could you identify that book if you saw it?"

"Certainly! Besides, you would find it full of his notes and figures."

"That will do for the present, Mr. Nettleton, unless my friend here wants to examine you. No? Then recall Superintendent Hawthwaite for a moment. Superintendent, you have just heard of a certain pocket-book which belonged to the late Mayor. Was it found on his dead body, or on his desk, or anywhere, after the murder? No? Not after the most careful and thorough search? Completely disappeared? Very good. Now let us have Louisa Speck."

A smartly-dressed, self-possessed young woman came forward, and Tansley, nudging Brent, whispered that this was Mallett's parlour-maid and that things were getting deuced interesting.

CHAPTER XXII

THE PARLOUR-MAID

That the appearance of Louisa Speck in the witness-box came as something more than an intense surprise to at any rate two particular persons in that court was evident at once to Brent's watchful eye. Mrs. Mallett, a close observer of what was going on, started as her parlour-maid's name was called, and lifting her eye-glass surveyed the girl with a wondering stare of prolonged inspection. And in the dock Krevin Crood also let a start of astonishment escape him; he, too, stared at Louisa Speck, and a frown showed itself between his eyebrows, as if he were endeavouring to explain her presence to himself. Suddenly it cleared, and he indulged his fancies with a sharp laugh, and turning to Simon made some whispered observation. Simon nodded sullenly, as if he comprehended; from that point forward he kept his small eyes firmly fixed on the witness. Tansley, too, noticed these things, and bent towards his companion with a meaning glance.

"This young woman knows something!" he muttered. "And those two chaps in the dock know what it is!"

The young woman upon whom all eyes were fixed was perhaps the most self-possessed person present. She answered the preliminary questions as coolly as if she had been giving evidence in murder cases as a regular thing. Louisa Speck. Twenty-six years of age. Been in the employ of Mrs. Mallett, of the Bank House, for three years. Still in that employment, as far as she knew. What did she mean by that? Well, that Mrs. Mallett had left the house some days before, and that since yesterday afternoon Mr. Mallett had not been there, and, accordingly, neither she nor the other servants knew exactly how things stood.

"Just so," observed Meeking. "Somewhat uncertain, eh? Very well." He paused a moment, glanced at his papers, and suddenly leaned forward towards the witness-box with a sharp, direct look at its occupant. "Now then!" he said. "When did you first hear of the murder of the late Mayor, Mr. Wallingford?"

Louisa Speck's answer came promptly:

"The night it happened."

"What time—and who told you of it?"

"About nine o'clock. Robertshaw, the policeman, told me. I was at the front door, looking out on the market square, and he was going past."

"I see. So you remember that evening very well?"

"Quite well."

"Do you remember the previous evening—equally well?"

"Yes!"

"Were you at the Bank House that evening—the evening before the murder?"

"I was."

"What was going on there that evening? Anything that makes you particularly remember it?"

"Yes."

"What, now?"

"Well, Mrs. Mallett went away that day to visit her sister, Mrs. Coppinger, for a day or two. About noon Mr. Mallett told me and cook that he wanted to have some gentlemen to dinner that evening, and we were to prepare accordingly."

"I see. Sort of special dinner, eh?"

"Yes."

"Did the gentlemen come?"

"Yes."

"Who were they?"

"Mr. Coppinger and Alderman Crood."

"What time was that?"

"Between six and half-past."

"What happened after their arrival?"

"They went into the morning-room with Mr. Mallett. I took some brown sherry in there and glasses. Soon after that, Mr. Mallett went out. I was just inside the dining-room as he crossed the hall. He told me there'd very likely be another gentleman to dinner, and I must lay another cover. He went out then, and was away about ten minutes. Then he came back with Mr. Krevin Crood."

"Came back with Mr. Krevin Crood. Did you see them come in together?"

"I let them in."

"Did you hear anything said as they entered?"

"Yes, I heard Mr. Krevin Crood say that he wasn't dressed for dinner-parties. Mr. Mallett then told me to take Mr. Krevin upstairs and get him anything he wanted."

"Did you take Mr. Krevin upstairs?"

"Yes. I took him up to Mr. Mallett's dressing-room. I showed him the hot water arrangement, got him clean towels, and asked him what he wanted. He said he wanted a clean shirt, a collar, and a handkerchief."

"A handkerchief?"

"Yes, a handkerchief."

"Did you get him these things?"

"I showed him where to get them. I opened the drawers in which Mr. Mallett's shirts, collars and handkerchiefs are kept, so that he could help himself. Then I asked him if there was anything more I could get him. He said there was nothing but a clothes brush. I got him that, and left him."

"When did you see him next?"

"About twenty minutes after, when he came downstairs and went into the morning-room to the other gentlemen."

"Was he smartened up then?"

"He was smart enough—smarter than the others, I should say."

"Had he taken one of Mr. Mallett's shirts?"

"Yes, one of his very best white ones."

"Very good. Now then, talking about shirts, who looks after the laundry affairs at the Bank House?"

"I do."

"You send the linen to the laundry?"

"Yes."

"And receive it and put it away when it comes back?"

"Yes."

"Always?"

"Always!"

"When does it go, and when does it return?"

"It goes on Monday morning and comes home on Saturday afternoon."

"Do you put it away on Saturday afternoon?"

"Not finally. It goes into a hot cupboard to air. Then on Monday, some time, I put it away in the proper place—sort it out."

115

"I see. Do you remember sorting it out and putting away the different articles in their proper places on the Monday before this little dinner-party?"

"Yes, I do."

"Did you notice the presence of any article which didn't belong to the Mallett family?"

"Yes—at least, I was doubtful."

"Doubtful, eh? Well, what was it?"

"A gentleman's handkerchief."

"You weren't sure that it was Mr. Mallett's?"

"I wasn't sure that it wasn't. And I didn't think it was."

"Why were you uncertain?"

"Well, this wasn't like Mr. Mallett's handkerchiefs. He has dozens of them, nearly all fancy ones, with coloured borders. This was a very fine cambric handkerchief—I'd never seen one like it before. But, still, I wasn't certain that it wasn't Mr. Mallett's after all."

"Why?"

"Because sometimes when Mr. Mallett was away for the day he'd buy a spare handkerchief—he's a lot of odd handkerchiefs that he's brought home in his pockets. I thought this might have been got that way."

"You didn't mention its presence to anybody?"

"No—I didn't think of it."

"Well, what did you do with the handkerchief about which you were doubtful?"

"I laid it on top of one of several piles of handkerchiefs that were in Mr. Mallett's handkerchief drawer in the dressing-room."

"Why did you put it on top?"

"In case any inquiry was made about it from Marriners' Laundry."

"Was any inquiry made?"

"No."

"Now was that drawer you have just spoken of the drawer that you pulled open for Mr. Krevin Crood?"

"Yes."

"Was the handkerchief there then?"

"Yes, it was there!"

"You saw it?"

"I saw it."

"Have you ever seen it since?"

"Never!"

"Do you know if Mr. Krevin Crood took it out of the drawer?"

"No!"

"Did you see it in his possession that evening?"

"No! I didn't. But it wasn't in the drawer next morning."

"You are sure of that?"

"Positive. I went into Mr. Mallett's dressing-room very early next morning, and I noticed that Mr. Krevin had left the drawers half-open. The handkerchief drawer stuck a little, and I pulled it right out before pushing it in. I noticed then that the handkerchief had gone."

"Did you conclude that Mr. Krevin had taken it?"

"No, I don't think so. I didn't conclude anything. If I thought anything, it would be that Mr. Mallett had taken it. Mr. Mallett would think nothing of taking half a dozen handkerchiefs a day."

"But the handkerchief was there when you opened the drawer for Mr. Krevin that evening, and it wasn't there when you looked into the drawer next morning early? That so?"

"Yes, that's so."

"Very well! Now then, about this little dinner. Mr. Mallett had three guests, Mr. Simon Crood, Mr. Krevin Crood, Mr. Coppinger? Nobody else?"

"No; no one else."

"Was it a nice dinner?"

"It was a very good dinner."

"Wine?"

"There were several sorts of wine."

"What time was dinner?"

"About a quarter-past seven."

"And what time did the gentlemen rise from table?"

"They didn't rise from table. When dinner was over, Mr. Mallett decanted some very special port that he has in the wine-cellar, and they settled down to it round the dinner-table, talking."

"I see. Did you hear any of the conversation?"

"No, I didn't. I carried two decanters of the port into the dining-room for Mr. Mallett, and got out port glasses from the sideboard, and after that I never went into the room again."

"Until what hour did Mr. Mallett's guests remain with him?"

"Well, Alderman Crood and Mr. Krevin Crood left at about a quarter to eleven. They went away together. Mr. Coppinger stopped till about half-past eleven."

Meeking paused at this point, put his hand underneath the papers which lay in front of him and produced a cardboard box. From this, after slowly undoing various wrappings, he took the fragment of stained and charred handkerchief which had been found in the Mayor's Parlour, and passed it across to the witness.

"Take that in your hand and look at it carefully," he said. "Now, do you recognize that as part of the handkerchief to which I have been referring?"

"It's the same sort of stuff," replied Louisa. "I should say it was part of that handkerchief. It's just like it."

"Same material?—an unusual material?"

"I think it is the same handkerchief. It's an unusually broad hem—I noticed that at the time."

"To the best of your belief is that the handkerchief you've been talking about?"

"Yes," declared Louisa Speck, this time without hesitation. "It is!"

Meeking sat down and glanced at Simon Crood's solicitor. Stedman accepted the challenge and, rising, threw some scornful meaning into his first question to the witness.

"Who got you to tell all this tale?" he asked satirically. "Who got at you?"

Louisa Speck bridled.

"Nobody got at me!" she retorted. "What do you mean by such a question?"

In the Mayor's Parlour

"You don't mean to tell their Worships that you haven't been induced to come forward and tell all this?" suggested Stedman incredulously. "Come, now! Who helped you to refresh your memory, and to put all this together?"

"Nobody helped me," replied Louisa Speck, with rising indignation. "Do you think I'm not capable of doing things on my own? I can use my eyes and ears as well as you can—and perhaps better!"

"Answer my question!" said Stedman, as a laugh rose against him. "Who got you to go to the police?"

"Nobody got me to go to the police! I went to the police on my own account. I read the newspaper about what took place at the inquest—the last inquest, I mean—and as soon as I heard about the handkerchief, I knew very well that that was the one I'd noticed in our laundry, and so I went to see Mr. Hawthwaite. Mr. Hawthwaite's known what I had to tell you for a good while now."

Stedman was taken aback. But he put a definite question.

"On your oath, did you see that handkerchief in Mr. Krevin Crood's possession that night he was at Mr. Mallett's?" he asked.

"I've already told him I never did," retorted Louisa Speck, pointing at Meeking. "I didn't see him with it. But I'm very certain he got it!"

Stedman waved the witness away, and Meeking proceeded to put in the depositions taken before the Coroner in regard to the finding of the fragment of handkerchief and its ownership, and called evidence to show that the piece just produced was that which had been picked up from the hearth in the Mayor's Parlour on the evening of the murder, soon after the finding of the dead man, and to prove that it had remained in the custody of the police ever since. The fragment went the round of the bench of magistrates, and Tansley whispered to Brent that if Meeking could prove that Krevin Crood had taken that handkerchief out of Mallett's drawer, and had thrown it away on the following evening in the Mayor's Parlour, Krevin's neck was in danger.

"But there's a link missing yet," he murmured. "How did Krevin get at Wallingford? They've got to prove that! However, Meeking's evidently well primed and knows what he's after. What's coming next?"

What came next was the glancing of the barrister's eye towards a venerable, grey-bearded man who sat in the front row of spectators, leaning on a gold-headed cane. He rose as Meeking looked at him, and came slowly forward—a curious figure in those sombre surroundings.

CHAPTER XXIII

THE CONNECTING WALL

From a certain amount of whispering and nodding that went on around him, Brent gathered that this ancient gentleman was not unknown to many of those present. But Tansley was turning to him, ready as always with information.

"That's old Dr. Pellery," he whispered. "Old Dr. Septimus Pellery. Tremendous big pot on antiquarianism, archæology, and that sort of stuff. Used to live here in Hathelsborough, years ago, when I was a youngster. I should have thought he was dead, long since! Wonder where they unearthed him, and what he's here for? No end of a swell, in his own line anyway."

Meeking seemed determined to impress on the court the character and extent of Dr. Pellery's qualifications as an expert in archæological matters. Addressing him in an almost reverential manner, he proceeded to enumerate the witness's distinctions.

"Dr. Pellery, you are, I believe, a Fellow of the Society of Antiquaries?"

"I have that honour."

"And a member of more than one archæological society?"

"I am."

"And a corresponding member of various foreign societies of a similar sort?"

"For many years."

"You are also, I think, a Doctor of Civil Law of the University of Oxford?"

"Yes."

"And the author of many books and articles on your pet subject—archæology?"

"That is so."

"Am I right, Dr. Pellery, in believing that you are thoroughly well acquainted with the archæology, antiquities, and ancient architecture of this town?"

"Quite right. I lived here for several years—ten or eleven years."

"That was—when?"

"It is about twenty years since I left this place."

"You made a close study of it while you were resident here?"

"A very close study. Hathelsborough, from my point of view, is one of the most deeply interesting towns in England. While I lived here I accumulated a vast mass of material respecting its history and antiquities, with the idea of writing a monograph on the borough. But I have never made use of it."

"Let us hope that you will still do so, Dr. Pellery," said Meeking, with a suave smile and polite bow.

But Dr. Pellery shook his head and stroked his long beard. A cynical smile played round his wrinkled eyes.

"No, I don't think I ever shall," he said. "Indeed, I'm sure I shan't!"

"May I ask why?"

"You may! Because there aren't twenty people in Hathelsborough who would buy such a book. Hathelsborough people don't care twopence about the history of their old town—all they care about is money. This case is a proof!"

"I think we'll get back to the case," said Meeking, amidst a ripple of laughter. "Well, we may consider you as the greatest living expert on Hathelsborough anyway, Dr. Pellery, and eminently fitted to give us some very important evidence. Do you know the ancient church of St. Lawrence at the back of this Moot Hall?"

"Ay, as well as I know my own face in the glass!" answered Dr. Pellery with a short laugh. "Every stone of it!"

"It is, I believe, a very old church?"

"It is the oldest church, not only in Hathelsborough, which is saying a good deal, but in all this part of the county," replied the witness with emphasis. "St. Hathelswide, the parish church, is old, but St. Lawrence ante-dates it by at least five hundred years. The greater part of St. Lawrence, as it now stands, was complete in the eighth century: St. Hathelswide was built in the thirteenth."

Meeking produced a large chart, evidently made for the occasion, and had it set up on the table, in full view of the bench and the witness-box.

"From this plan, Dr. Pellery, it appears that the west tower, a square tower, of St. Lawrence immediately faces the back of the Moot Hall. And between the outer wall of the tower and the outer wall of the Moot Hall there is a sort of connecting wall——"

"Not a sort of," interrupted Dr. Pellery. "It is a connecting wall, thirty-six feet long, ten feet high, and eight feet in width, forming an arch over the street beneath—the narrow street called St. Lawrence Lane."

"It is an uncommon feature, that wall?" suggested Meeking.

"Comparatively—yes. I know of other places where ancient buildings are so joined. But there are few examples."

"Well, I want to ask you a very important question about that connecting wall. Is there a secret way through that wall from St. Lawrence tower to the Moot Hall?"

Dr. Pellery drew himself up, stroked his beard, and glanced round the court. Then he gave Meeking an emphatic nod.

"There is! And I discovered it—years ago. And I have always thought that I was the only living person who knew of it!"

Meeking let this answer soak into the mentality of his hearers. Then he said quietly:

"Will you tell us all about it, Dr. Pellery?"

"Enough for your purpose," replied the witness. "You have there, I believe, a sectional drawing of the tower—give it to me. Now," he continued, holding up a sheet of stout paper and illustrating his remarks with the tip of his forefinger, "I will show you what I mean. St. Lawrence tower is eighty feet in height. It is divided into three sections. The lower section, the most considerable of the three, forms a western porch to the church itself, which is entered from it by a Norman arch. Above this is the middle section; above that the upper section, wherein are three ancient bells. The middle and upper sections are reached from the lower by a newel stair, set in the south-west angle of the tower. Now the middle section has for many centuries been a beamed and panelled chamber, from which the bells are rung, and wherein are stored a good many old things belonging to the church—chiefly in ancient chests. During the years that I lived in Hathelsborough I spent a great deal of time in this chamber—the then vicar of St. Lawrence, Mr. Goodbody, allowed me to examine anything I found stored there—it was amongst the muniments and registers of St. Lawrence, indeed, that I discovered a great deal of valuable information about the history of the town. Well, I have just said that this chamber, this middle section of the tower, is panelled; it is panelled from the oak flooring to within two feet of the oak beams in its ceiling, and the panelling, though it is probably four hundred years old, is in an excellent state of preservation. Now, about the middle of the last year that I spent in this town, I began to be very puzzled about the connecting wall between St. Lawrence tower and the Moot Hall. I saw no reason for making an arch at that point, and the wall had certainly not been built as a support, for the masonry of the tower and of the hall is unusually solid. I got the idea that that wall had originally been built as a means of communication between tower and hall; that it was hollow, and that there at each extremity there was a secret means of entrance and exit. I knew from experience that this sort of thing was common in Hathelsborough; the older part of the town is a veritable rabbit-warren! There is scarcely a house in the market-place, for instance, in which there is not a double staircase, the inner one being very cleverly concealed, and I know of several secret ways and passages, entered, say, on one side of a street and terminating far off on another. There is a secret underground way beneath the market-square which is entered at the Barbican in the Castle and terminates in St. Faith's chapel in St. Hathelswide's church; there is another, also underground, from St. Matthias's Hospital to the God's House in Cripple Lane. There are others—as I say, the old town is honeycombed. So there would be, of course, nothing unusual or remarkable in the presence of a secret passage between St. Lawrence tower and the Moot Hall. The only thing was that there was no record of any such passage through the connecting wall; no one had ever heard of it; and there were no signs of entrance to it either in the tower or in the Moot Hall. However, I discovered it—by careful and patient investigation of the panelling in the chamber I have mentioned. The panelling is divided, on each wall of the chamber, into seven compartments; the fourth compartment on the outer wall slides back, and gives access to a passage cut through the arch across St. Lawrence Lane and so to the Moot Hall."

"There's one man here who knows all this!" whispered Tansley in Brent's ear. "Look at Krevin Crood!"

Krevin was smiling. There was something unusually cynical in his smile, but it conveyed more than cynical amusement to Brent. There was in it the suggestion of assurance—Krevin, decided Brent, had something up his sleeve.

But the other people present were still intent on the old antiquary. Having come to the end of his explanation he was passing back the chart to Meeking, and seemed satisfied with what he had said. Meeking, however, wanted more.

"To the Moot Hall!" he repeated. "Well, Dr. Pellery, and where does this passage emerge in the Moot Hall?"

"Just so," said Dr. Pellery. "That, of course, is important. Well, the wall or arch between St. Lawrence tower and the Moot Hall, on reaching the outer wall of the latter, is continued within, from that outer wall along the right-hand side of the corridor off which the extremely ancient chamber known as the Mayor's Parlour is situated. If close examination is made of that wall you will find that it is eight feet thick. But it is not a solid wall. The secret passage I have mentioned runs through it, to a point half-way along the length of the Mayor's Parlour. And access to the Mayor's Parlour is had by a secret door in the old panelling of that chamber—just as in the case of the chamber in the church tower."

"You investigated all this yourself, Dr. Pellery?"

"Discovered and investigated it."

"And kept the secret to yourself?"

"I did. I saw no reason for communicating it to anyone."

"However, as you discovered it, it was not impossible that others should make the same discovery?"

"It is very evident that somebody has discovered it!" replied the witness with emphasis.

"Now, you say that it is about twenty years since you made this discovery. Have you been in St. Lawrence tower since?"

"Yes. Superintendent Hawthwaite has been in communication with me—privately—about this matter for some little time. I came to Hathelsborough yesterday, and in the afternoon he and I visited the tower and I showed him the secret way and the doors in the panelling. We passed from the tower into the Mayor's Parlour—as you or anyone may, just now, if you know the secret of the sliding panels."

"Is it what you would call a difficult secret?"

"Not a bit of it—once you have hit on the exact spot at which to exert a pressure. The panels are then moved back quite easily."

"Your evidence, then, Dr. Pellery, comes to this—there is a secret passage through the apparently solid arch in St. Lawrence Lane which leads direct from the middle chamber in St. Lawrence tower to the Mayor's Parlour in the Moot Hall? Is that correct?"

Dr. Pellery made an old-fashioned bow.

"That is absolutely correct!"

"I am sure the court is greatly obliged to you, sir," said Meeking, responding to the old man's courtesy. He looked round, and seeing that Stedman made no sign, glanced at the policeman who stood by the witness-box. "Call Stephen Spizey!" he commanded.

Spizey moved ponderously into the box in all the glory of his time-honoured livery. He looked very big, and very consequential, and unusually glum. Meeking, who was not a Hathelsborough man, glanced quizzingly at Spizey's grandeur and at the cocked hat which Spizey placed on the ledge before him.

"Er—you're some sort of a Corporation official, aren't you, Spizey?" he suggested.

"Apparitor to his Worshipful the Mayor of Hathelsborough," responded Spizey in his richest tones. "Mace-bearer to his Worship. Town Crier. Bellman. Steward of the Pound. Steward of High Cross and Low Cross. Summoner of Thursday Market. Convener of Saturday Market. Receiver of Dues and Customs——"

"You appear to be a good deal of a pluralist," interrupted Meeking. "However, are you caretaker of St. Lawrence church?"

"I am!"

"Do you live in a cottage at the corner of St. Lawrence churchyard?"

"I do!"

"Do you remember the evening on which Mr. Wallingford was murdered?"

"Yes."

"At seven o'clock of that evening were you in your cottage?"

"I was!"

"Did Mr. Krevin Crood come to your cottage door about seven o'clock and ask you for the keys of St. Lawrence?"

"He did!"

"Did he say why he wanted to go into the church?"

"Yes, to write out a hinscription for a London gent as wanted it."

"Did you give him the keys?"

"I did."

"Did you see him go into the church?"

"Yes, and hear him lock himself inside it."

"Did he eventually bring the keys back?"

"Not to me. My missis."

Meeking waved Spizey's magnificence aside and called for Mrs. Spizey. Mrs. Spizey, too, readily remembered the evening under discussion and said so, with a sniff which seemed to indicate decided disapproval of her memories respecting it.

"What were you doing that evening, Mrs. Spizey?" asked Meeking.

"Which for the most part of it, sir, I was a-washing of that very floor as you're a-standing on, sir, me being cleaner to the Moot Hall. That 'ud be from six to eight."

"Then you went home, I suppose?"

"I did, sir, and very thankful to!"

"Was your husband at home?"

"He were not, sir. Which Spizey had gone out to have his glass, sir—as is his custom."

"Did Mr. Krevin Crood come to you with the keys of the church?"

"He did, sir. Which the clock had just struck eight. And remarked, sir, that the light was failing, and that his eyes wasn't as strong as they had been. Pleasant-like, sir."

"I see! Had Mr. Krevin Crood any papers in his hand?"

"He had papers in his hand, sir, or under his arm."

"And that was just after eight o'clock?"

"The clocks had just struck it, sir."

Meeking nodded his dismissal of Mrs. Spizey. It was plain that he was getting near the end of his case and his manner became sharp and almost abrupt.

"Call Detective-Sergeant Welton," he said. "Welton, were you present when Superintendent Hawthwaite arrested the prisoner Krevin Crood, and afterwards when the other prisoner, Simon Crood, was taken into custody?"

"I was, sir."

"Did you afterwards, on Superintendent Hawthwaite's instructions, search Krevin Crood's lodgings and Simon Crood's house?"

"I did, sir."

"Tell their Worships what you found."

"I first made a search at the rooms occupied by Krevin Crood in Little Bailey Gate. I there found in an old writing-case kept in his bedroom a quantity of papers and documents in the handwriting of the late Mayor, Mr. Wallingford. I handed these over to Superintendent Hawthwaite. I now produce them. There are fifty-six separate papers in all. I have gone through them carefully. All relate to Corporation accounts and to the financial affairs of the borough. Several are blood-stained."

There was a shiver of horror amongst the women present as the witness handed over a sheaf of various-sized papers, indicating where the stains lay. But the even-toned, matter-of-fact, coldly-official voice went on.

"Later, I made a search of the prisoner Simon Crood's house at the Tannery. In a desk in a room which he uses as a private office I found more papers and documents similar to those which I had found at Krevin Crood's lodgings. I produce these—there are seventeen separate papers. All are in the handwriting of the late Mr. Wallingford. I also discovered in a drawer in Simon Crood's bedroom a memorandum book, bound in red leather, the greater part of which is filled with notes and figures made by the late Mayor. I produce this too. I also identify it as a book which the late Mayor was in the habit of carrying about with him. I have frequently seen him make use of it."

While every neck was craned forward to catch a glimpse of the memorandum book, Tansley suddenly saw Krevin Crood making signals to him from the dock. He drew Brent's attention to the fact; then went down into the well of the court and over to Krevin. Brent watched them curiously; it seemed to him that Krevin was asking Tansley's advice, and that Tansley was dissuading Krevin from adopting some particular course. They conversed for some minutes, while the magistrates were examining the memorandum book and the papers. Simon Crood joined in, and seemed to agree with Tansley. But suddenly Krevin turned away from both with a decisive gesture, and advanced to the front of the dock.

"Your Worships," he exclaimed in a loud, compelling tone, "I have had quite enough of this farce! I desire to make a full and important statement!"

CHAPTER XXIV

BEHIND THE PANEL

D espite the admonitions of the presiding magistrate, and the stern voices of sundry officials, posted here and there about the court, a hubbub of excited comment and murmur broke out on Krevin Crood's dramatic announcement. Nor was the excitement confined to the public benches and galleries; round the solicitors' table there was a putting together of heads and an exchange of whisperings; on the bench itself, crowded to its full extent, some of the magistrates so far forgot their judicial position as to bend towards each other with muttered words and knowing looks. Suddenly, from somewhere in the background, a strident voice made its tones heard above the commotion:

"He knows! Let him tell what he knows! Let's hear all about it!"

"Silence!" commanded the chairman. "If this goes on, I shall have the court cleared. Any further interruption——" He interrupted himself, glancing dubiously at Krevin. "I think you would be well advised——"

"I want no advice!" retorted Krevin. Simon had been at his elbow, anxious and pleading, for the last minute: he, it was very evident, was sorely concerned by Krevin's determination to speak. "I claim my right to have my say, at this stage, and I shall have it—all this has gone on long enough, and I don't propose to have it go on any longer. I had nothing to do with the murder of Wallingford, but I know who had, and I'm not going to keep the knowledge to myself, now that things have come to this pass. You'd better listen to a plain and straightforward tale, instead of to bits of a story here and bits of a story there."

The chairman turned to those of his brother magistrates who were sitting nearest to him and, after a whispered consultation with them and with the clerk, nodded not over graciously at the defiant figure in the dock.

"We will hear your statement," he said. "You had better go into the witness-box and make it on oath."

Krevin moved across to the witness-box with alacrity and went through the usual formalities as only a practised hand could. He smiled cynically as he folded his fingers together on the ledge of the box and faced the excited listeners.

"As there's no one to ask me any questions—at this stage, anyway—I'd better tell my story in my own fashion," he said. "And to save time and needless explanations, let me begin by saying that, as far as it went, all the evidence your Worships have heard, from the police, from Louisa Speck, from Dr. Pellery, from Spizey and his wife, from everybody, I think, is substantially correct—entirely correct, I might say, for I don't remember anything that I could contradict. The whole thing is—what does it lead up to? In the opinion of the police to identifying me with the actual murder of John Wallingford, and my brother there with being accessory to the crime. The police, as usual, are absolutely and entirely at fault—I did not kill Wallingford, and accordingly my brother could not be an accessory to what I did not do and never had the remotest intention of doing. Now you shall hear how circumstantial evidence, brought to a certain point, is of no value whatever if it can't be carried past that point. Hawthwaite has got his evidence to a certain point—and now he's up against a blank wall. He doesn't know what lies behind that blank wall. I do! And I'm the only person in this world who does.

"Now listen to a plain, truthful, unvarnished account of the real facts. On the evening of the day before Wallingford's murder, I was in the big saloon at Bull's Snug between half-past six and seven o'clock. Mallett came in, evidently in search of somebody. It turned out that I was the person he was looking for. He came up to me and told me that his wife was away and that he was giving a little dinner-party to my brother Simon and to Coppinger. They were already at his house, and he and they were anxious that I should join them. Now, I knew quite enough of my brother Simon, and of Coppinger, and of Mallett himself to know that if they wanted my company it was with some ulterior motive, and being a straightforward man I said so there and then. Mallett admitted it—they had, he said, a matter of business to propose to me. I had no objection and I went with him. What the girl, Louisa Speck, has told you about what happened after I entered the Bank House is quite correct—she's a reliable and a good witness and gave her evidence most intelligently. She took me up into Mallett's dressing-room, showed me where I could get what I wanted, and left me to make my toilet. I helped myself to clean linen, and I have no doubt whatever that the handkerchief which I took from one of the drawers which the girl had opened for me was that of Dr. Wellesley's of which we have heard so much in this case. I say, I have no doubt whatever about that—in fact, I am sure of it.

"Having made my toilet, I went downstairs and joined my host and his other guests. We had a glass or two of Mallett's excellent sherry, and in due course we dined—dined very well indeed. When dinner was over, Mallett got up some of his old port, and we settled down to our business talk. I very quickly discovered why I had been brought into it. What we may call the war between Wallingford, as leader of the reform party, and the Town Trustees, as representatives of the old system, had come to a definite stage, and Mallett, Coppinger, and my brother, Simon, realized that it was high time they opened negotiations with the enemy. They wanted, in short, to come to terms, and they were anxious that I, as a lawyer, as a man thoroughly acquainted with the affairs of the borough, and as a former official of high standing, should act as intermediary, or ambassador, or go-between, whatever you like to call it, in the matter at issue between them and Wallingford. Of course I was willing.

"Mallett acted as chief spokesman, in putting matters plainly before me. He said that Wallingford, since his election as Mayor of Hathelsborough, had found out a lot—a great deal more than they wished him to know. He had accumulated facts, figures, statistics; he had contrived to possess himself of a vast amount of information, and he was steadily and persistently accumulating more. There was no doubt whatever, said Mallett, as to what were the intentions of Wallingford and his party—though up to then Wallingford's party did not know all that Wallingford knew. There was to be a clean sweep of everything that existed under the Town Trustee system. The Town Trustees themselves were to go. All pensions were to be done away with. All secret payments and transactions were to be unearthed and prohibited for the future. The entire financial business of the town was to be placed in the care of the Corporation. In short, everything was to be turned upside-down, and the good old days to cease. That was what was to happen if Wallingford went triumphantly on his way.

"But it was the belief of Mallett, and of Coppinger, and of my brother, Simon, that Wallingford's way could be barred. How? Well, all three believed that Wallingford could be bought off. They believed that Wallingford had his price; that he could be got at; that he could be squared. All three of them are men who believe that every man has his price. I believe that myself, and I'm not ashamed of voicing my belief. Every man can be bought—if you can only agree on a price with him. Now, the Town Trustees knew that Wallingford had ambitions; they knew what some of his ambitions were, and of one in particular. They proposed to buy him in that way, and they commissioned me to see him privately and to offer him certain terms.

"The terms were these. If Wallingford would drop his investigations and remain quiet for the remaining period of his mayoralty, the Town Trustees would agree to the making and carrying out of certain minor reforms which should be engineered by and credited to Wallingford in order to save his face with his party. Moreover, they would guarantee to Wallingford a big increase in his practice as a solicitor, and they would promise him their united support when a vacancy arose in the Parliamentary representation of Hathelsborough, which vacancy, they knew, would occur within the year, as the sitting member had intimated his intention of resigning. Now, this last was the big card I was to play—we all knew that Wallingford was extremely desirous of Parliamentary honours, and that he was very well aware that with the Town Trustees on his side he would win handsomely, whoever was brought against him. I was to play that card for all it was worth. So then the proposal was—Wallingford was to draw off his forces, and he was to be rewarded as I have said. Not a man of us doubted that he would be tempted by the bait, and would swallow it."

Brent leapt to his feet and flung a scornful exclamation across the court.

"Then not a man of you knew him!" he cried. "He'd have flung your bribe back into the dirty hands that offered it!"

But Krevin Crood smiled more cynically than ever.

"That's all you know, young man," he retorted. "You'll know more when you're my age. Well," he continued, turning his back on Brent and again facing the bench, "that was the situation. I was to act as ambassador, and if I succeeded in my embassy I was to be well paid for my labour."

"By the Town Trustees?" inquired the chairman.

"By the Town Trustees, certainly," replied Krevin. "Who else? As my principals——"

"I think you will have to tell us what fee, or payment, you were to have," interrupted the chairman. "If——"

"Oh, as the whole thing's come to nothing, I don't mind telling that," said Krevin. "I shall never get it now, so why not talk of it? I was to have a thousand pounds."

"As reward for inducing the Mayor to withhold from the public certain information which he had acquired as regards the unsatisfactory condition of the borough finances?" asked the chairman.

"Y-es, if you put it that way," assented Krevin. "You might put it another way, as regards the Mayor. He was to—just let things slide."

"Go on, if you please," said the chairman dryly. "We understand."

"Well," continued Krevin cheerfully, "we settled my mission over Mallett's port. The next thing was for me to carry it out. It was necessary to do this immediately—we knew that Wallingford had carried his investigations to such an advanced stage that he might make the results public at any moment. Now, I did not want anyone to know of my meeting with him—I wanted it to be absolutely secret. But I knew how to bring that

In the Mayor's Parlour

about. Wallingford spent nearly every evening alone in the Mayor's Parlour—I knew how to reach the Mayor's Parlour unobserved. The secret of which Dr. Pellery has just told you was also known to me—I discovered the passage between St. Lawrence tower and the Moot Hall many years ago. And I determined to get at Wallingford by way of that passage.

"About seven o'clock of the evening on which Wallingford was murdered, I called at Spizey's cottage in St. Lawrence churchyard and got the keys of the church from him, on the excuse that I wanted to copy an inscription. I locked myself into the church, and went up to the chamber in the tower. I spent some little time there, considering the details of my plan of campaign, before going along the secret passage. It would be about half-past seven, perhaps more, when I at last slipped open the panel, and crossed over to the Moot Hall. The panel at the other end of the passage, which admits to the Mayor's Parlour, is the fifth one on the left-hand side of that room; I undid it very cautiously and silently. There was then no one in the parlour. All was silent. I looked through the crack of the panel. There was no one in the place at all. Incidentally, I may mention that when I thus took an observation of the parlour I noticed that on an old oak chest, standing by the wainscoting and immediately behind the Mayor's chair and desk, lay the rapier which was produced at the inquest, and with which he, undoubtedly, was killed.

"I suddenly heard the handle of the door into the corridor turned, then Wallingford's voice. I slipped the panel back till it was nearly closed, and stood with my ear against it, listening. Wallingford was not alone. He had a woman with him. And I made out, in their first exchange of words, that he had met her in the corridor just outside the door of the Mayor's Parlour and that they were quarrelling and both in high temper. I——"

"Stop!" exclaimed the chairman, lifting his hand as an excited murmur began to run round the court. "Silence! If there is any interruption—Now," he went on, turning to Krevin, "you say you heard Mr. Wallingford come into the Mayor's Parlour and that he was accompanied by a woman, with whom he was having high words. Did you see this woman?"

"No, I saw neither her nor Wallingford. I only heard their voices."

"Did you recognize her voice as that of any woman you knew?"

"I did—unmistakably! I knew quite well who she was."

"Who was she, then?"

Krevin shook his head.

"For the moment—wait!" he replied. "Let me tell my tale in my own way. To resume, I say they—she and Wallingford—were having high words. I could tell, for instance, that he was in a temper which I should call furious. I overheard all that was said. He was wanting to know as they entered the room how she had got there. She replied that she had watched Mrs. Bunning out of her house from amongst the bushes in St. Lawrence churchyard, and had then slipped in at Bunning's back door, being absolutely determined to see him. Wallingford answered that she would get no good by waylaying him; he had found her out and was done with her; she was an impostor, an adventuress; she had come to the end of her tether. She then demanded some letters—her letters; there were excited words about this from each, and it was not easy to catch all that was said; at times they were both speaking together. But she got in a clear demand at last—was he or was he not going to hand those letters over? He said no, he was not—they were going to remain in his possession as a hold over her; she was a danger to the community with her plottings and underhand ways, and he intended to show certain of those letters to others. There was more excited wrangling over this—I heard Dr. Wellesley's name mentioned, then Mallett's: I also heard some reference, which I couldn't make head or tail of, to money and documents. In the midst of all this Wallingford suddenly told her to go; he had had

127

enough of it, and had his work to attend to. Once more she demanded the letters; he answered with a very peremptory negative. Then I heard a sound as of his chair being pulled up to his desk, followed by a brief silence. Then, all of a sudden, I heard another sound, half-cry, half-groan, and a sort of dull thud, as if something had fallen. A moment later, as I was wondering what had happened, and what to do, I heard the door which opens into the corridor close gently. And at that I pushed back the panel and looked into the Mayor's Parlour."

It seemed to Brent that every soul in that place, from the grey-haired chairman on the bench to the stolid-faced official by the witness-box was holding his breath, and that every eye was fastened on Krevin Crood with an irresistible fascination. There was a terrible silence in the court as Krevin paused, terminated by an involuntary sigh of relief as he made signs of speaking again. And, in that instant, Brent saw Mrs. Elstrick, the tall gaunt woman of whom he had heard at least one mysterious piece of news from Hawthwaite, quietly slip out of her place near the outer door and vanish; he saw too that no one but himself saw her go, so absorbed were all others in what was coming.

"When I saw—what I did see," continued Krevin, in a low, concentrated tone, "I went in. The Mayor was lying across his desk, still, quiet. I touched his shoulder—and got blood on my fingers. I knew then what had happened—the woman had snatched up that rapier and run him through. I pulled out my handkerchief—the handkerchief I had taken from Mallett's drawer—wiped my hand, and threw the handkerchief in the fire. Then I took up a mass of papers and a memorandum book which Wallingford had laid down—and went away by the passage. And that's the plain truth! I should never have told it if I hadn't been arrested. I care nothing at all that Wallingford was killed by this woman—not I! I shouldn't have cared if she'd gone scot-free. But if it's going to be my neck or hers, well, I prefer it to be hers. And there you are!"

"Once again," said the chairman, "who was this woman?"

Krevin Crood might have been answering the most casual of casual questions.

"Who?" he replied. "Why—Mrs. Saumarez!"

CHAPTER XXV

THE EMPTY ROOM

Brent was out of his seat near the door, out of the court itself, out of the Moot Hall, and in the market-place before he realized what he was doing. It was a brilliant summer day, and just then the town clocks were striking the noontide; he stood for a second staring about him as if blinded and dazed by the strong sunlight. But it was not the sunlight at all that confused him—though he stood there blinking under it—and presently his brain cleared and he turned and ran swiftly down River Gate, the narrow street that led to the low-lying outer edge of the town. River Gate was always quiet; just then it was deserted. And as he came to half-way down it, he saw at its foot a motor-car, drawn up by the curb and evidently waiting for somebody. The somebody was Mrs. Elstrick, who was hastening towards it. In another second she had sprung in, and the car had sped away in the direction of the open country. And Brent let it go, without another glance in its direction.

He turned at the foot of River Gate into Farthing Lane, the long, winding, tree-bordered alley that ran beneath the edge of the town past the outer fringe of houses, the alley wherein Hawthwaite had witnessed the nocturnal meeting between Mrs. Elstrick and Krevin Crood. Brent remembered that as he hastened along, running between the trees on one side and the high walls of the gardens on the other. But he gave no further thought to the recollection—his brain was not yet fully recovered from the shock of Krevin Crood's last words, and it was obsessed by a single idea: that of gaining the garden entrance of the Abbey House and confronting the woman whom Krevin had formally denounced as the murderer of Wallingford. And as he hurried along he found himself saying certain words over and over again, and still again....

"I'm not going to see a woman hang!—I'm not going to see a woman hang! I'm ... not ... going ... to——"

Behind this suddenly aroused Quixotic sentiment he was sick with horror. He knew that what Krevin Crood had told at last was true. He knew, too, that it would never have come out if Krevin himself had not been in danger. A feeling of almost physical nausea came over him as he remembered the callous, brutal cynicism of Krevin's last words, "If it's going to be my neck or hers, I prefer it to be hers!" A woman!—yet, a murderess; the murderess of his cousin, whose death he had vowed to avenge. But of course it was so— he saw many things now. The anxiety to get the letters; the dread of publicity expressed to Peppermore; the mystery spread over many things and actions; now this affair with Mallett—there was no reason to doubt Krevin Crood's accusation. The fragments of the puzzle had been pieced together.

But as he ran along that lane, and as his mental faculties regained their normality Brent himself did some piecing together. Every word of Krevin Crood's statement had bitten itself into his intelligence. Now he could reconstruct. It seemed to him that he visualized the Mayor's Parlour on that fateful evening. An angry, disillusioned, nerve-racked man, sore and restive under the fancy, or, rather, the realization of deceit, saying bitter and contemptuous words; a desperate, defeated woman, cornered like a rat—and close to her hand the rapier, lying on the old chest where its purchaser had carelessly flung it. A maddened thing, man or woman, would snatch that up, and——

"Blind, uncontrollable impulse!" muttered Brent. "She struck *at* him, *at* him—and then it was all over. Intentional, no! Yet ... the law! But, by God, I won't have a hand in hanging ... a woman! Time?"

He knew the exact location of the door in the garden wall of the Abbey House and presently he ran up to it, panting from his swift dash along the lane. Not five minutes had elapsed then since his slip out of the excited court. But every second of the coming minutes was precious. And the door was locked.

The garden wall was eight feet high, and so built that on all the expanse of its smoothed surface there was no foothold, no projection for fingers to cling to. But Brent was in that frame of mind which makes light of obstacles: he drew back into the lane, ran, gathered himself for an upward spring at the coping of the wall, leapt, grasped it, struggled, drew up his weight with a mighty effort, threw a leg over, and dropped, gasping and panting, into the shaded garden. It was quiet there—peaceful as a glade set deep in the heart of a silent wood. He lay for a few seconds where he had dropped; then, with a great effort to get his breath, he rose and went quickly up the laurelled walks towards the house. A moment more and he was abreast of the kitchen and its open door, and in the presence of print-gowned, white-aproned women who first exclaimed and then stared at the sudden sight of him.

In the Mayor's Parlour

"Mrs. Saumarez?" said Brent, frightened at the sound of his own voice. "In?"

The cook, a fat, comfortable woman, turned on him from a clear fire.

"The mistress has not come in yet, sir," she said. "She went out very early this morning on her bicycle, and we haven't seen her since. I expect she'll be back for lunch."

Brent glanced at the open window of the room in which he had first encountered Mrs. Saumarez and to which he had brought her the casket and its contents.

"Can I go in there and sit down?" he asked. "I want to see Mrs. Saumarez."

"Certainly, sir," answered cook and parlour-maid in chorus. "She can't be long, surely."

Brent went further along and stepped into the room. Not long? He knew very well that that room would never see its late occupant again! She was gone of course.

The room looked much the same as when he had last seen it, except that now there were great masses of summer flowers on all sides. He glanced round and his observant eye was quick to notice a fact—beneath the writing-table a big waste-paper-basket was filled to its edges with torn-up papers. He moved nearer, speculating on what it was that had been destroyed—and suddenly, behind the basket, he noticed, flung away, crumpled, on the floor, the buff envelope of a telegram.

Brent, picking this up, expected to find it empty, but the message was inside. He drew out and smoothed the flimsy sheet and read its contents. They were comprised in five words: *Lingmore Cross Roads six-thirty.*

Of course that was from Mallett. He glanced at the post-marks. The telegram had been sent from Clothford at seven o'clock the previous evening, and received at Hathelsborough before eight. It was an appointment without doubt. Brent knew Lingmore Cross Roads. He had been there on a pleasure jaunt with Queenie. It was a point on a main road whence you could go north or south, east or west with great facility. And doubtless Mrs. Saumarez, arriving there early in the morning, would find Mallett and a swift motor awaiting her. Well....

A sudden ringing at the front-door bell, a sudden loud knocking on the same door, made Brent crush envelope and telegram in his hand and thrust the crumpled ball of paper into his pocket. A second later he heard voices at the door, heavy steps in the hall, Hawthwaite's voice.

"No," said the parlour-maid, evidently answering some question, "but Mr. Brent's in the study. The mistress——"

Hawthwaite, with one of his plain-clothes men, came striding in, saw Brent and closed the door, shutting out the parlour-maid.

"Gone?" he asked sharply.

"They say—out for a bicycle ride," answered Brent, purposely affecting unconcern. "Went out very early this morning."

"What did you come here for?" demanded Hawthwaite.

"To ask her personally if what Krevin Crood said is true!" replied Brent.

Hawthwaite laughed.

"Do you think she'd have admitted it, Mr. Brent?" he said. "I don't!"

"I think she would," answered Brent. "But——"

"Well?" inquired Hawthwaite.

"I don't suppose I shall ever have the chance of putting such a question to her," added Brent. "She's—off!"

Hawthwaite looked round.

"Um!" he remarked. "Well, it only means another hue-and-cry. She and Mallett of course. There's one thing in our favour. She doesn't know that Krevin Crood knew anything about it."

"Are you sure of that?" suggested Brent.

"Oh, sure enough!" affirmed Hawthwaite. "She hasn't an idea that anybody knows. So we shall get her!"

"What about Krevin Crood—and Simon?" asked Brent.

"Adjourned," replied Hawthwaite. "There's no doubt Krevin's told the true story at last, but he and Simon are still in custody and will be until, perhaps, to-morrow. We want to know a bit more yet. But I'll tell you what, Mr. Brent, this morning's work has broken up the old system! The Town Trustees and the ancient regime, as they call it—gone! Smashed, Mr. Brent——"

"What are you going to do about this?" interrupted Brent, glancing round the room.

"Set the wires to work," answered Hawthwaite half-carelessly. "Unless she and Mallett have laid their plans with extraordinary cleverness, they can't get out of the country. A noticeable pair too! Went out very early this morning, cycling, did she? I must have a talk to the servants. And that companion, now—Mrs. Elstrick—where's she got to? I noticed her in court."

"Left, sir, just before Krevin Crood finished," said Hawthwaite's companion. "I saw her slip out."

"Ay, well!" observed Hawthwaite. "I don't know that that matters! If any of them can get through the meshes of our net ... Mr. Brent!"

"Well?" asked Brent.

"We've got at the truth at last about your cousin," continued Hawthwaite, with a significant look. "It's been a case of one thing leading to another. And two things running side by side. If we hadn't cornered Krevin Crood we'd never have had his revelations about the Town Trustees. Talk about your Local Government Board inquiry!—why, five minutes of Krevin's tongue-work did more than half a dozen inquiries. I tell you, sir, the old system's dead—the Crood gang was smashed to pieces in that court this morning! Somehow, it's that that interests me most, Mr. Brent. But—business!" He turned to the plain-clothes man, and nodded towards the door. "Fetch those servants in here," he said. "They've got to know."

Brent went away then, carrying certain secrets with him. He put them away in a mental vault and sealed them down. Let Hawthwaite do his own work, he would give him no help. He foresaw his own future work. Wallingford, dead though he was, had won his victory and in his death had slain the old wicked system. Now there was building and reconstruction to be done, and it was his job to do it. He saw far ahead as he trod the sunlit streets of the old town. He would marry Queenie and they would settle into the slow-moving life of Hathelsborough, and he and men who thought with him would slowly build up a new and healthy state of things on the ruins of the old. So thinking he turned mechanically towards Mrs. Appleyard's house, in search of Queenie. Queenie, said Mrs. Appleyard, was in the garden behind. Brent went through the house, and out into the garden's shade. There he found Queenie. She sat in a summer-house, and she was shelling peas for dinner.

THE END.